FINDING *beauty in the* DARKNESS

Sometimes loving someone means setting them free.

Finding the Beauty in the Darkness

Originally titled Bordello @ 2017 Nikki Ash

2nd edition 2021 Nikki Ash

Cover Design and formatting by Jersey Girl Design
Cover Photograph by Sara Eirew Photography

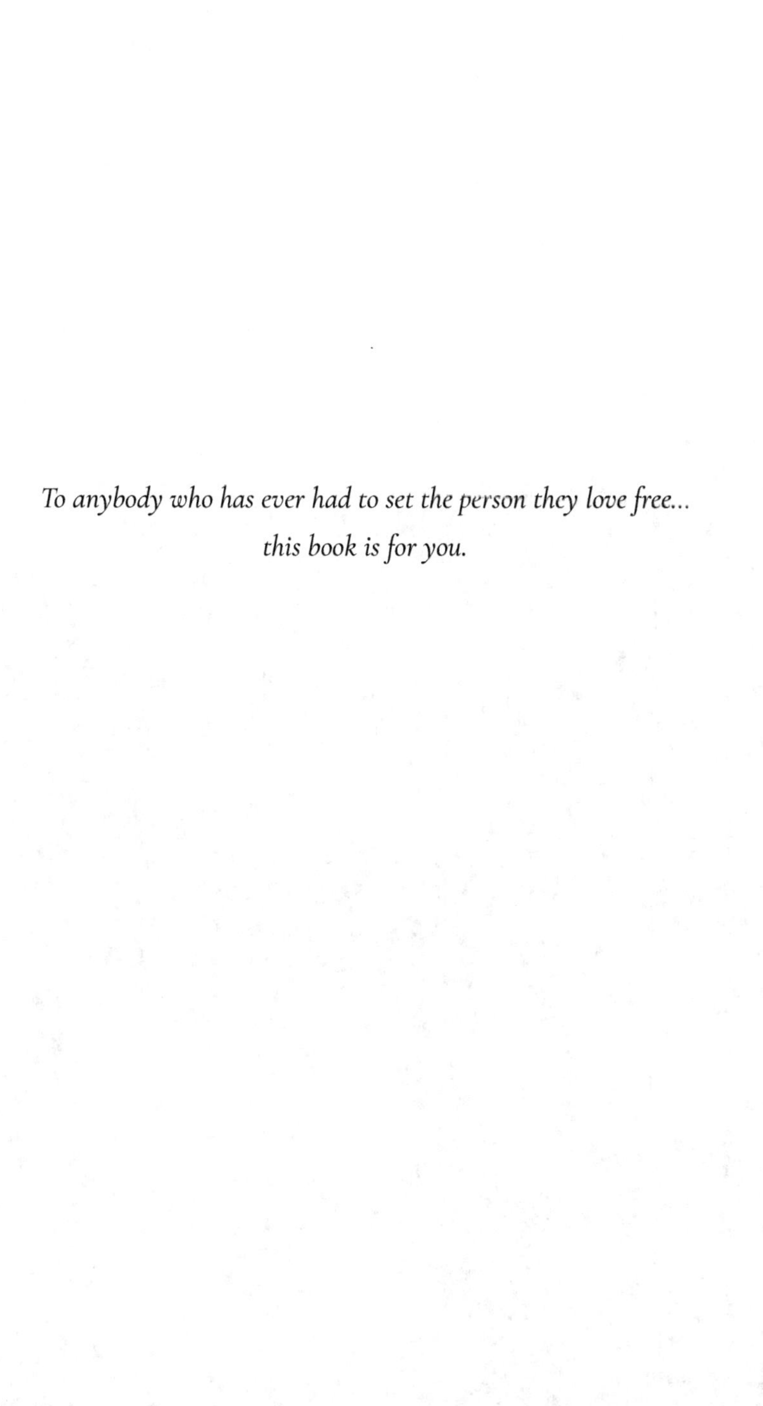

To anybody who has ever had to set the person they love free...
this book is for you.

Chapter One

GIOVANNI

"LISTEN, DON, YOU AND MY FATHER GO WAY BACK, SO IF this girl has the balls to show up here and ask for the loan, I'm going to give it to her. But I just had Johnny look her up and she isn't worth shit. You know I don't normally deal with people like this."

I'm sitting at my desk in my office, checking my watch for the time...again. I've got too much shit to handle today, and dealing with a little girl who needs money to pay off her overdue credit card bills isn't my top priority, that's for damn sure.

"I understand, Giovanni. Like I said, I'm calling in a personal favor. This girl, Ashley, she's a tough cookie, but she just can't seem to catch a break. Single mom, working at my strip joint to make ends meet. She isn't like the usual women. She doesn't do drugs. She's got her head screwed on right. She wouldn't be asking for thirty grand unless she's desperate for it."

Don is the owner of Double D's strip club here in Las Vegas. For many years, Don and my father have done business together. Our family owns the club, but we are what you call a silent partner. My father has been using the club to launder money for years. I, on the other hand, have more productive ways to do business.

"You know the chance of me getting my money back from her is slim, right? Which means you'll be paying me back if she can't." Don knows I don't lend money to people who have nothing to lose.

"I told her if she can't pay you back, she'd have to work for you."

I laugh at that. There's no way I'm forcing some woman to work for me. The reason everything runs so smoothly is because the women who work here *choose* to be here.

"You know that's not happening."

Don sighs. "I know, but I'm hoping she'll be scared enough, she'll pay you back. She's responsible. She's just going through a tough time."

There's a knock on my door, and Johnny—my right-hand man— enters. "Boss, there's an Ashley Myers here to see you. Edgardo asked me to see what she wants, but she only wants to speak to you. Are you expecting her?"

Edgardo is one of my bouncers here at the club. His job is to keep an eye on who's coming and going and to make sure shit stays on the up and up. When you're in the business I'm in, it's easy for shit to go bad quick. The key is to always be one step ahead.

"Send her back here." Johnny nods once and heads back out, closing the door behind him. "Listen, Don, apparently your girl has some brass fucking balls because she just got here."

"Thank you, Giovanni. Like I said, I owe you one."

"Yeah, you do." *And I always fucking collect.*

I hang up the phone and wait for Johnny to walk this girl back to my office so I can handle this before I leave to meet my mom for lunch. I check my cell for any messages and notice one from Cecilia.

Cecilia: Senator Hightower hurt Natalie. Can you please come here asap?

Me: Is Rome holding him?

Cecilia: Yes

Me: Be there in twenty. Do we need to call Dr. Fox?

Cecilia: Already did. It's not good.

Jesus fucking Christ! This isn't the first time the Senator's put his hands on one of my girls. I gave him a second chance because of his affluence in the community, but it won't be happening again—not at my damn club. I look down at my watch and make a mental note to let my mom know I won't be making it to lunch today.

There's a knock at my door and Johnny enters. "Boss, Ashley Myers."

"Thank you. You can close the door behind you."

He exits, leaving a pretty brunette with a banging fucking body, and my first thought is she would make a fabulous addition to the women here. While she's probably almost thirty years old, she screams innocence and maturity in her royal blue wrap around dress. Don was right—she isn't your typical stripper. She hasn't been in this life long enough for it to corrupt her, but it will. It always does.

I stand to greet her, and as I'm assessing her, I notice she's doing the same to me. Her eyes are telling. She's trying to figure out if she can trust me, which is ironic since I'm the one lending her the money. Her eyes roam over my face then descend to my chest. While I start my day in a three-piece suit, as the morning progresses, articles of clothing tend to get shed, piece by piece. My jacket's thrown over the back of my chair and my tie undone with the top buttons of my shirt unbuttoned.

Her eyes stop at the tattoo peeking out of my shirt. It's a saying in Italian.

Dalla nascita. Per sangue. Famiglia. By birth. By blood. Family.

My grandfather, my father, and my brothers all have the same tattoo. We were taken to get the ink done the day we turned eighteen, when we were officially brought into the organization. The moment she realizes I'm watching her check me out she blushes an adorable shade of pink. The men that frequent this place would eat her alive.

I motion for her to have a seat, then sit down as well. "How may I help you?" My tone comes across as *let's get straight to the damn point* instead of polite, and she looks down at her hands for a moment, taken aback by my bluntness. Maybe she was hoping I'd offer her some coffee and pastries. As cute as she is, I don't have time to fuck around. I have a girl who's been hurt and a Senator who's going to pay for hurting her.

Ashley looks up at me, her shoulders squared, back straight. "I need a loan for thirty thousand dollars and I was told by Don you could help me." I gotta give this girl credit. She's holding her own.

"Hmm...Did he now? Did he tell you what I accept for collateral?" I hold back my smirk because really, I'm just fucking with this woman, but she doesn't need to know that. She doesn't own shit other than a house that will more than likely be foreclosed on in a few months, which is why Don threatened her with working for me, hoping it'll motivate her to pay me back.

"Yes, women," she chokes out, and I've immediately gained respect for her. You can see it written all over her face she's scared shitless, yet she's still here, with her chin up, asking for a loan, knowing if she can't pay me back, she'll be working as an escort here at my bordello: *La Stella Gentleman's Club*. Stella was my nonna's name, which translates to Star. When my father came over here from Italy and opened the bordello forty years ago, he named it after his mother—my grandmother—who died in a shooting shortly after my father was born.

"So, you understand, if at any time you can't pay me back the set monthly payment you'll be required to work it off here at my gentleman's club?"

"Yes, I do." Her voice wavers, but she keeps her chin up.

I have Johnny run a more thorough background check on her, and once she checks out, I lend her the money. She argues about the interest rate, and for a second I almost feel bad because I can pretty much guarantee this woman won't be able to make these payments, but at the end of the day that's not my fucking problem. My job is to bring in money, not give it away. Twenty percent interest is considered low with the people I deal with, but no matter how confident this woman is, she's playing a game she has no business being a part of. What she doesn't know is that by Don vouching for her, if she doesn't pay up, he'll end up taking over her loan.

Once she has the money in her hands, I have Johnny see her out. More than likely I'll see her again, when I'm forced to go after her for the money she owes me, until I know she has nothing left to give. Will I actually drag her here to work for me? Hell no. I prefer all my woman to come willingly, but if she knows that, she won't even bother to attempt to pay me back. More than likely, she'll lose her house then she'll sell her car. Soon after that, she'll rack up whatever credit cards she has. After she's gone down all those avenues, she'll borrow money from her family or a close friend, and once she's out of options and she's hit rock bottom—because they always do—Don will have to take over. Either way, I'll be getting my money back with interest. Because unlike Ashley, who has no idea what she got herself into, Don knows I don't fuck around. I have a reputation to protect, and in the business I'm in, your reputation is all you have.

I'm Giovanni Valentino, and my family runs one of the most powerful crime organizations in Italy as well as Nevada, and I run one of the most exclusive brothels in the United States. I am also one of the biggest loan sharks on the West Coast.

My grandfather, Joe Valentino, is now retired and lives in Italy with my younger brother, Mario, who runs a hotel and restaurant over there. My other brother, Nico, runs the hotels and casinos here in Las Vegas while my father and his adopted brother Stefan, who is Cecilia's dad, deal with the underground aspects of the business, which includes the illegal gambling as well as the exporting and importing of various contraband. We knew from an early age our grandfather and father were powerful men. This life we live is not for the weak.

My brothers and I are spaced two years apart. Me, the eldest at thirty-two years old, Mario at thirty, and Nico is the youngest at twenty-eight. Our poor mother had her hands full raising three boys growing up in the organization while trying to be the perfect mob boss's wife, but she knew from the beginning what she was getting herself into. She was working in one of the bordellos my father owned in Italy before he sold them and moved here. According to her, he saved her life and in return, she keeps her ears covered, eyes closed, and cheek turned pretending my father is the perfect husband. When the truth is, while he might be the perfect boss and businessman, he is a horrible fucking husband by normal standards. I don't doubt he loves my mother in his own fucked up way, but he has no idea how to be faithful, and she chooses to let it all go and accept him the way he is because he makes sure she's taken care of the only way he knows how.

My mother wants for nothing when it comes to materialistic possessions. She belongs to country clubs and takes vacations whenever she wants to. But it's all given to make up for the fact that my father's only true loyalty is to the Valentino organization. While she's busy being the perfect wife at their home in Summerlin, a community in between the bordello and Vegas, he's out running the organization and getting his dick wet all over Vegas. Her life is put at risk every day, and everywhere she goes, she's accompanied by bodyguards—we all are. It's always been our way of life, and I don't know any other way.

Which is why I made the decision early on to never get married. My mom claims I'm being dramatic. She says I'm still young and will change my mind one day, but when I see the emptiness in her eyes she's in denial of, I know I'm making the right decision. I could never do that to someone. The people we bring into our lives are always at risk. My grandmother was shot going to the corner market in Italy by another organization. My mother has been in life threatening situations too many times to count. I would never want someone I love to be in harm's way for choosing to be with me. Just because it's the life I was born into doesn't mean I'm going to willingly bring someone else into this life.

Besides, why would I want to settle on one piece of ass forever when I can have any woman I want, any time I want? Who wants to eat the same food every day? It's human nature to want variety. My dad chose to get married so he could have a family, but instead of spending his life being the man my mom deserves, he's spent their entire marriage cheating on her. I'd rather stay single and not have to remain faithful to any one woman or be responsible for her wellbeing. I'll leave it up to my brothers to pass down the Valentino name.

I grab my jacket from the back of my chair, throw it on, and head to the holding cell to deal with the senator. Caesar—one of my bodyguards—joins me on my way down the hall. "I saw her, Boss. She's pretty fucked up." My fists tighten at my sides as I stalk toward the holding cell. *I'm going to kill this motherfucker.*

It's as if he reads my mind. "You know you can't kill him." Caesar grabs ahold of my shoulder, pulling me back before I open the door.

"What do you mean I can't kill him?" I'll be damned if this piece of shit lives to hurt another fucking woman.

"This shit needs to be handled properly. He's the senator and running for reelection, and he owes you a shit ton of money."

"I don't give a fuck about the money!"

"You make him disappear and questions will be raised. You don't want that attention, especially while you're in the middle of negotiations with the Lorenzo family." He's right about that. I have enough cops in my pocket to make shit go away if need be, but I'd be pushing my luck if shit goes down with the Lorenzos. We're in the middle of renegotiating the terms of our agreement and they aren't exactly known for compromising.

I swing the door open to find Rome—another one of my

enforcers—standing over Senator Weston Hightower. Weston's fists are raised and bound together with a steel chain that's hooked in the ceiling. For a man in his late fifties, he's in decent shape. Gray hair trimmed neatly, probably from the stress of trying to keep control of a state which can't be controlled. He's shirtless and there are several nail markings covering his chest. The entire room is nothing but concrete and is completely empty.

"I heard you hurt one of my girls tonight, Hightower." I get in his face, looking him right into his frightful eyes.

"I—I didn't mean to..." He stutters over his words, terrified. Bet he wasn't stuttering when he was hurting Natalie. It's so easy for a man to exude his power and strength over a woman, but just because you can, doesn't mean you should.

"Didn't mean to do what, exactly?" Placing my hand on his throat, I squeeze his jugular just enough so it cuts off his airflow.

"Hurt her." His voice is raspy from the lack of oxygen and that has me grinning on the inside.

"Rome, what *exactly* did the senator do to my girl?" I squeeze his throat tighter, causing his face to turn a light shade of red. Most people don't know this, but it takes more than a good squeeze to kill someone. It takes several minutes of completely cutting off their oxygen before the body gives up and the heart stops pumping.

"He choked her with his belt, Boss."

I look down at his pants and see his belt is missing. "And?"

"A gun, Sir."

My head whips around to Rome, keeping my hand around the senator's throat. "What the do you mean, a gun? Did he shoot her?" I take my gun out from the back of my waistband and point it directly at Weston's forehead, while choking him harder. His chest is rising and falling faster than before, his heart working overtime to keep him alive since he's lacking the oxygen needed to breathe properly.

"No, he shoved it inside of her and it tore her up. The doctor's checking her out now for internal bleeding." I warned this motherfucker about doing this shit at my club. The last time he used a champagne bottle to fuck her. Tore her pussy and ass up. I gave him a second chance because Natalie asked me to. She swore she agreed to what he wanted to do, but things escalated too quickly and he couldn't control himself. I call bullshit because I don't give a fuck how in the moment you are, you can always control yourself. I'm almost certain Natalie has unhealthy feelings for the senator, but this shit stops now. Her safety comes first.

"Where's the fucking gun now? Get me the damn gun and the fucking belt!" I roar. Rome bolts out of the room. "Did you enjoy pushing metal fucking objects into my girl?" Weston doesn't say anything, so I squeeze his throat tighter, pushing the barrel of the gun harder into his forehead. I can feel the hardness of his skull against the barrel of the gun, and it takes every ounce of restraint I have not to pull the trigger and blow this asshole's brains out.

Weston shakes his head emphatically, his eyes wide with fear.

"I think you did enjoy it."

Rome comes back into the room with the belt and gun. I remove my gun from his head and tuck it back into my waistband. I release my hand from the senator's throat, and he inhales a huge gulp of air as he tries to catch his breath. Taking the belt from Rome, I wrap it around the senator's throat, tightening it past the smallest hole. He begins gasping for a breath once again. *Good! Now you'll know what she felt like.*

"Please, Giovanni. I'm sorry. Please, I won't be that rough again."

"It's Mr. Valentino to you. You don't get the right to use my first name you piece of shit. And damn right you won't be that rough with her again because you aren't welcome in my club anymore."

Grabbing Weston's gun from Rome, I push it up against Weston's lips, forcing them apart. He tries to fight against me, but when I tighten my grip on the belt, his face goes pale and he has no choice but to open wide. Pushing the barrel of the gun down his throat, I begin to fuck his throat with the gun. He's choking and gagging on the barrel, his face turning a light shade of grey.

"Does that feel good? Huh? How does it feel having a metal object shoved inside of you?" Weston's head shakes and his body starts to convulse from the lack of air. A few more minutes and he'll be dead. I hear one of my men clear his throat, and reluctantly, I let go of the belt. None of my men would dare tell me what to do, but they have my back, and they know killing the senator right now wouldn't be in my best interest.

Shoving the gun down farther, I feel it bottom out as he gags and chokes. Then I move it out of his throat, and with the same gun he just deep throated, I point it right between his eyes.

"You are *never* to step foot in my club again, and our deal... consider it void effective immediately. You have thirty days to pay me back with interest. Don't make me fucking hunt you down." And unlike the idle threat I made to that stripper a little while ago, I *will* follow through on this one.

Dropping the gun and belt to the floor, I walk away from that piece of shit before I change my mind and end his life right here. "Get him off my property and get rid of his gun." Just as I'm about to exit the room, I hear Weston take a deep breath of relief. I stop and turn back around.

"On second thought, undo those chains." I nod toward the ceiling. Rome pulls the lever on the chains and the senator's hands come flying down, still cuffed together. Taking the gun back from Rome, I grab ahold of his right hand. Jerking it toward the wall and splaying his hand out, I smash his fingers with the gun over and over again. He screams in agony as the bones shatter. "Next time you consider hurting a woman who has put her trust in you, remember these broken fingers are nothing compared to what I'll do to you if I find out about it."

I get to Natalie's room and knock softly. "Come in," I hear through the door. I walk in and see Natalie lying on the bed, the doctor sitting next to her, and Cecilia standing next to Natalie, holding her hand. Cecilia is like the madam of the club. Her entire job is to take care of the women and make sure they're safe. She ensures they're all on birth control and are tested regularly, as well as makes sure they are happy. Not a single woman is here against her will, and every one of the women are more than compensated for their services.

When my father first moved our family here, my mom was the madam of the bordello. When I took over the club ten years ago, she passed the torch to Cecilia.

I know my parents are hoping one day Cecilia and I will get married. Cecilia's dad, Stefan Ricci, is as close to a brother as it gets for my father. My grandfather took him under his wing years ago, and it would give the family great pleasure to have us marry and make everyone legally related. A grandchild together would make us family by blood. While she's a decent fuck, it's not happening.

"How's she doing, doc?" I direct my question at Vivian Fox, the on-call doctor for the mansion, but I give Natalie my full attention. I don't like to see my girls hurt, especially by a piece of trash corrupt senator like Weston Hightower.

"She has some tearing in her vaginal walls but no internal bleeding. I'm giving her an antibiotic to be on the safe side because of what he put in her."

I run my fingers over her neck where that asshole choked her. There's a bright red ring around the entire length of her throat that's already turning purple, the first hint of a bruise forming. "Does your throat hurt?" Natalie nods softly, tears filling her eyes. "I made sure he was punished, and he'll never be back here again. Take a few days off and get some rest, okay?"

"Okay." I can see the hurt and betrayal shining through in her eyes over the fact a man she cared about used his power and strength to hurt her.

"I want you to speak with Dr. Simone before you go back to work." Gladius Simone is a therapist all the women see. According to my mom, a woman selling her body for money can make even the strongest crumble, so I make sure every woman who works for me sees the therapist. If she doesn't feel they are in the right mind, they don't work here.

I walk Vivian out and thank her for coming so quickly. I can see the disdain evident in her eyes—she wants to say something but the amount of money she gets paid keeps her from speaking her mind.

"I'll make sure everyone knows Senator Hightower is forbidden to step foot on these grounds," I say to Cecilia after the doctor leaves.

"Thank you, *amore*." Cecilia gives me a kiss on my cheek, her hands run up my body, and her perky tits rub against my chest. She lingers a little too long, her wet lips remaining on my flesh, then she moves her mouth over to kiss my lips.

"Not out here, Cecilia." She pouts but nods in understanding. She knows I don't fuck around where everyone can see. I have a reputation to uphold. Touching and fucking stays behind closed doors.

Taking her hand in mine, I pull her into my office. It's on the first floor, along with the restaurant, the bar, and the common area, as well as the private rooms. On this floor, there is also the staff kitchen. All the ladies, including Cecilia, sleep on the second floor. The east wing is for the women who work as escorts, and the west wing is for the rest of the staff. My living quarters are on the third floor by itself, and I never bring anybody to my room. Bedrooms are intimate, and nothing about what I do with Cecilia or any woman is meant to be intimate. It's nothing more than a fuck, and whoever I'm with, especially Cecilia, needs to remember that.

Once we get to my office, I don't bother to remove her clothes. She's been getting too emotionally attached lately and needs to remember she'll never be anything more than a fuck.

Pulling her dress up to her waist, I push her underwear to the side and stick two fingers inside her to make sure she's wet. She quickly undoes my pants, pushing them to the ground, then she reaches into my briefs to pull my dick out.

Grabbing her by her hair, I turn her around and bend her over the edge of my desk, her face pressed against the wood, her ass up in the air. I rip open a condom, roll it over my hard length, then shove my cock into her cunt, fucking her relentlessly until we both find our release.

Once we've both come, I tuck myself back into my briefs and pull my pants up. Cecilia turns around with hearts in her eyes. At some point, I'm going to have to stop fucking her. She wants all types of shit I can't give her. Shit I'm not *willing* to give her.

"I need to get back to work." I open the door, making it clear it's time for her to leave. Money doesn't get made on its own after all.

Chapter Two

ARIA

THE ROOM IS DARK AND QUIET. EVEN THOUGH I KNOW at least one person is home, it's calm. I try to stay relaxed, but it's hard. It's during quiet moments like now, my heart starts beating erratically and I know if I don't get what I need soon, I'll have a full-blown panic attack. You would think I'd welcome the quietness, but the problem with the quiet is, it's like the calm before the storm. My brain goes into overdrive, wondering what will happen once the storm arrives. With each storm, I'm destroyed little by little, and one day the storm will be so strong, it'll leave nothing but destruction in its wake.

Lying in my bed—which is nothing more than a mattress on the ground with a single sheet and pillow—with a worn-out copy of my favorite romance novel open, I try to focus on the words, but I can't. My hands are shaking and my heart feels like it's going to beat out of my chest. It's been quiet for too long.

I read the same line three more times and give up, closing the book. I remember when I begged for the book, saying I needed something to do down here in the quiet isolation. He forced me to earn that book in ways I can't bring myself to think about. Now I can't even concentrate long enough to finish reading a book I have read dozens of times. At first, I lived in fear, my brain conjuring up the worst-case scenarios. Now that I've lived them, it's hard to switch my brain off.

The drugs help. I know I've become addicted to them, but when it's the only way to shut your body down, the addiction doesn't matter. Survival is all I know now.

I hear the front door slam shut and know he's home, and by the way he's stomping around there's a good chance he's pissed about something. I close my eyes and pray he won't come down here. There's nothing he can give me that's worth the consequences of him coming down here.

His assistant, Derek, is the only person I need. He gives me the drugs I crave to calm my nerves. He'll make my hands stop shaking, my heart stop thumping, and my body and mind shut off. Derek gives. Weston, on the other hand, takes. He takes and takes from me, and at this point, I feel like I have nothing left to give.

The door creaks open and a bright light shines through. I quickly cover my eyes, unable to recall the last time I saw light other than through the small slats in the windows that give off just enough natural light for me to read my book. My world, which used to be a bright canvas, has been stripped of all color. The heavy footsteps make each step creak as a shadow makes its way down. When I see it's Weston, my heart plummets.

Take.

He's here to take.

Not give.

"Spread your fucking legs." He stalks toward me. Then roughly grabbing ahold of my ankles, he pulls my body toward the edge of the bed, my head hitting the cement wall then getting dragged down.

"I—I need something." It's stupid to beg for what I need, knowing he doesn't care, but I'm desperate. He only drugs me to make me stop screaming, stop fighting him. He prefers me almost comatose so he can do whatever he wants to me.

"You need to shut your fucking mouth!" He backhands me so hard I almost blackout. "I can't wait until you turn twenty-two so I can get rid of your fucking whore ass!" Twenty-two seems to be the magic number. For what? I have no clue, and while I have no clue how long I've been down here, I imagine I have at least another year or so until I turn twenty-two.

I close my eyes and wish for the drugs he refused to give me. If he would've given them to me, I would be somewhat numb during this horrific nightmare.

Take.

Take.

Take.

Even without the drugs, I've trained myself to escape my mind during his torture. For several long moments, I'm free.

Free from the pain. Free from the darkness. Free from him.

Smack!

My escape has been short-lived. With one hard slap, I'm right back with him.

Weston is done with me, though. The essence of his crimes against me are smeared against my inner thighs, a sticky reminder that I'll never fully escape.

He grabs my face and turns me to face him. He smacks me again across my face and then walks back up the stairs. Once the door is shut, I go to the small bathroom that's down here to rinse off. I use a small amount of soap, unsure if Weston will replace it once it's all gone. I've had the same bottle of soap since he kidnapped me and locked me down here.

Once I'm done rinsing off, I dry my body with the one towel I have. I don't have any clothes, so I can't get dressed. I take a few sips of the sink water to wet my parched throat then go back to bed. Closing my eyes, I try to imagine my future, what my life will be like if I make it out of here alive, only my visions are no longer clear. The longer I'm down here, the blurrier my future looks.

A little while later, the door opens again and I hold my breath, praying it's Derek. Hearing the soft footsteps padding downward, I know it is, and for a short-lived moment, I allow myself to sigh in relief.

"Do you have something for me?"

Derek looks at me with sadness in his eyes. He's never said it, but I don't think he wants to be a part of Weston's plans—that doesn't stop him from carrying out the orders, though. I don't necessarily blame him for what his boss is doing, but at the same time, he hasn't stopped him or turned him in, either.

"I do." He places the pills on the nightstand. There are five pills total. He usually brings me the pills twice a day, but this morning he didn't come down, leaving me shaking and in need of the numbness— the escape I crave more and more each day.

"Anything else?" Sometimes Derek will bring me down some coke—not often enough, but when he does, I'm able to escape for a bit longer than I do with the pills. It kicks in quick—only a minute after I snort the white powder into my nostrils, I can feel myself floating away to a place where I'm no longer held prisoner.

"Not today."

"Thank you, Derek." I grab all the pills and swallow them dry. I have no idea what they are and I never question it. I know Weston isn't going to give me something that's going to kill me. At least not until I turn twenty-two that is. I imagine they're Xanax or Oxy. I'm not sure, but they work. For a little while, my body and mind can escape the reality of this nightmare.

He leaves the room, and I stare at the ceiling, at the fan whirring around and around, until I finally fall asleep.

Rialto

Chapter Three

GIOVANNI

I VALET PARK MY CAR AND WALK TO THE RESTAURANT inside one of the hotels my family owns here in Vegas, immediately spotting my family at the back table that is permanently reserved for us.

"Oh, Giovanni, how is it we live in the same town, yet I feel like I never see you." My mother, Claudia Valentino, is a beautiful Italian woman, especially for her age. With shoulder-length brown hair, dyed to keep her true age a mystery, steely matching brown eyes with thick fake lashes, and makeup drawn on to hide any flaw one would find to be natural at her age, my mom looks like a woman who has been bred from luxury. She hides her true story well.

She is also the most suffocating mother you will ever meet. She has taken the void from her marriage and used her three sons to fill it. Not a day goes by that I don't receive several calls and messages from my mom attempting to meddle in my life.

Grabbing my biceps, she leans in and gives me a motherly kiss on my cheek then wipes off her lipstick. "I'm sorry, Mom. I've been busy with work."

"That's no excuse to go weeks without visiting your mother, Son." My father pulls me in for a hug, patting me on my back before we sit down at the table. It is then, I notice there are three empty seats. "Who's joining us?" I motion toward the empty chairs, annoyed. I don't like surprises.

"Your brother, Cecilia, and Stefan."

I groan on the inside. My mother does this shit every few months. Calls for a family lunch where she tries to play matchmaker with Cecilia and me. I've told her countless times it's not happening, but she refuses to listen. Typical Italian woman, stubborn as hell.

My brother Nico arrives next, followed by Cecilia and her father. After we all say hello, we order drinks and appetizers from the waiter. He looks scared and I don't recognize him.

"New waiter?" I nod toward the man currently tripping over his own feet.

"Yes, but I'm not sure if he is going to work out. He's the son of Giuseppe." Giuseppe is a business associate of Dad's, in Italy. His son must have moved here and needed a job.

"I hear the senator is giving you some issues," Stefan says, getting straight to business. My mother frowns but doesn't say a word.

"He hurt one of my girls, again. I'll be collecting the debt he owes in full at the end of the month. I'm done doing business with him." My blood starts to boil just thinking about what he did to Natalie a couple weeks ago.

"That's understandable. Just make sure you keep it civil. With him running for another term as senator, we don't want any trouble."

"Understood," I bite out too harshly, even to my own ears.

While my father is reckless, Stefan is levelheaded. He is always looking out for the organization's best interests. My father trusts him with his life, and as a result, so does everyone in my family. Any time we aren't sure what decision to make, we go to Stefan. His daughter, on the other hand, is the opposite of levelheaded. Cecilia is cutthroat when she wants something. She doesn't think about the consequences of her actions. She's so used to her dad cleaning up her messes, she knows nothing about ramifications of one's actions in the real world. She comes across as pure and innocent in front of her father. All she has to do is bat her fake eyelashes and he does everything in his power to make sure she gets what she wants. If the man knew I was banging his daughter with no intention of putting a ring on her finger, he might not be so levelheaded.

"He's been falling behind in the polls," Stefan continues. "Ever since his wife passed away, he's been known to have some anger issues, even slipped a few times in public."

"His anger issues are now irrelevant," I quip, already over this conversation.

"Doesn't he have a stepdaughter?" Nico joins in. "I saw some pictures of her a while back. She's smoking fucking hot."

"Nico," our mom scolds. "Watch your language."

"I don't give a fuck about his personal life or his hot daughter. As long as he pays me back every goddamned last penny he owes me, his business is his business."

"Giovanni," my mom chides at the use of my language.

"I read she went missing," Nico adds.

"Yes, right after her mother died. The press questioned the senator, but he asked for his personal life to remain private, saying his stepdaughter needed to grieve," Stefan informs us. As much of an asshole as Hightower is, it wouldn't surprise me if that girl ran for the hills. All this talk about Hightower makes me realize I haven't heard from him since the day he ran out of my club with his balls in his hands.

My mom cuts in, changing the subject. "I am thinking of doing a family vacation this summer. Maybe May or June, all of us in Atlantis." She smiles excitedly.

My father nods, returning her smile. "Anything you want, Claudia." You'd think, with the way he treats her, she hangs the moon. But if so, then why does he seek pussy elsewhere?

"That sounds good, Mom. Just let me know when."

"Yeah, a trip to the Bahamas sounds good. Maybe Mario can join us." Nico pulls out his phone, most likely texting our brother.

"Cecilia, would you be able to go?" *Real subtle, mom...*

"I think so. As long as Giovanni doesn't mind me taking off at the same time as him." Cecilia bats her eyelashes at me, and Nico chuckles under his breath. I give him a pointed look, telling him silently to shut the hell up.

Thankfully, the topic of conversation switches back to work. "I heard from Don you lent one of his girls money." My dad gives me an appreciative smile.

"Yeah, as a personal favor toward him. If she doesn't pay me back on time, he'll owe me the money...or she can work at the club to pay it off. She would definitely be a money maker."

I see Cecilia straighten, and I know I hit a nerve. If it were up to her, there would be no club. She detests the thought of all these women taking attention away from her. I've never admitted it, but I haven't fucked any of the women who work for me. I'd rather her assume I do. If I'm not fucking her, I usually just pick up a woman at one of our hotel bars or clubs. It's just easier that way. My father taught me a long time ago, not to shit where you eat. Fucking the women who work for me would only create an unnecessary shit storm. And yes, I'm aware I'm fucking Cecilia who works for me, but that shit started before she worked for me, and trust me when I say, I've learned my lesson.

"I appreciate you doing him that favor. I know it's not your usual modus operandi." He reaches over and gives me a squeeze on my shoulder. "The bordello is bringing in good money, Son. Nico and I were going over the books recently and I am pleased with the way things are going. The hotels, restaurants, and casinos are all thriving. The economy is improving, and we are in the black.

My only concern is with the Lorenzo family in New Jersey. Mario has been having some issues with shipments going through." He lets out an exhausted sigh. "Last thing I heard, they are wanting to buy back the waterfront property they lost and it's been rumored they're going to try to stop the shipments from coming in. I might need you to go to New Jersey soon. I have some important shipments that'll need to get through without issue and I can't take a chance."

"Whatever you need, Dad." And that's the truth. I would do anything for my family. You don't get to where we are by not remaining loyal to those in your circle.

"*Grazie*, my boy."

After lunch is over, we all go our separate ways. Cecilia asks if I want to take a cab back with her, but I have other things to take care of, so I tell her I'll see her back at the club later.

Half an hour later, I'm standing in the senator's office requesting to speak with him.

"I'm sorry, Sir. He's not seeing anyone without an appointment," his secretary says.

I smile and give her a wink. "Let him know Giovanni Valentino is here to see him. He will make the exception."

She picks up the phone and calls her boss. After a bunch of "yes sirs," she puts the phone down, and giving me a pointed look, huffs out, "He will be with you momentarily."

I smile and walk toward the sitting area. There are several pictures along the walls. A couple of the senator at ribbon ceremonies, one of him shaking an old President's hand. The last one looks like a family picture at a charity event. There are two women with Weston. The woman on his right is beaming brightly, but it looks fake as hell. She's pretty for an older woman. She's clearly younger than Weston but older than the other woman in the picture, who is standing on Weston's other side. This girl is a mini-version of the older woman. She has chocolate brown hair, olive skin, and bright bluish-green eyes. She must be her daughter.

"Such a shame." I turn to face the secretary to give her my attention. "His wife. She was killed in a car accident...well geez, it must have been almost nine months ago. Time sure flies." She frowns.

"The girl in the picture? Is that their daughter?" I point to the one I was just examining.

"That's his stepdaughter. I guess it's a shame about her as well. After her mom died, she dropped out of college at the end of her sophomore year and took off." *Hmm...guess she's not missing.*

"Thank you, Margaret." Weston's voice is clipped. Cold. Not like a man who lost his wife tragically and it hurts to hear about her. More like a man who is hiding something. I tilt my head just a tad and give him a knowing smirk. *I see you, Weston Hightower. Game on.* Extending my hand, I go in for a shake just to fuck with him. He takes my hand in his, his fingers bandaged.

"What happened to your hand, Senator? Looks bad." He pulls his hand back without answering my question and mutters to his secretary to hold all his calls.

The office door closes behind us and I cut right to the chase. "I haven't heard from you. I'm assuming you are busy collecting my money from God knows where."

"I need some more time. Give me two months."

"You have two weeks to pay me in full. I want a percentage now, though."

His one good hand balls into a fist at his side. He's used to being the one in charge and he's holding back from going off on me. He stalks to his desk and opens the safe hidden underneath, taking out a stack of bills. "This is all I have right now."

I take the two stacks of wrapped hundreds and place one into each of the inside of my jacket pockets. "I'll take this, for now. But you owe me the rest in the next two weeks. Don't make me have to look for you, Hightower."

He grimaces but keeps his mouth closed. *Wise choice, Senator.*

Chapter Four

ARIA

THERE'S SHOUTING UPSTAIRS. I SHOULD CARE, BUT I don't. Nothing matters anymore besides taking the drugs that numb me. I can't even tell you how long I have been down in this pit of hell, but it's been long enough that I have been trained like Pavlov's dog to drool over the goods. Popping those pills means temporarily numbing the pain and shame I feel. It means forgetting I'm in a basement with no way out. That I'm being held hostage by my mom's ex-husband, who has lost his damn mind. It means I don't have to remember my mom is dead. That my life will never be the same.

I'm due for a fix, but instead of Derek coming downstairs, he's arguing with Weston. My body is freezing. I'm shivering and I need some damn pills or powder. My head is pounding and my thoughts are running wild and loud. I need something to dim them, to shut them up. I can feel an anxiety attack coming on. Grabbing the thin blanket that doubles as a fitted sheet, I wrap it around me, trying to warm myself up, trying to find comfort.

It's not working.

More shouting.

Can't they argue later? Like after Derek brings me the damn drugs? I mean, seriously, it would take two minutes to come down here, hand me the pills, and walk back upstairs.

The shouting stops.

The door to the basement swings open and I sit up like Pavlov's dog with my hands out, mouth dry, waiting for the drugs to numb me once again.

It's not Derek. It's Weston. *Just great.*

"Get on your fucking knees!" He barks out orders before he even makes it all the way down the steps. I want to argue and beg for my fix, but it'll do no good. If anything, he'll just withhold the drugs to torture me. I drop to my knees, close my eyes, and wait for whatever he has in store for me this time. Since I've been here, it seems Weston comes down once every few weeks, but recently he's been coming down more often.

I can't see him with my eyes closed, but I know when he's in front of me because his hands fist my hair. I try to think about something else—finding my escape, grasping at every fond memory that still lingers.

My mom, our visits to the Hoover Dam, our hiking trips in Red Rock Canyon. I focus on my good memories instead of what's happening to me in this moment, what he's forcing me to do. The pictures I used to take of the scenery during our hikes. How my mom used to stop at various locations and insist I take selfies of us. I swear she did it just to drive me nuts.

"People ruin the photos," I used to tell her. She would laugh and tell me I was wrong, it's the people who make them. I try to hold on to the memories, cling to them like they're my lifeline, but they're getting harder to recall.

Those happy memories melt away like a skillet full of bright crayons all mixing together to make something black and ugly. It matches my heart. I'm decaying and lost.

He grunts, and I shudder away the last of the color in my world.

"Up." He's finished with me and forces me to stand. I open my eyes to see Weston tucking himself back in his pants. "I have company tonight and you're going to entertain them. You understand?" He asks like I really have a choice. It's not often he forces me to have sex with other, but when he does, he usually drugs me up first with the good stuff. While I hate that I've become dependent on drugs, I prefer it that way.

"I..." I close my mouth quickly. I almost slipped.

"You what?" Weston glares at me. "You what?" *Smack!* His palm strikes me across my cheek.

"I need drugs...please," I beg.

"You need drugs?" He looks at me incredulously. "You *need* drugs?" Now he's laughing humorlessly. "You don't *need* shit. I tell you when you need something. And if you ask again, I'll make you wait even longer. Tonight, you'll be sober. You'll entertain these men, and every time you feel them inside of you, you'll remember what a whore you are." He grabs my face with his hand and squeezes my cheeks. "And if you speak one single word, I will tear you apart after they leave."

Leaning down, he gives me a soft kiss on my lips that has me wanting to throw up all over him. "Let's go."

"Upstairs?" Entertaining someone always means them coming down here. I haven't been upstairs since I was forced down here.

"Shut the fuck up. What part of not speaking a single word are you not understanding?"

I follow him upstairs and I'm met with bright lights. My head pounds and I immediately feel dizzy. I haven't eaten in hours, and I'm in desperate need of the drugs to calm me down.

I follow Weston to the living room of the home I have lived in since I was a little girl, and when I look around, I'm shocked at what I see. All the family portraits have been removed, and in their place are cheap looking paintings. I glance at the shelves and see all my mom's knickknacks are gone. It's like he wiped everything of my mom and me from this home.

A myriad of emotions hit me all at once. Anger. Grief. Sadness. Confusion. This was my mother's home. My home. It was our home before it was his, yet he has taken it over and has eliminated any proof that we ever existed. A man who supposedly at one time loved my mother has destroyed any evidence she was ever alive. Who is this man? How did he manage to fool everyone around him?

"Get her cleaned up," Weston whispers to Derek angrily. Derek grabs me by my arm and pulls me into the guest bathroom. The picture frames that used to sit on the sink are gone as is the toothbrush holder I made for my mom when I took art in middle school.

"Jump in the shower and rinse off. Make sure you shave. Do it quickly."

Once I'm done showering and shaving, I step out and dry off, waiting for further instruction. My body is shaking and my head and heart feel like they're going to explode. Derek notices and sighs. "You need to chill out, Aria. Weston isn't going to give you anything until after you're done. Be a good girl and he'll probably give you more."

Chill out? Seriously? I didn't even want this shit! They did this to me. They came into the basement and day after day drugged me to calm me down. Every time I screamed and cried and begged for them to stop and let me out, they shoved pills down my throat or gave me a bump of coke. They did this to me. They made me this way and now I'm supposed to *chill out?*

I don't bother arguing. It's no use. I just need to do as they say. I need to get this over with so I'll get my drugs and be allowed to go back to my room. *My room.* The fact that I'm calling the basement my room sickens me. It's a reminder that I've officially lost hope. That I've accepted I'll most likely spend the rest of my life in that basement.

Derek guides me to the library where there are several men sitting around in the oversized reading chairs my mom and I picked out. They're drinking liquor and smoking cigars, stinking up our once perfect reading room. I remember the nights I used to curl up with my book and read while my mom wrote. She was a mystery romance author and would write for hours. Sometimes she would stop and read me her scenes and ask for my opinion. I shake the memory off because now is not the time to remember. When I remember, I feel, and when I feel, I hurt, and hurting right now isn't going to do me a bit of good.

Taking a closer look, there are four men all over fifty years old. I recognize two of them from the dinners my mom and Weston used to throw. I know for a fact one of them is married with kids, and this knowledge puts the final nail in my coffin. These men have reputations to protect. There isn't a single man in this room who would risk his reputation in order to save me.

"Aria, I think Mr. Nelson would like some attention." Weston points to the fat, slimy-looking man sitting in my favorite reading chair. The man smiles at me, causing me to throw up a little in my mouth.

All the men sit around the room discussing next year's election, the poll numbers, and the campaign donations, like a young woman isn't servicing a man three times her age. My hands continue to shake, still needing something to take the edge off. As my brain tries to find its escape, I hear a door swing open.

"What are you doing here?" Weston's voice sounds different—nervous, shaken. The man forcing himself on me pushes me away while the entire room goes quiet. I hit the floor flat on my butt before turning around to see who's entered.

When I look up, the most beautiful man lock eyes with me. From head to toe, he is the epitome of perfection. Messy chestnut brown hair that looks like he's been running his fingers through it all day, soft brown eyes like milk chocolate that's been warmed up. He's in a three-piece suit, which hugs every inch of his body perfectly. It looks like it was designed just for him. He's tall, well over six feet. But what catches my attention is his smile. It's probably capable of being sweet, but it's not. It's filled with contempt with a bit of humor like he's in on some private joke nobody else is privy to. He towers over Weston, exuding power and confidence. He's sure of himself and of his place in this world. I remember when I had that same feeling, knowing the world was at my fingertips. When I had a bright future.

Normally Weston is the one in control, but right now he's scared. He's cracking his neck like he used to do when my mom would catch him in a lie and he wasn't sure how to get himself out of it. His uninjured hand is opening and closing into a fist, but he's not towering like he usually is, instead he's cowering. Whoever this man is holds more power than Weston.

Then it hits me. I need to speak up, try to save myself. If it doesn't work, I'll be in a world of hurt, but what if it does work? Before I can say something, the man speaks. His eyes leaving mine.

"I heard you were holding an investment meeting tonight, so I figured I would drop by and check on my money. Your time is almost up."

"Weston, I think it would be best if we go." The man who just had his nasty hands on me is now trying to run.

"I think you all should stay. I would imagine what I have to say will interest you. Mr. Nelson, is it?" Mystery man smiles sardonically at the guy who pushed me to the ground, causing him to shut up and frown, and it sends chills straight up my spine. "I could be wrong, but I believe you have invested with Mr. Hightower. Am I right?"

"Well, yes you are. I did."

"Giovanni, there's no need to involve these men. Let's speak in private." Weston's voice is shaky. He's freaking the fuck out, and it kind of makes me smile a little on the inside.

The man Weston just called Giovanni quirks one brow up and tilts his head just slightly to the left, silently shutting Weston up. If I weren't scared of the repercussions, and without any clothes on, I would stand and cheer him on.

"Are you aware that Mr. Hightower owes me a significant amount of money?"

"Weston, is this true?" One of the other men speaks up.

"Gentleman, I can explain."

"You absolutely can explain, Mr. Hightower, right after you show me the progress you've made on getting me my money. I hope you aren't planning to wait until the last second to obtain that amount of money." Giovanni never raises his voice. The way he speaks you'd think he was placing a to-go order at a restaurant, yet his voice is strong and assertive. Every emotion is made known without even needing to yell. This man means business.

"I can pay you back some more of it. I don't have it all. Come with me into my office."

"Rome, Caesar." Giovanni says two names and instantly two big burly men enter the room. They are similar to Giovanni in appearances, both in suits which fit them perfectly—great physique and good looking—but they don't hold the room like Giovanni does. They aren't calm like he is. They must be his backup, his enforcers. They look angry and seem to lack the patience Giovanni has.

The two men grab Weston by his arms to escort him to his office, making me realize I need to speak up now before it's too late.

"I need your help, please." My voice comes out hoarse from recently gagging, so I clear my throat and say it clearer. "I need your help, please."

"Shut the fuck up, Aria." Weston tries to get out of the men's hold, but they just tighten their grip on him. It gives me the confidence to stand. This might be my only chance to be set free.

"H-He...Weston...He's holding me captive. Please, can you call the police?" I stand, and then remembering I'm naked, I wrap one arm around my chest to cover my breasts, and with my other hand,

I try to cover my sex the best I can.

Giovanni assesses me for a few moments. "Who are you?"

"She's nobody! Don't worry about her!" Weston's outburst has Giovanni smirking. Weston just showed his cards.

Moving closer to Weston, Giovanni lets out a soft humorless chuckle. "I think I will worry about her because you seem extremely worried about her. Now shut your mouth." He walks over to me until we're only a few inches apart. "Who are you?"

"I—I'm Aria. My mom died...well, I'm not sure how long ago. But he's been holding me captive in the—"

"Shut the fuck up, Aria!" Weston bellows, effectively cutting me off, and for the first time Giovanni shows a hint of anger. He stalks over to Weston and punches him right in the face. His head jerks to the side and blood instantly pours from his mouth. "I told you to shut up."

"Can you please call the police?" I beg.

Giovanni walks slowly back toward me. Instinctively, I tighten my arms around myself. He studies me for a moment before he raises his hand to my face. I flinch out of habit, fearful he's going to strike me, but instead he wipes a falling tear from my cheek, his face completely devoid of all emotion. "Please," I repeat.

"No, I'm sorry but I can't do that." His hand leaves my cheek, taking its warmth with it.

"No." The word is meant to be a question, but I heard him correctly. It hits me that this man isn't going to save me. More tears well up in my eyes, and my chin trembles. My hands are shaking, and I'm about to lose it. A sob escapes and tears of hopelessness gush down my cheeks.

"No." I repeat the word one more time to force myself to accept it.

"Maybe I'll just take her as payment." *He'll what? Did this guy just volunteer to take me as Weston's payment?*

"Boss."

"No fucking way."

One of Giovanni's men and Weston both speak at the same time, sounding as confused as I feel, but Giovanni ignores them both, keeping his eyes on me for a beat longer. I think maybe he's going to save me, but then he turns his back on me and walks out of the room with Weston and his men.

"Please!" I implore as the door closes, leaving me in a room with Weston's associates. I drop to my knees at how cruel life can be.

Chapter Five

GIOVANNI

"IT'S A PLEASURE DOING BUSINESS WITH YOU." I STAND and shake the hand of a high-power defense attorney. He's married with two kids and he's just paid a small fortune to be an exclusive member of La Stella's Gentleman's Club. Just another example of a man not being faithful. But who the hell am I to judge when it means more money in my pocket.

"Thank you, Mr. Valentino."

I walk him out of my office and down the hall to the common room to meet Cecilia, so she can help him pick out the woman he'd like to spend time with. *I'm looking for a companion. It's not about sex,* he said. If I had a dollar for every man who walked through my doors and tried to convince me and themselves that it's not about sex, I would be even richer than I already am.

"Cecilia, this is Mr. Steele. Please show him around. He's looking for a companion."

"Will do, Sir." She beams at Mr. Steele, giving him a flirtatious wink.

I walk over to the bar and have a seat on one of the cushioned stools, in need of a drink. "Emilio, whiskey neat."

"Sure thing." He makes my drink and sets it on the bar top.

As I sip the whiskey, enjoying the warmth it brings, my mind can't get off the beautiful woman at the senator's house. When she begged me to save her, it took everything in me not to pick her up and take her out of that house. And the fact I even considered it, scares the ever-loving shit out of me. What got me was the desperation in her eyes. I've been raised around whores my entire life. For God sakes, I lost my virginity to a whore at this bordello, courtesy of my father when I had barely hit puberty, who told me it was time to become a man.

But the difference is, every one of those women choose to spread their legs. The women I employ make the choice to have sex with men for money. No woman here is ever forced to do anything she doesn't want to do. While a member has the right to request a particular woman, she in return has the right to deny him.

And watching that girl—who I recognized from the picture in the senator's office—looking so helpless in the living room, gutted me. When she informed me he was holding her captive, I saw red. But taking her then would have made me look weak. I'm a businessman, and my only business with Weston is the money he owes me.

I tried to ignore her. I tried to deal with the issue at hand, but when she stood and looked at me with such pleading, broken eyes, there was no ignoring the beautiful woman. Shiny golden-brown hair came down in waves along the outline of her face. When she looked up at me as I wiped the falling tear from her cheek, her eyes nearly knocked me on my ass. Deep sea-green, clear and luminous, with a darker blue rim around the outer part of the iris—in contrast to her brown hair and bronzed skin—had me in a trance.

But what got me the most was how dim her eyes were as she pleaded with me. The light in her eyes had been switched off. As she stood in front of me—naked and vulnerable—trying to cover her clearly malnourished self, I knew right then and there I would give this woman anything she asked for. And so, I had no choice but to turn my back on her. If I took her, I would have to keep her. She would be Weston's payment and I wouldn't be able to let her go. She would be forced from one prison to another, so to speak. *But at least here, she would be fed properly and taken care of.*

My chest tightens as I think how beautiful she'd be if her eyes were lit up once again. *How badly I want to be the reason her eyes light up, again.* How defeated she looked when she realized I wasn't going to be her savior. *How badly I want to be her savior.* Fuck! But I wouldn't be her savior. I would be her capturer. Sure, I'd be taking her out of that shitty situation but only to bring her into another one. But on the other hand, she's better off being held captive here than with that piece of crap senator.

Without thinking another thought, I put my drink down and

text Johnny to bring the car around. It's time to pay the good senator one last visit. It's been thirty days. I'll be getting paid today one way or another.

We get to the senator's house and his car isn't in the driveway, so I knock and wait. When nobody answers, I give Johnny a nod. "Let's take a look around."

Johnny chuckles and goes about breaking into the house. Once the door is open, I start searching through the house. I check the living room, reading room, kitchen. Nobody appears to be home. Then I hear water running.

"Do you hear that? Where's that water coming from?"

Johnny looks around. "I think from here." He points to a door off the kitchen.

"I'm going down to check it out. Wait here. Text Rome and Caesar and tell them to meet us here."

"You got it, Boss."

Opening the door, I notice a dark staircase. Looking back into the kitchen, I see a light switch next to the door. I flip it on and the stairs illuminate. I pull my gun out just in case and walk cautiously down the steps. When I get to the bottom, the water is being turned off and out stumbles the woman from before. Only this time, her face is completely bruised. She's sporting a fat lip and two black eyes. She's naked once again and there are black and blue marks marring her body. She's hunched over and limping slowly to her bed. She looks up and sees me, her eyes going wide for a split second.

"Great. You here to cause more trouble?" she hisses, wrapping herself up in the nasty looking blanket on her bed. She isn't even phased by the fact I'm holding a gun in my hand. I place the gun back into my waistband and advance toward her.

"Trouble?" I question.

"Yeah, trouble. When you came here the other day and I opened my mouth. As you can see, Weston wasn't too thrilled with me begging for you to save me."

My heart squeezes and my breath catches. I'm the reason for her looking like she was run over by a train several times. I didn't even think about the fact that Weston would punish her. When I saw her, she was giving old man Nelson head. They weren't beating her. Fuck! I should have seen this coming. He brutalized Natalie twice. I was so busy trying to get Aria out of my head, I ignored what was going on right in front of me.

"Johnny!" I call up the stairs.

"Are you guys going to rape me?" The woman who was just giving me lip suddenly looks at me with fear that just about has me dropping to my knees.

"No, sweet girl. I'm about to get you out of here."

For the first time, she smiles, and the way it fucks with my heart, I know I'm the one in trouble.

Chapter Six

ARIA

They are the sweetest words I've heard in a long time. He's going to get me out of here. With the dirty blanket still wrapped around me, I try to stand but my body isn't cooperating. I have been beaten and taken advantage of every which way over the last week to the point that I have blacked out several times. I'm convinced I have several broken ribs, and the blood coming from my vagina can't be a good thing. On top of all that, I haven't been given a single drug in days, so I'm feeling every ounce of pain and I'm pretty sure my body has been detoxing cold turkey.

Taking the blanket off of me, he removes his jacket and wraps it around my body. It's thick and warm and smells clean with a bit of a woodsy scent to it. Carefully, he picks me up and, holding me bridal style, walks us up the stairs. There's a man holding the door open, the one he called Johnny. He gives me a sad smile, one that looks a lot like pity, but I ignore it. I'm getting out of here. They can look at me however the hell they want to. We get upstairs and make it to the foyer when the door swings open and in walks Weston along with Derek, and behind them are the two men I saw with Giovanni the last time he was here.

Giovanni sets me down, still holding onto me, but I'm already planning my escape. There's no way I've made it this far, only to be shoved back down in that basement. I see the side door leading off the kitchen and wonder how long it would take me to hobble to it and try to make a run for it. I know realistically I wouldn't get past all these men, but at this point I'm so desperate, I'm willing to chance it.

Like he can hear my thoughts, Giovanni leans down and whispers, "If you run, I will catch you. You're mine now." The heaviness of his words spread goosebumps down my arms.

Weston must hear him because he starts to freak out. "You can't take her. She's not yours!" He stalks toward us, and just as I'm about to make a run for it, Giovanni picks me back up in his arms. His men grab Weston and hold him back. He starts bucking his body, attempting to flee the men. Giovanni holds me tighter, walking around Weston and his men.

"I'll meet you back at the club," he says to his men. "Just make sure his heart is still beating when you're done with him."

"She's mine, Valentino!" Weston spits out.

Giovanni turns around and gives him that same smile I fell for the other night. "Consider your debt paid in full. You're welcome. And if you so much as breathe near her, I will personally end your life. She's mine now." Then he walks us out of the house, Johnny opening and closing the door behind us.

The cold air hits my face and I shiver. It's been months since I've been outdoors. I take a moment to inhale the fresh air before Johnny opens the passenger door to the Cadillac sitting in the driveway. Giovanni places me on the seat then waits for me to move over before he edges in next to me, closing the door.

"Where to, Boss?"

"To the club," Giovanni confirms.

"You got it."

After a few minutes of silence, I get up the courage to speak. I don't know how far it is to this club, but I know I only have a short time to convince him to let me go. Where I'll go? I have no clue. I have no money, no clothes, and I'm in desperate need of medical attention. I need something to take the pain away. At this point, I'll take anything. My heart rate starts to pick up, my body going into emotional overdrive as I work myself up. An anxiety attack is building quickly, and I can't do anything to stop it. "Can y-you please let me go?" I'm freezing cold and my teeth are chattering. My hands are shaking and I'm on edge, needing something to calm me before I hit rock bottom. I need something to numb me before my body goes into full-on panic mode. My head's pounding and it feels like I'm having a heart attack.

Giovanni looks up from his phone and puts it back in his pocket, twisting to face me. Framing my face between his hands, he locks eyes with me. "What drugs are you on?"

Pulling out of his grip, I look down, ashamed of what my life has become. "I'm not a druggie. Can you please just let me go?"

"You're coming off of something. Don't lie to me." With his thumb and forefinger, he lifts my chin, so I'm forced to look at him.

"You are mine now. What drugs are you on?" *Mine.* That one word causes me to slip over the ledge. I yank my face from his touch. My hand goes to the door handle in an attempt to escape, not even caring that if I jump out and the car is going too fast, I'll likely hit the concrete and die. I'd rather my life end now and join my mom in heaven than live another day in this hell on earth.

Hands grab my waist and suddenly I'm being pulled into Giovanni's lap. My brain and body finally snap. "I'm not yours! I'm nobody's! You can rape me and drug me and force me into another basement, but I will *never* be yours!" A great tremor overtakes me as sobs break free from the deepest part inside me. My fists pound against his chest as I beg him to let me go. Streams of fear and devastation flow faster than my elevated heartbeat as I release every pent-up emotion I've had to keep down. I have no idea what this man is going to do to me for my outburst, but I can't stop. It's like being in the middle of a tornado—the basement door has been swung open and there's no closing it. All I can do is ride out the storm and pray I make it through alive.

"It's okay," he says soothingly as he rubs my back. "It's okay, sweet girl. Let it out." And I do. I yell and scream and continue using his chest as a punching bag. I cry and beg, and when my body and mind and heart can't take it anymore, I shut down and everything goes black.

Chapter Seven

GIOVANNI

WHAT THE HELL DID I JUST DO? I'M NOT SAYING I'M A standup guy because that would be a boldfaced lie. I'm in the fucking mob for crying out loud. I own a bordello—a fucking whorehouse! Albeit a high class one, but still a whorehouse, nonetheless. I've killed when necessary and sometimes just because it's what I felt should be done. But never have I resorted to kidnapping a young woman—or any woman for that matter.

I went into the senator's house with the intention of finding her, but I wasn't prepared for what I would do once I found her. I wasn't prepared to see her beaten and bruised and broken...so fucking broken. One look at her and my heart felt like it was put through a grinder and was bleeding out. The look of pain in her eyes nearly brought me to my knees. Without even thinking about the repercussions of my actions, I picked her up and took her. Taking her as payment means she's mine and there's no going back on that.

Not for her own safety and sure as fuck not for my reputation.

At first, when I took her, she was quiet. I knew she was hurt, but I figured she'd be okay until we got to the club and I could have Vivian come check her out. But then when she tried to jump out of my car, which was doing at least seventy down the highway, I realized she wasn't okay. I pulled her into my arms and listened to her while she lost it until she finally blacked out from exhaustion.

Now, as she lies against my chest, passed out in the back of the car, I contemplate all the ways I'm going to torture Senator Weston Hightower before I bury him alive for physically and emotionally hurting this woman.

"Boss, is she okay?" That's a loaded fucking question, but I'm assuming he's simply referring to her going from losing it on me to being deathly quiet. I can feel her chest rising and falling so I know she's alive.

"I think she had a nervous breakdown and she appeared to be coming off drugs. I'm going to need to get Dr. Fox to come out. I think she's in pain. It looks like her ribs might be broken."

"Umm...Boss..."

"Yes?"

"I don't want to overstep..."

"Just spit it out." We've been friends for damn near our entire lives. The guy never cares when he oversteps.

"Are you kidnapping this woman? Because if you are, you know I have your back. I just need to know what to expect. Will someone be looking for her other than the Senator?"

"Her mom was killed in a car accident and from what my brother told me, everybody assumed she took off to grieve for her mom. I don't know all the details, but it seems the Senator has been holding her captive, drugging her and forcing himself on her, as well as sharing her with other men."

Johnny swears under his breath. His eyes meet mine in the rear-view mirror and we both silently agree. As soon as it's possible, the senator is fucking dead.

A few minutes later Johnny speaks up again. "You didn't answer my question. Are you kidnapping her?" He quirks his eyebrow up, his telltale sign that he needs the truth. I can't bring myself to say the words, so I look out the window. I've never lied to him and I'm not about to start now. Am I kidnapping her? I would like to say no. I'm saving her from the senator. But is it saving someone when you're forcing them into a situation just as dangerous? Johnny lets out an exasperated sigh and the rest of the drive is made in silence.

When we arrive back at the mansion, Aria is still sleeping. Johnny opens the car door and carefully I carry her inside. "Let's bring her around the side," I suggest. It's early evening, and with all the cars lined up, there will be several people in the common room and bar. No need to draw attention to myself and the semi-naked woman I'm carrying in who looks to be half-dead.

"Where are you bringing her?" Johnny walks ahead to open the door to the side of the club. There are several available rooms in the workers' wing and a couple empty ones where the girls stay, but my chest tightens at the thought of her being so far away from me in her fragile condition. "My room."

Johnny's steps falter a moment. "Your room, Boss?"

"Yes, my room," I snap at him, irritated he's questioning my choice. Aria stirs in my arms before her face goes back to nuzzling against my chest. "She's hurt and I need to get her checked out." I get her into my room and gently lay her down on my bed. I notice she has some dried blood on the insides of her thighs, but I don't want to touch her there, so I grab a towel and lay it down under her, then pull the blankets over her to keep her warm. "Call Dr. Fox and tell her I need her immediately," I demand before Johnny leaves.

After changing out of my suit and into a pair of sweatpants and a shirt, I use the bathroom, brush my teeth, and get ready for Dr. Fox to arrive. I grab one of my shirts and a pair of boxers for her to put on once she wakes up since she's still in only my jacket. Then I grab the garbage can from the bathroom. Once Aria wakes up, we'll have a long night ahead of us. Hell, depending on how badly she's hurt and how bad her addiction is, we might have a long couple weeks ahead of us.

Quickly grabbing my laptop from my office, I settle into my reading chair in the corner of the room to work while I wait for the doctor to arrive. Nico sent over the quarterly earnings for La Stella and as usual I'm in the black. The gentleman's club makes more money than most of the business ventures my family owns. When I took it over, I made significant changes and obviously for the better. I made it more exclusive by requiring a membership and allowing only powerful and wealthy men access.

When I told my father I was gutting the place and renovating it completely, he thought I was crazy. My mom thought it was a wonderful idea and it feels damn good that in the last ten years since I took over, I've always been in the black with my numbers steadily increasing.

I attempt to read over the reports probably ten times before I accept I'm not in any place to deal with work. Instead, I send an email to my housekeeper requesting for her to order clothes, under garments, and toiletries for Aria. Not knowing her size, I have her order a couple different sizes.

There's a soft knock on my door and I check on Aria to make sure she hasn't woken yet. After setting my laptop down, I open the door to find Cecilia and Dr. Fox standing together. "Giovanni, I didn't know Dr. Fox was needed." Cecilia gives me a perplexed look then tries to peer around me to see who is in my room. I block her view, closing the door behind me and stepping out into the hallway.

"Thank you for coming, Dr. Fox. The woman I need you to take a look at is sleeping right now. I'm not sure when she'll wake up. If you could wait inside, I just need to speak to Cecilia for a moment alone." After letting Vivian into the room, I close the door. "I'm going to be occupied for a few days, so I am going to need you to be on your A-game with the club. Go to Johnny first, but if you need me, I'll be here."

"What's going on, Giovanni?" she questions. Sooner or later, I'm going to need to tell Cecilia about Aria since she'll be here for the foreseeable future, but at the same time, my business isn't her business, and she needs to understand that.

"I'm helping a woman get well. She was drugged and beaten badly."

Cecilia looks at me baffled. "At the club? How was I not aware?"

"No, not in the club. Elsewhere, but she'll be staying here while she's healing."

Cecilia looks past me at my closed door. "In your room? You don't let anyone in your room." Her hand goes to her hip, angrily. Looks like I'm going to have to nip this shit in the bud right now.

"Who I let in my room isn't any concern of yours. Your job is to take care of the escorts, that's it. Nothing more." Cecilia flinches before composing herself. She steps close to me, running her hand down my arm, flipping her switch from angry to sweet.

"Don't act like that, Giovanni. You know I just want to help." Her voice is meant to be seductive, but it doesn't work on me because I'm immune to her fake-ass charm.

I remove her hand from my body. "You can help by making sure the front end is running smoothly and there are no issues with the women or members." I turn my back on her and go into my room, closing the door on her face.

When I step inside, Aria is awake and in tears. Dr. Fox is holding her on the bed while she sobs in her arms. "I- I need something. Please. I-I'm in so m-much pain," Aria hiccups through her gut-wrenching sobs.

"What do you need?" I ask, sitting on the edge of the bed next to the women.

Aria swipes away the falling tears, taking deep breaths until she composes herself. Then she narrows her glossy eyes at me, shooting me a glare like I'm the devil incarnated.

"Are you in the mob?" she seethes. I try to hide my smirk. This woman has some sass to her and she's not stupid. She guessed right on the first try.

"What do you need?" I repeat, ignoring her question. I'm not going to give her drugs, but I need to know what she was on so we can help her kick that shit.

"Xanax or Oxy, please...or..." She contemplates what she's going to say next, her bright red nose scrunching up like she's not sure whether to say what she wants. After a moment of hesitation, she murmurs, "Since you're in the mob, maybe you can get me something stronger. I'm sure you have access to the good stuff."

Holy shit, this woman has no filter. Dr. Fox is quietly listening, her eyes volleying back and forth between Aria and me. "There are no drugs on this property," I growl out. "Whatever the doctor says you can take is what you'll get."

Aria rolls her eyes and scoffs, "Fine. Give me whatever you can and then I need to get out of here." I don't bother to let her know she isn't going anywhere. The doctor might have signed an NDA, but I can't imagine her holding to it if she knew that technically Aria is being held here against her will.

"Sweetie, I'm here to check you out and then we'll see what we can give you for the pain. Can you tell me what happened to you? How long you were in this condition?" Dr. Fox pushes Aria's hair from her face and speaks soothingly to her.

"I'm not sure. I don't even know what today is." I tell her the date and her eyes go wide in shock.

"Oh my God! That asshole had me locked up for nine months! My mom was killed in an accident in May. He took me right before my finals, only a couple weeks after she died, and it's already February! Nine goddamned months!"

Her head drops into her hands as she shakes her head back and forth, mumbling incoherent words through her hands as she chokes on her sobs. I've never felt so helpless in my life. My first thought is that I want to find that piece of shit and kill him. It's the only way I know to try to right this wrong, consequences be damned. But realistically, I'm aware it's not going to make Aria better. Only time will heal her, and even then, she'll never truly be okay. Open wounds eventually heal, but wounds as deep as the ones she's sporting will leave thick scars as a reminder of what she went through.

"Giovanni, can you give us some privacy so I can examine Aria, please?"

As much as I don't want to leave her, I reluctantly get up and go to my sitting room, which is attached to the bedroom, to give them privacy without leaving.

Chapter Eight

ARIA

I WAKE UP IN A SOFT BED, ONE I'VE NEVER SEEN BEFORE, and for a second I get lost in the comfort of the plush pillows and down comforter I'm wrapped up in, wondering how I ended up in this comfy bed. Then everything comes back to me. The basement. Giovanni taking me. Attempting to throw myself out of the moving vehicle. I try to sit up but the pain in my abdomen forces me to stay still.

"Careful, sweetie. I need you to tell me where it hurts." I jump at the sound of a female's voice and see a woman sitting on the edge of the bed next to me.

"Who are you?" I look around to see where I am. I'm in a large room, most likely a master bedroom. The entire room is decorated in dark browns and creams. I'm lying in a king-sized four-poster bed. All the furniture, including the bed, is made of what looks like real mahogany wood. The drapes are closed, leaving the room without light, save for a single lamp next to me. On the wall across from the bed is a roaring fireplace which spans from floor to ceiling with a flat screen television hanging over the mantle.

"My name is Vivian Fox. I am the on-call doctor here at the club. Giovanni asked for me to check you out. Can you tell me what hurts?" Something about the way this woman speaks and smiles softly at me, has me feeling suddenly at ease. She looks to be in her late forties, beautiful sandy blond hair pulled up into a low ponytail with comforting brown eyes that remind me of my mother. She patiently smiles at me and my heart craves the love of my mom.

Ignoring the pain, I sit up to give her a hug, hoping her touch will feel like my mom's. Her being here is the first sense of hope I've had that I will finally be free...or at least safe. After a few minutes of crying in her arms while she simply hugs me without saying a word, I hear the door open, causing me to jump back.

Giovanni walks in, no longer in his suit but in a pair of sweatpants and a shirt that make him look just as alluring as the suit does but in a completely different way. This man screams power no matter what he's wearing.

They ask me some questions and I'm shocked to learn Weston has been holding me captive for close to nine months. In less than two months I'll be turning twenty-one. It felt like I was in the basement for so much longer and to think Weston would have been holding me there for another year, until I turn twenty-two, send shivers straight down my spine.

"Giovanni, can you give us some privacy, so I can check out Aria, please?" Dr. Fox asks. He doesn't appear to be thrilled about leaving me alone, but he gets up and walks out and into what looks like an extension of his room. Maybe a sitting room? I'm not sure. She hands me a mug and I take a large sip. It's cold water and it feels soothing going down my throat.

"Can you tell me what hurts?" she queries.

I put the now empty mug back on the nightstand. "My face. I think my ribs are broken, my stomach is aching, and I'm bleeding heavily from my vagina."

She gives me another soft smile and I appreciate the fact that she doesn't look at me with pity.

"Giovanni, come here, please," she requests.

He walks back into the room. "Everything okay?"

"I'm going to need some equipment. Can you have one of your men bring me the equipment from my trunk, please?"

After Giovanni leaves, Dr. Fox helps me remove Giovanni's jacket and hands me the clothes that are next to the bed. "Go ahead and slip this shirt on for now. I want to check you out before you put on your shorts, though."

"Okay, thank you."

She gently helps me slip the shirt on over my head.

Giovanni knocks once before walking in, and following him inside the room are the three men who work for him, carrying several pieces of medical equipment. "Aria, in case you don't remember.

This is Rome..." He points to a good-looking, dark-haired man who is slightly less built than Giovanni and a few years younger but just as handsome. "...and Johnny."

The man I recognize as Giovanni's driver tilts his head up. He's carrying a piece of what looks like heavy equipment. His biceps are bulging out with veins running downward. His hair is a light brown and longer than the other men. It's slicked back but not greasy. His eyes are a beautiful shade of icy blue and he's sporting a neatly trimmed beard. I must be appraising Johnny too long because Giovanni makes a noise in the back of his throat, which causes the guy he hasn't formally introduced me to yet, to laugh.

"This is Caesar," Giovanni finishes, his words coming out harsher than before.

"If you need anything, please let me know," Caesar says as he sets down the medical bag he's holding and steps over to me, taking my hand in his and giving the top of my knuckles a soft kiss. I flinch from his touch, but I don't pull back.

While Giovanni, Johnny, and Rome all look like men straight out of the Godfather, Caesar gives off a more playful approach. His hair is jet black and curly, and his face is clean shaven making him appear younger than the others. They all have faint accents, which if I had to guess are Italian, but they all speak English perfectly.

Caesar's kiss lingers for a few seconds before Giovanni growls out, "Okay, set the equipment down and get back to work."

The three men all chuckle but do as he says. It's obvious that while they work for Giovanni, they are all friends on some level.

"While you are here, if you need anything. you come to me first. But if I'm not available, you can go to any of those three men. You can trust them, got it?" While I'm here? Does that mean he's going to let me go?

I give Giovanni a small smile and thank the guys. Even though I'm almost ninety-nine percent sure he's going to force me to stay here, I appreciate him trying to make me feel comfortable and safe, especially after having gone so long without feeling either one. Wow! You know your life has reached new levels of craziness when you're thankful your new kidnapper is nicer than your previous kidnapper.

The three men leave, shutting the door behind them, and Giovanni goes back to the sitting room.

"I'm going to do an ultrasound first to see if we can find out why you're bleeding." Dr. Fox lifts my shirt and squirts blue gel on the lower part of my stomach. I flinch from the pain I feel when she presses down. "I'm sorry, sweetie, because of the bleeding, I don't want to go in vaginally unless I have to."

She switches on a monitor, and a black and white screen comes into view. "This is your uterus." She points to the screen. She moves the transducer across my stomach continuing to spread the gel, not saying anything more. The silence is killing me, but I'm trying to let her do her job without asking a million questions.

"What's wrong?" I finally ask.

She turns her face to me, and for the first time since I met her a short time ago, she gives me a look of pity—or maybe sympathy. "You're pregnant. Well, you were. There's no heartbeat. The bleeding you are experiencing is your body naturally miscarrying. I'm so sorry."

The thought of my body carrying a baby from one of the men who have raped me hits me hard. I lurch forward and, grabbing the first thing I can find—the mug I drank my water from—I vomit.

Giovanni rushes to me, holding the trashcan out for me just in time as I hurl again and again until there's nothing left inside my stomach. My abdomen screams in pain, but it's the least of my concerns right now.

"What happened?" His voice stays calm, but I can hear the worry in his tone.

I finally stop heaving and answer him, knowing Dr. Fox won't. "I was pregnant and I'm losing the baby." *Baby.* The thought of a helpless little baby in my uterus brings tears of devastation to my eyes. The baby might have been half one of them, but the other half was me. It was my job to protect it and I didn't. I should have known there was a baby in me. I should have protected my stomach better.

"Do we need to get her to a hospital?" Giovanni sounds worried.

"No," Dr. fox says, answering Giovanni's question, then directs her words towards me. "Aria, your body is currently doing what it's made to do. I'm going to prescribe you something for the pain and a prescription to prevent infection. I'm also going to prescribe you a small dose of Xanax. But I'm going to have Giovanni give them to you. I don't want you taking too much. Those drugs are highly addictive and we need to slowly ween you off them. Don't worry, I'll help you. I'll come back in a few days to check on you." Dr. Fox put her hands softly on my cheek. "I'm sorry for your loss, sweetie." And then as if she can hear the thoughts running through my head, she adds, "This was not your fault."

"I should have protected it." A single drop of grief wells up in the corner of my eye. I'm so sick of crying but the blows keep coming one after the next. When will it stop?

"You were just under twelve weeks along. Your body knows how to protect itself. I know you are thinking this miscarriage was caused from you getting beat up, but you can't know that. Miscarriages happen every day. It's the body's way of saying something isn't right. There's nothing you could've done differently."

I know deep down miscarrying is for the best, especially given the circumstance, but it still hurts to know there was something precious inside of me. Even if created from rape, it was still a baby with a beating heart. I'm not sure if I would have been able to make the decision to abort the baby or if I was still with Weston, if he would have given me the choice one way or another, so maybe it was fate's way of handling the situation for me.

She digs into her briefcase and pulls out a couple sanitary pads. "Mr. Valentino, please give us some more privacy, and can you please make sure Aria gets more sanitary pads as well as underwear? She will be bleeding for a few more days."

Giovanni looks from the doctor to me, his eyes haunted. He nods in understanding, and after placing the waste basket outside, goes back to the sitting room. Once he's gone, Dr. Fox helps me place a sanitary pad along the inside of the boxers Giovanni left out for me since I have no clothes.

"Let's look at the rest of you." She begins to feel across my torso, and I jump once she gets to the right side. "Take a deep breath for me."

I breathe in and out, the pain in my stomach radiating through me. "That hurts," I yelp when she hits a super sensitive area.

"It looks like you have a couple bruised ribs on your right side. Let me check to make sure they aren't broken." She walks over to a large suitcase and opens it up, pulling some weird looking machine out.

"What is that?" I question.

"A portable x-ray machine." After she's done setting it up, she has me lie still while she takes pictures. After assessing them, she says, "They aren't broken which is encouraging. I don't want to wrap them up because it can make breathing more difficult." She grabs something from her briefcase and snaps it in half. "Keep this icepack on you." Wrapping a small towel around it, she places it on my side, then tapes it on gently.

"It's like you're the doctor's version of Mary Poppins," I joke, trying to make light of this entire horrendous situation.

"Yes, I guess I am." She laughs and I join in as well—the sound foreign to my ears—causing my ribs to ache in pain.

"Careful. I don't want you to get up unless you must. I know you're going to want to shower and you'll need to use the bathroom, but make sure someone helps you." Dr. Fox moves up the bed to look at my face. I can't even imagine how bad I look. If my pain is any indication, I most likely look like a truck ran me over then reversed to do it all over again.

After running a cleaning wipe over my forehead and face, which stings like a bitch, Dr. Fox says, "This should have gotten stitches, but it's too late. I'll glue it the best I can." She works on my face for a few minutes then gets up to throw the garbage away.

"I want to check your vaginal walls. I know you're bleeding and normally I would wait, but I want to make sure nothing has been damaged. I did an image test while doing the ultrasound so I know there's no internal damage, which is a good sign."

After putting gloves on, she gently pushes my legs apart and begins to check me out. My vagina is extremely sore and I feel myself wincing at her touch. I had assumed the bleeding was from the rough sex I experienced a few days ago—it didn't start until after Weston and his friends left me in the basement.

"Okay, everything seems normal. I didn't feel any tears. I'll check you again once you're done bleeding." She takes the gloves off and throws them away. She's gone for a few minutes, during which time I hear the sink turn on. She must be washing her hands. Knowing we're about done and she's about to leave me, my hands begin to shake, my heartbeat going erratic. I feel another anxiety attack coming on. Dr. Fox walks back inside the room and starts putting her equipment into her suitcases.

"Dr. Fox, I know you're prescribing a low dose of Xanax, but do you think maybe you can give me a little more?" My voice wavers as my heartbeat picks up speed.

She comes over next to me and, taking both my hands in hers, smiles softly. "You've been given drugs for quite some time, sweetie. You don't want to be dependent on them. I am going to recommend you begin to see a psychiatrist as soon as possible. She can be someone for you to talk to, to work through what you've been through, and she can also put you on the appropriate medications and doses. I'll let Mr. Valentino know of a couple I recommend. Ones who specialize in what you've been through."

"Okay, but my heart hurts right now." I try to grip my chest. I'm working myself up, but I can't stop it once it starts. Everything that's happened these last several months is weighing down on me. It's like I'm drowning and can't come up for air. With each breath I try to take, another weight is added, sinking me further down, suffocating me. I sit up, starting to freak out, beginning to hyperventilate, needing to take a breath. My hands clutch my chest, but it's no use. The weights are too heavy. I can't push them off. I can't come up for air.

Dr. Fox's soothing voice breaks through. "Breathe slowly, Aria. Copy me." She takes a deep breath in, then lets it out, and I follow her lead, focusing on her breathing. We do this for a few minutes, slowly taking deep breaths in, then just as slowly breathing out, until my body begins to calm down, each weight being removed one by one, the heaviness slowly leaving my chest, allowing me to finally come up for air and take a much needed, calming breath.

"Good, there you go." I continue to breathe slowly, copying her motions. Once my heart has slowed back to its normal pace, she opens a pill bottle. "You see. You calmed yourself down without taking a pill. We're going to get you on the right dose, but until then, take one of these to help you get some rest."

Giovanni walks over to Dr. Fox and begins to pick up the equipment, moving it to the side. "Just leave that machine here, so I can check her in a few days," she instructs him. Then turning to me, she says, "Aria, if you need anything at all, you call me, okay?" She hands me her card.

"Thank you." I lean over and give her a hug.

Giovanni and her both leave, closing the door behind them. Snuggling up into the sheets, my body starts to feel numb. It must be the pill she gave me to help me sleep. For the first time in a long time, I fall asleep without the fear of what I might wake up to.

Rialto

Chapter Nine

GIOVANNI

ARIA HAS BEEN SLEEPING ON AND OFF THE LAST FEW days. The sleeping pills, anti-anxiety meds, and painkillers Vivian left for her have helped tremendously to get her through the miscarriage and bruised ribs. I've been sleeping in the chaise lounge in the corner of the room because I couldn't bring myself leave her. I'm almost positive my neck has a permanent kink in it, but leaving her to sleep somewhere more comfortable wasn't an option. When Vivian informed Aria that she had miscarried, my heart broke for her. She can't be more than twenty-one, maybe twenty-two years old, but she has experienced more loss than any young woman should ever have to. Loss of her mom. Loss of her life when she was taken. Loss of her baby. Shit, probably loss of her sanity. I placed a call to a psychiatrist who is willing to make house calls and have her scheduled to come out next week.

The first twenty-four hours on the low dose of the anti-anxiety drugs had Aria freaking out when she was awake. I watched Vivian bring her down from her potential anxiety attack when she was here, so when one started, I did what the doctor did and was shocked that it actually worked.

Aria asked for something to read, so I had Johnny go to the store and pick her up an iPad. I installed all the book apps and set up her account with one of my credit cards. I'm not sure of the situation with Weston yet, but as far as I can tell, Aria doesn't have any access to money. We haven't talked about anything as I don't want to overwhelm her with too much too soon. She's been through enough as it is.

Knowing I just gave her a sleeping pill and it'll keep her knocked out for at least a few hours, I shower and throw on a suit to check on the club. When I get to my office and begin going over the books, there's a knock on my door. "Come in."

Cecilia saunters in, her high heels clacking against the marble floor. "Nice of you to join society again. Does that mean whatever *situation* you had going on in your room is taken care of?"

Not liking the fact that she's referring to Aria as a situation, my voice takes on a harsher tone than intended. "My *situation* isn't any concern of yours. Her name is Aria and until I get things figured out, she will be staying here."

"In your room?" Cecilia's voice comes out in an annoying whine.

"Jealousy is not a good look on you." I raise a brow, silently ending this conversation.

"Fine. Your mother has invited us to dinner later in the week. Shall we ride together?"

Shit. I received the text yesterday from my mom requesting we do a family dinner at her house. "I'm not sure if I'm going. Plan to drive yourself." Cecilia huffs out in annoyance but doesn't argue. "Close the door on your way out," I say, dismissing her. She stomps out, slamming the door shut behind her.

A few minutes later, there's another knock. This time it's Rome. "Who peed in Cici's cereal this morning?" Like most people who know Cecilia on a more personal level, Rome calls her by her nickname. I never gave into it, not wanting anything between us to ever get too personal. Rome has a seat in front of my desk, laughing at his own joke.

"She's pissed because I have a woman in my room and she hasn't met her."

"Can you blame her?" Rome chuckles.

"Who I have in my room isn't anybody's fucking business."

"But that's just it. You never have anyone in your room. And while you and Cici aren't technically exclusive, you sure as hell fuck her like you're a couple. But even then, you never let her in your room. You have something more going on with Aria?"

"There's nothing going on between Cecilia and me besides fucking, and as far as Aria goes, she's nothing to me." But even as I say those words, I feel the lie deep within me. I'm not sure what Aria is to me. Hell, I don't even know her. But saying she's nothing makes my chest ache. Something tells me, a woman like Aria could never be considered nothing. Fuck...I need to nip these thoughts in the bud.

"She was my payment from Weston Hightower." I shrug nonchalantly.

"So, what? You own her?" Rome gives me a knowing smirk, which pisses me off.

"Are we done gossiping like women? I'm assuming you're in here to go over something business related."

Rome throws his head back with a laugh then quickly sobers. "Caesar and I have searched high and low for that pussy senator. It's like he's disappeared into thin air. Caesar had a couple of guys stake out his home and office, but nothing. I called his office and his secretary said he had to go out of town for business but wouldn't tell me where he went. He never put his personal number on his file."

"Motherfucker, I should have known his bitch-ass was going to run. I need to find out why he was holding Aria captive. Something's not kosher. Weston could have hired any prostitute he wanted. Why would he hold her in a basement for almost a year with no intention of letting her go?"

"What the fuck?" Rome's voice booms through the office. I've been so busy keeping an eye on Aria, I haven't had time to catch him and the other guys up to speed.

"According to Aria, nine months and counting."

"How is she not freaking the fuck out?" Rome shakes his head.

"Vivian has her on some sleeping pills and is keeping her on the Xanax she's been on. When she first got here, she was begging for drugs. Luckily it seems the worst of it is behind her."

"What are you going to do with her once she's feeling better?"

"She's mine," I blurt out, a myriad of emotions hitting me with those two spoken words. First, regret for saying them out loud. Then confusion for realizing how badly I want them to be true. Frustration at the fact I can't force her to be mine. Anxiousness when it hits me that once she's healed, she's going to leave. And lastly, determination, knowing I'm not going to let it happen.

"Giovanni...you can't seriously be considering holding her captive."

I dismiss his statement because that's exactly what I will be doing if I try to keep her here and I'm not ready to deal with that reality.

I change the subject. "Anything else I should know about?"

"That stripper you lent the money to..."

"Ashley?"

"Yeah. She's a week late on her payment. Want me to pay her a visit?"

Saw that shit coming. "No, I'll do it myself. I told Don I'd handle it. Anything else?"

"Benjamin Fields will be arriving tonight to check out the club."

"Call me when he gets here. I'll handle his tour personally." Benjamin and I go way back. He owns a few clubs in Vegas and we run in similar circles.

"You got it, Boss."

After checking on a few more memberships and replying to several emails, I go back upstairs to check on Aria. Seeing her still sleeping, I go to the kitchen and ask Maggie, my head chef, to make us both lunch and have it delivered. Then I go to the stock room where the playroom toys are kept and find what I need.

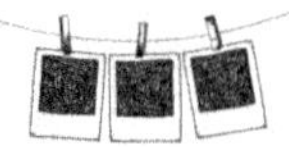

"GOOD AFTERNOON," I SAY CALMLY AS ARIA ATTEMPTS TO stretch her arms over her head, lightly flinching when only one arm is able to stretch fully. She squints and blinks a few times before frowning as she looks up at the handcuffs—one handcuff attached to her wrist and the other attached to the thick wooden headboard.

"Good afternoon? What the fuck, Giovanni! Why am I attached to the goddamned headboard?"

"Well, since you're feeling better, I can't take the chance of you running, so I figured it was my best option to ensure you don't try to." Aria glares at me then tries to rip the handcuffs through the wood. "Please stop before you hurt your wrist. That wood is a good two inches thick. You aren't breaking it."

"So, what...you kidnapped me from my kidnapper?" Her furious glare disappears, fear taking its place.

"I wouldn't call it kidnapping. Weston owed me a shit ton of money. It's obvious you're important to him, so I took you since he couldn't pay up. Now you're safe. You should be thanking me."

"Are you fucking serious? I should be thanking you for saving me only to hold me captive? Do you even hear yourself? I'm not collateral. You can't keep me here because he didn't pay you!"

"Speaking of which, do you have any idea why he was keeping you in that basement?"

"No, all he said was once I turn twenty-two, he would be getting rid of me." Hmm...interesting.

"How old are you?"

"I'll be twenty-one April twenty-ninth."

"All right. I have my guys trying to find him. Until we figure out why he needs you so badly, you will be safe here."

Aria's glare returns. "Un. Lock. Me." The words come out of her mouth slowly and with such conviction, I have to hold back my grin. She's cute as fuck when she's mad. Like a pissed off cat with her claws out.

"Not happening." I shrug. "For now, and until further notice, you're mine. Once I know you won't run, we can work on giving you more freedom."

"I'm not yours, and can't you just have one of your goons stand guard?" Not a bad idea. Why didn't I think of that? Oh, yeah...because the idea of Aria trussed up in handcuffs had my dick twitching.

"I'll think about it."

She huffs out in annoyance and this time I can't hold back my grin.

"I'm glad you find this all so funny. Could you possibly help me to the shower today? I feel so gross. And maybe if you could get me some clean sheets, I can change them. Oh, wait! I'm locked up. You can change them," she says dryly.

"I'll have the housekeeper bring up the sheets and change them." I text Donna, one of the housekeepers, and put in the request. "Why don't I have one of the women help you shower and once you're done, lunch should be here. I requested chicken noodle soup and deli sandwiches."

"You sure you don't want her to just give me a sponge bath right here in the bed? Then you can keep me locked up." My dick perks up at her attitude, but I mentally tell it to stand down. Now is not the time to be thinking with the head below.

Texting Cecilia, I ask her to send up Natalie. She's close in age to Aria and one of the sweetest women I know. After Celia asks why, I tell her to just do it. She and I are going to need to have a conversation soon. I text Rome and tell him he needs to stand guard outside Aria's room to ensure she doesn't run.

"I'm going to unlock your cuffs so you can shower. Rome will be standing guard, so it wouldn't be wise to try to run." Aria gives me another death glare, mumbling what sounds like swear words under her breath. There's a soft knock on the door and when I open it, Natalie is waiting timidly on the other side.

"Good afternoon, Mr. Valentino. How may I help you?"

"Natalie, thank you for coming up. My guest, Aria, is in pain but needs to shower. Would you be willing to help her?" I hear Aria grumble something about not being a guest, which causes me to chuckle, only for her to shoot daggers at me in return, which has me laughing harder. Natalie eyes me, confused as to what is happening. *That makes two of us, sweetheart.*

Natalie smiles warmly at Aria, then says, "Absolutely, sir. My first date isn't for a couple hours."

Natalie and I walk over to the bed, and after I unlatch the handcuffs—Natalie pretending like she isn't seeing any of this—we each take one of Aria's arms and slowly raise her until she's on her feet. Aria tries to shake my hand off her arm, which only makes me hold on to her tighter.

"Do you think I could borrow another shirt and boxers?" she quietly asks, reminding me that I ordered her some clothes.

"I have some clothes for you. I wasn't sure of your size so I had a couple different sizes delivered. I'll place them in the bathroom. Just let me know which sizes fit best and I can order you more. I also had the housekeeper put some toiletries in the shower for you. Shaving cream, a razor, shampoo...If you prefer any certain brand just let me know and I'll have her pick them up."

Aria stares at me for a moment like she's trying to figure out my motive. Then she shakes her head and mumbles out a "thanks."

After both women are inside the bathroom, I head out to give them some space. Rome, who is guarding the door, gives me a curt nod as I walk downstairs.

"Emilio, my usual." The bartender goes about making me a whiskey neat and places it on the bar top with a napkin.

"*Grazie.*"

Sitting at the bar, I sip my drink and scroll through emails and texts on my phone. Several men come and go. Some stop to say hello and others just nod. I spot Cecilia speaking to one of the members while tapping away on her iPad, most likely scheduling him in. Several women who work for me smile at me as they meet with the men they are scheduled to escort, either to bed or out somewhere.

One of the women sits on a gentleman's lap in the common room. She's laughing at whatever he's saying and I recognize him immediately. He gave a hefty sum to one of the organizations Weston took part in. Now that I think about it, I remember seeing them at several dinners together.

I walk over and stop in front of them. "Kelly, would you mind giving Mr. Wentworth and me a moment?"

"Yes, Sir." She gets off Phillip Wentworth's lap and makes herself scarce.

"What can I do for you, Mr. Valentino?"

"I'm sorry to interrupt your time with Kelly. I'm hoping you can help me locate someone. I have some unfinished business with Senator Hightower but it seems we keep missing each other. It's an urgent sensitive matter."

Phillip frowns. "The last I heard, he was looking for his stepdaughter. He wasn't sure when he would be returning.

Apparently, he's concerned because he hasn't heard from her since she took off after her mom died." *So that's what that fucker is saying...*

"You wouldn't happen to have a way to contact him, would you? I have his business number on file, but it seems he didn't leave me his personal one. Must have been an oversight on one of our parts." I've spoken to Cecilia about this. I don't give a shit how powerful the man is, she needs to get every damn number available in the future.

Pulling out his cell phone, he gives me the senator's personal number and I program it into my phone. "I appreciate it. Are you enjoying yourself?"

"Yes, Kelly is such a delight. It's too bad my wife can't be more like her." It no longer shocks me when I hear comments like this. What I don't understand is why when a man isn't happy in his marriage, instead of trying harder to make it work, he would rather stray with new pussy. If that's the case, why get married at all? Just stay single and fuck anyone you want.

I chuckle softly. "Good, I'll let you get back to her. If you need anything, please let me know."

"Will do." I shake Phillip's hand and then find Kelly to let her know she can rejoin him.

Closing the door to my office, I dial the senator's number to see if he answers.

"Hello."

"Senator, I'm so glad you answered."

"Who is this?"

"I'm the man who has the woman you are supposedly out looking for."

"Giovanni, how did you get this number?"

"That's not of importance. What is important, however, is whether the rumors are true. Are you out searching for Aria?"

"N-no, I'm not. But it would be wise of you to return her to me."

"Is that a threat I hear?"

"I'm not threatening you. But this is a family matter and it would be best if Aria is returned." His words grate me.

"Family? How would the people of Nevada feel about how you treat your family? I'm not sure they would be too pleased to know you've been holding your dead wife's daughter captive for almost a year while raping her."

"What did that bitch tell you?" Weston screams, losing his cool. I ignore his question and the fact that he just called Aria a bitch. This fucker will get his in due time.

"What I want to know is why."

"Why what?" he booms.

"Why have you been holding her captive? Why do you want her back so badly? What are you hiding, Senator?"

The phone line goes dead. I've hit a nerve. Senator Hightower is hiding something and I'm going to figure out what it is.

Me: Aria is no longer your family. If you come anywhere near her, I will personally end your life. She's mine.

I'm not expecting him to answer, but I know he got my message.

Now I need to have Johnny start looking into Aria's past and why Weston Hightower so desperately wants her in his possession until she's twenty-two.

Rialto

Chapter Ten

ARIA

"THANK YOU FOR HELPING ME SHOWER AND GET dressed." The woman Giovanni brought in, Natalie, has been such a godsend. She helped me shower, shave my legs and arm pits, wash my hair, and blow dried it so it's not soaking wet. I can't remember the last time my body and hair felt so clean...Oh wait. Yes, I do. Nine fucking months ago! I take a deep, calming breath before I work myself up.

Natalie is holding out Victoria's Secret sweatpants for me to step into. The bleeding has finally reduced to light spotting, the clotting all behind me, and it feels good to be able to put on a pantyliner and regular underwear instead of living in Giovanni's boxers.

I pull the pants up, then reach for the matching tank top. My ribs are still sore, but at least now I can walk a bit more and reach over my head when necessary. Natalie helps me put on my tank top.

"Do you work for Giovanni?" I ask, making conversation. It's been a long time since I've had anyone to converse with. She gives me a nervous look. "I'm sorry. I didn't mean to pry. I was just trying to make conversation. I've been stuck in a basement with no social interaction for almost a year."

Natalie's eyes bug out, and I note not to start off my conversations like that in the future.

"Yes, I work for Mr. Valentino."

"What do you do here?" I remember she said something about going on her first date...Could that be work related?

"I think you should probably ask Mr. Valentino that."

"Ask me what?" Giovanni walks in, looking like the powerhouse businessman I first met. I haven't seen him in a suit since I arrived, making me forget how sexy he looks when he's dressed to impress. I really need to tame down these thoughts. This is the same guy who handcuffed me to the damn headboard earlier, trying to make a claim on me like it's the 1800s. He is not someone I need to be attracted to, especially if my suspicions are correct and he's in the mob.

"Sir, Aria was just wondering what I do for you...for work."

"You look beautiful all cleaned up, Aria." It doesn't go over my head that he's changed the subject without responding to what Natalie's said. "The clothes fit good. Very...pink." He points to the bright pink Victoria's Secret sweats I'm sporting with an equally pink tank top. "Do you need anything else from Natalie before she heads back downstairs?"

"Nope. Thank you, Natalie." I shoot her a grateful smile.

"My pleasure. If you end up staying around, come find me. We can hang out."

She exits the bathroom, leaving Giovanni and me alone. "So…"

"So, what?" He tilts his head to the side, confused.

"What does Natalie do as your employee?"

Giovanni frowns, taking my arm in his, and helps me back to bed. There's a tray of food waiting on the nightstand for us. Helping me sit in bed, he pulls the fresh sheets up and places the tray of food on my lap before sitting in his usual chair with his food. "I run a high-class gentleman's club. Natalie works for me entertaining the men." The words come out carefully like he's trying to gauge my reaction.

"Gentleman's club like with old fat men sitting around smoking cigars and chilling together in a sauna?"

Giovanni laughs heartily, the sound making me smile. "Well, they range in age and body type, and while many do smoke cigars, there is no sauna. However, we do have a bar, several hot tubs, and an outdoor and indoor pool."

"So…she hangs out with them? Waitresses?" Why is he making me practically beg for answers?

"Natalie, as well as several other women who work for me, hang out with the men, yes. But no, she's not a waitress."

"Okay…so what do they do with them? I don't get it." Geez! It's like pulling teeth with this guy. Then it hits me…Holy shit! A gentleman's club. A sex club. No way!

Giovanni rubs the stubble on his chin. He looks frustrated, so I try a different approach, needing to know if my suspicions are correct. "Are we at your house?"

"I live here, yes."

"But is it your house?"

"Usually we refer to it as the club."

"Okay, is the club where you live?"

"Yes."

Now I'm desperate to know if I'm living in a damn sex club. Taking the tray that's on my lap, I set it aside and pull back the blankets.

"What are you doing?" He stands, looking perplexed.

"You obviously aren't going to answer me, so I'm going to go check this place out myself. I was stuck in a basement for almost a year. I'd like to know where I'm being forced to stay." Slowly standing, I use the edge of the bed to help me.

"Sit down, please, or I'm going to be forced to handcuff you again," Giovanni says in a demanding tone, which only makes me want to leave that much more. I've spent the last year being held down. Nobody is ever going to tell me what to do again, if I have anything to say.

"No, thank you." I walk as fast as my broken body can go toward the door. Giovanni beats me there, putting his hand over the handle. My body tenses, suddenly feeling claustrophobic.

"Move. Now." My heart begins to beat faster.

"Calm down." Giovanni puts his hands out and palms up in a placating motion when he sees me starting to freak out. "If I have to lock you up in here, I will. You need to understand your place in this."

"My place?" I bite out.

"For now, and until further notice, you'll be staying here. You will go nowhere without one of my men or me."

"And if I run?" I challenge.

"I will find you and bring you back here and you will regret it." Giovanni's voice is cold, detached. It reminds me of the night he showed up wanting to talk to Weston. "And if I don't find you, which I will, Weston will be after you. Would you rather go back to the basement?" His brow quirks up in a challenging manner.

Oh, hell no. "Don't you dare threaten me with going back there!" I jab my finger into his chest to emphasize my point and he looks down at it in shock then back up at me.

"Okay, I'm sorry. I shouldn't have said that." he concedes.

"Thank you. Don't let it happen again." He grants me a lopsided grin, but I remain serious. "Why don't you want me knowing what you do for a living?" I come back around to my initial question, refusing to let him off the hook.

"It's not that I don't want you knowing..." Giovanni runs his hands over his face in frustration. "I will explain it to you and then I'll show you."

With my hands on my hips, I raise my eyebrows. "Okay, tell me.

But move away from the door."

Giovanni moves out of the line of my exit. Smart move, buddy. "Rome is outside the door anyway." He smirks. *Fucker.* "This type of gentleman's club allows sex." *I knew it!*

"Like a whorehouse?"

"I prefer the term *bordello.*"

"What's a bordello?"

"I suppose in Italian it means whorehouse, but these women aren't whores in the negative use of the term. They are escorts."

"Do they get paid to have sex?"

"Yes, extremely well."

"So, they are high-class prostitutes?"

"Escorts."

"Are they here by choice?"

"Of course. Did Natalie look like she's being held here against her will?"

I blanch at his words. "No, I didn't mean to insinuate you are forcing them into sex, but you are holding me here against my will."

Giovanni sighs. "Why don't we sit down and eat lunch? We can talk, and afterward, I can give you a tour of the place."

"Okay." Instead of sitting on the bed, I take my soup and sandwich to the sitting room to eat at the table. "I feel like I've been in that bed for months," I say as way of explanation.

Giovanni sits across from me with his food. After a few minutes of eating in silence, he starts talking. "Have you thought anymore about why Weston had you locked up?"

I swallow a bite of my delicious turkey sandwich. "I've thought about it, but I have no idea. He just kept saying once I turned twenty- two he could get rid of me."

"When your mom died, did she leave you any money?" *Where is he going with this?*

"She had a life insurance policy, but it was only a couple million. I had the money from it in my bank account, but one day I went to pay for groceries and was declined. I looked at my account and it showed every cent had been withdrawn. Before I could investigate it, I was taken from my dorm by a masked man who delivered me to Weston. He drugged me and put me down in the basement, where you found me nine months later. Are you thinking he took the money? And if so, why would he take me? The money was taken before I was."

Giovanni takes a large bite of his sandwich, then washes it down with a sip of his water. "Your mom's husband is in a lot of financial trouble."

"Please don't call him that." The thought of that evil man being linked to my mom or me in any way, including marriage, makes my skin crawl. "I don't know why he would take me, though. Like I said, if he's the one who emptied my bank account, he already got every cent in my name. The house was put in his name before my mom died. I have nothing!"

"There has to be something else. You said the magic number is twenty-two, right? When is your birthday, again?"

"I turn twenty-one in April."

"All right. My men are looking into all this. If you think of anything else, you need to let me know. Your step—Weston has gone under the radar. He ran scared after I took you, but he'll eventually come out of hiding. He made it clear when I spoke to him, he wants you back. I'm going to have my men search your house. Anywhere in particular he might keep important documents?"

"There's a safe in his office and another one in the master bedroom. I don't know the combinations, though."

"Don't worry about that. I'll handle it. What were you doing when he took you? You said you were in your dorm?"

"I was in my sophomore year of college, majoring in photography." Thinking about my life before I was taken makes me smile. Then I think about everything I've lost. Everything Weston has taken from me, and I suddenly feel depressed.

"I know you don't understand why I have to keep you here, but the truth is, it's for your own good, until we figure out what Weston wants from you. If he was willing to hold you captive, I imagine he's desperate. I can keep you safe here."

"I understand that, I do. But I'm sick of having my choices taken away from me. It should be my choice whether I stay here or leave."

"Aria, you need to come to terms with the fact that you're staying here for the foreseeable future. The moment I told Weston I was taking you as payment, your fate was sealed."

"Life doesn't work like that!" I start to get worked up. "Before I was taken, I had a boyfriend and a best friend. I really need to contact them and let them know I'm okay. And I'm broke. I need to find a job. I need to earn money, so I can go back to school. You can't hold me here against my will!" I stand and get in Giovanni's face.

He gives me a soothing smile and takes my hand in his. "Breathe, Aria. We'll take it one step at a time, okay? Finish up your lunch and then I'll show you around."

I pull my hand out of his. How can he be so damn calm? He's holding me prisoner here while acting like I'm a house guest on an extended vacation. I sit back down and for the rest of lunch, we eat in silence. Once we are done eating, Giovanni is true to his word. He starts with his living quarters. He shows me the living room, the library, and the kitchen. Then he takes me outside onto the balcony to show me the Jacuzzi.

After he's shown me the entire floor, we go down the stairs to the second floor. Giovanni tells me it's split into two wings: the east and the west. Apparently, this place is so huge it needs to be labeled like a compass.

He walks me through the west wing where he tells me his staff sleeps. Staff such as his chefs, bodyguards, and housekeepers. Apparently, even his bartenders have rooms here.

"Emilio can make any drink you want," he jokes then frowns. "Shit, you aren't old enough to drink."

I roll my eyes. "You do realize I was in college, right? Drinking might as well be a college student's major their first couple years."

His breath escapes him on a laugh, making him look a hundred times sexier than when he looks mad and worked up. Giovanni Valentino laughing should be illegal. My insides tingle and I feel my nipples poke through my tank top reminding me I need to ask him to buy me a bra. "I'll have to take your word on that. I didn't go to college, so I wouldn't know. Just don't get too drunk." He attempts to give me a stern look that only makes me laugh.

We cross over to the other side as he explains the east wing is where all the women stay. I wonder if he'll ask me to move to this area. I imagine I'm overstaying my welcome, taking up his bed. Then I take that thought back. His ass is forcing me here. He deserves to be on the uncomfortable couch.

As we make our way through the floor, he introduces me to several women. Some are dressed up, others look like they're about to go to bed, but all of them are beyond stunning and none of them appear to be nervous in the presence of their boss.

"How did you come across owning a bordello?" I'm curious how a man who didn't even go to college became so successful. I haven't seen the entire place yet, but it's obvious this club is worth millions, and when I was looking out his bedroom window this morning, I could see it's on hundreds of acres. It looks more like a mansion than a club. Outside in the back, I spotted the most beautiful gardens and plan to explore them soon whether he likes it or not. Rome or Caesar will just have to join me.

"My parents moved us here from Italy when my youngest brother was born. My mom and dad used to run this place until I took it over about ten years ago. We also own a few hotels and casinos."

His mention of Italy gets me excited. Traveling to Italy is number one on my list of things to do and see. "Wow! Italy? My dream is to go to Italy one day to study art there. I bet it's beautiful in person. Have you ever been to any of the art museums there? Like the Uffizi Gallery? I have a list of places I want to explore all over Italy, places I want to take pictures of. Ugh! Have you ever visited Cinque Terre? The photos are amazing! I can't even imagine what it looks like in person. Oh! And the Piazzale Michelangelo, and the Frascati in Rome. If I ever make it there, I'm going to take a million pictures." Giovanni just stands there not saying anything, grinning at me. "What?"

"Nothing. I was just listening to you." His smile is amused.

"Were you planning to contribute to this conversation?"

He chuckles and shakes his head. "And interrupt your excitement?"

"Whatever. Have you been to Italy?"

"*Sì, e hai ragione. È più bella di persona.*"

"What did you just say?"

"I said, 'Yes, and you're right. It is more beautiful in person.' If you plan to visit Italy one day, you should start learning Italian." Giovanni taps me on my nose and winks. I don't bother telling him

I've taken several classes of Italian. I just can't understand it when spoken so quickly.

"Or I can just drag you with me. You can be my personal tour guide," I joke, and it shocks me that I just insinuated I'd welcome this man to join me on a trip to Italy.

"Your own personal tour guide to where?"

I turn to see where the feminine voice is coming from, and find the most exquisite woman gliding up the stairs from the first floor. From her ivory white dress that shows her perfect curves, to the high heels with the signature red sole, she screams class. She reaches us on the landing and up close, she's even prettier. She has midnight black hair that's pin straight, not a single hair out of place, and her makeup is done to perfection. She smiles at Giovanni, ignoring my presence. Her lips are full and plump, but look natural. The Kardashians have nothing on this woman's lips.

She and Giovanni seem to be having a silent conversation, and the longer they stare, the more fake her smile seems to get, like it's being forced.

"Hi! I'm Aria...you are?" I put my hand out to shake hers, trying to be polite and break the tension that seems to be building by the second. She looks down at my hand, not taking it, then slowly assesses me. I can feel the judgement pouring off this woman. *Okay, then....*

I make a mental note not to turn around so she can't see the words *Love Pink* across the back. For some reason, I don't think this woman has any pajamas with writing across the ass.

"Giovanni, where will you be guiding her?" *Huh?* Oh, right! The tour guide comment.

"To Italy," I answer her, since Giovanni has apparently gone mute. He sucks in his bottom lip, as if he's attempting to hold back a smile.

"Cecilia, this is Aria. She's my guest. Aria, this is Cecilia—" Great! How nice of him to join in.

"His girlfriend," Cecilia cuts him off. Oh, shit. His girlfriend? I've been sleeping in his bed—mentally undressing him—and he has a girlfriend. I mean, it's not like anything was going to happen. After what happened with Weston and all those assholes, I have no intention of having sex any time soon, plus there's the fact that he's holding me here against my will and I might still have a boyfriend, although it's been nine months since I've seen him. But there's no harm in looking, right? Especially when it's looking at that sexy-as-sin man. Shit! I'm doing it again. I can't be thinking about someone else's boyfriend like that.

That reminds me…I need to call Antonio. I'm assuming after almost a year of me being gone, he's no longer my boyfriend, but I should still call him to let him know I'm okay. He and Amber must be worried. I wonder what happened to my dorm room, my classes? Did anyone report me missing?

"Hey, you okay?" Giovanni lifts my chin and rubs his thumb down my cheek. For a brief second, I allow my face to nuzzle his hand, then I remember he has a girlfriend and is holding me captive.

Moving back too quickly, I bump into the railing, hitting my side on the wood. "Oww!" I grab my ribs and close my eyes, trying to will the pain to stop. The throbbing is so severe, I'm nearly brought to my knees.

I feel a pair of hands holding me up and my eyes open. "I'm okay, you can let go of me. I got it."

Giovanni looks at me confused, but doesn't let go of me. "I think you should lie down. I can show you downstairs once you've rested for a bit."

I look at Cecilia, and if looks could kill, I'd be six feet under. "I know my way back to the room. I can go myself. I'm sure you have Rome or whoever else following me around anyway." I wave my arms around. "Stay here with your girlfriend."

"I'm sure you can, and you're right, they are around. But I'd rather make sure you get there myself." Without saying a single word to Cecilia, Giovanni takes my arms and helps me back up the stairs to his room.

"Does Cecilia live here?" I ask once I'm back in his bed.

"Yes." Giovanni sits on the bed next to me. It's the first time he hasn't sat in the chair.

"I can sleep in one of the rooms on the second floor. I feel bad taking over your room. Your girlfriend doesn't seem too thrilled about it, either. You can just have your guard stand at attention in front of one of those rooms."

Giovanni lets out a deep breath. "You aren't sleeping anywhere else but right here, and Cecilia's not my girlfriend."

Huh. "Does she know that?"

Giovanni chuckles. "Yes, she does. She just thinks if she tells enough people otherwise, my stance on the topic will change."

"Do you have a girlfriend?"

Giovanni smirks at me. "Why? You want to apply for the position?"

"What? No! That's not what I meant."

"I'm just joking," he says between fits of laughter. "Plus, you're like twelve years younger than me."

"And I'm not even sure if I have a boyfriend," I add. "Hey! Wait a second. It's a proven fact, women mature ten years quicker than men. Technically, at thirty-one years old—"

"Thirty-two," he cuts me off.

"Fine. At thirty-two..." I emphasize the two, rolling my eyes. "... you're only twenty-two, which means you're technically only a year older than me since I'll be twenty-one soon."

Giovanni's entire body shakes with laughter. "If women mature ten years quicker, I think that means you're technically thirty-one, putting you at a year *younger* than me."

"Either way, we're only a year apart." I shrug.

"This supposed boyfriend of yours..."

"Antonio."

"Antonio...Were you guys serious?"

"Yeah, I guess. I don't know. It was mostly just hanging out. It's hard to take anything too seriously while in college. Do you think I could borrow your phone to call him? And to call my best friend, Amber."

Giovanni thinks on this for a moment. "Okay, but don't say anything stupid, Aria, or you won't be making any more phone calls." He hands me his phone from his pocket after typing in a code to unlock it.

I first dial Antonio's number, but it says it's not a working number. *Damn.*

"Not in service."

I dial Amber's number, and after several rings, I hear her voice. "Hello?"

"Amber?"

"Oh my God! Aria, is that you?"

"Yes, it's me!" Tears of happiness race down my cheeks.

Chapter Eleven

GIOVANNI

THIS GIRL IS GETTING TO ME. SHE'S MAKING ME JOKE around and laugh, and fuck, when she got excited about Italy, I wanted to call my pilot and fly her to Italy today. Then when she mentioned a boyfriend, my chest tightened and I wanted to lock her back up in the room and never let her out. I need to get myself together. What started as a way to fuck over Weston for nonpayment has turned into something more. I laugh to myself at the idea of seriously holding Aria captive because let's face it, the entire situation has turned into a damn joke. This woman has been out of bed less than a day and it's embarrassing the way she's running circles around me. I'm vomiting out information about my business, assuring her I don't have a girlfriend, and giving her tours of the place. I don't know what the hell she's doing to me but more shockingly, I don't think I mind.

I handed her the phone so she could call her boyfriend and

friend, but there was no way I was leaving. I played it off like I needed to make sure she didn't mention anything that would incriminate me, but with Weston already knowing I took her, I'm not really concerned. If he was going to turn me in, he would have already done so. And even if he did, the police aren't going to do shit about it. The truth is, I wanted to remain in the room to find out where she stands with her boyfriend.

Her boyfriend's number wasn't in service, but her friend answered her phone. Aria's first question was if anybody reported her missing. I can't hear what her friend is saying, but Aria's facial expression is one of confusion.

"What do you mean?" Aria's nose scrunches up, making me want to kiss the confusion away. Jesus, I need to get this girl out of my head. I can't be thinking this way about her. While the age difference might not be a problem for her, after everything she's been through, she deserves more than a guy who isn't capable of anything more than a fuck. Nothing can happen between us. I need to separate myself from her. She's here so I can keep her safe and find out what Hightower is up to, and I need to remember that.

"He told you I left by choice? Why the hell would he say that? I never told him I was going anywhere...Are you still at UNLV? Okay, hold on." Aria presses the mute button and turns to me. "Would it be possible for me to visit Amber? Like at a coffee shop near the university? I don't want to invite her here because...well..." I raise my eyebrows at her, and she huffs out, "I'm not going to run. You'll have someone with me. Please," her big green-blue eyes plead, and I give in.

"Fine, I can have Johnny drive you and stay with you."

"Okay, thanks!" Aria gives me a huge smile and my heart tightens. A thought pops into my head and it scares the fuck out of me. I don't want to see this woman sad. Her smile does something to me that I can't afford for it to do. I need to figure out what Weston is hiding so I can fuck him over and destroy him for fucking me over. Then once I do that, I can let Aria go, and we can both move forward with our lives.

"Is Saturday okay?"

"It should be fine, and it gives you a few more days to continue to heal."

"Saturday is good, Amber...I'll see you then. Bye."

She hangs up, frowning. "Amber said when I disappeared, she told Antonio they should report me missing, but he said I wasn't missing, that I told him I needed to take off to clear my head. She said my entire dorm was cleaned out and a few weeks later, Antonio disappeared. We're going to talk more on Saturday. It just doesn't make sense. I need to find Antonio."

"Do you know his last name?"

"Torino." *Why does that name sound familiar?*

"I'll have Johnny see if he can find anything out. We'll get this all figured out." I give her a small smile mentally vowing to myself to make sure this woman is safe if it's the last thing I do.

"Thank you...for getting me out of that hellhole and for making sure I got treated. I hate that you're keeping me here, but it's a thousand times better than what Weston was putting me through. I guess in a way I owe you." She shrugs.

"You don't owe me anything, Aria. This is business," I say, hoping to convince her and me of that fact. "Now what do you say you lie down for a nap and afterward I can show you the theater so you can watch a movie down there."

She beams excitedly. "I say, hell yes!"

After she gets comfortable in bed, I turn off the bedroom light and close the door so she can get some rest. Rome is standing outside my door. "Are we really holding her captive, Giovanni?"

"It's business," I say, just like I said to Aria. But as I say the words, I know there is no convincing anyone of this lie. I'm holding her here to ensure her safety, not to hurt her. As much as I should use her to fuck Weston over, I know I won't do that to her. The problem is, I can't admit any of this out loud. The woman is already running all over me. If I tell her she's not being held here against her will...Fuck! She'll trample right over me.

As I leave Rome to keep watch over Aria, I look for Johnny but don't see him, so I give him a call. "Johnny, where are you?"

"Helping Cici move some furniture downstairs. What's up?"

"Why is she moving shit around? Never mind, I'll be right down." I get downstairs and sure enough, Cecilia is having Johnny and Caesar move the couches around in the sitting room. "What are you doing?"

"Oh! Giovanni." Cecilia walks around the couches and leans in to kiss me. She knows better than to do this shit down here.

"Stop."

She gives me a small pout then looks around. "Where's your guest?"

"She's taking a nap. We aren't going to have a problem, are we? Aria is going to be staying here indefinitely. You telling her you're my girlfriend is unacceptable." I say it loud enough for the guys to hear, knowing it will embarrass her. She needs to be put in her place.

Cecilia's eyes widen and her cheeks turn pink, but she ignores my statement. "Will she be working here?"

The thought of Aria working here makes my blood boil. The idea of her fucking some stranger has my fists clenching, wanting to kill the fucker. Damn it, what the hell is wrong with me when it comes to this woman?

"No." I glance around the room, now agitated. "Put all the damn furniture back the way I had it. Don't move shit around," I bark out before walking away. "Johnny, my office now." I get to my office and sit at my desk, trying to calm the fuck down. Aria working here...no fucking way. Not happening.

"You okay, Boss?"

"Yeah, close the door and have a seat." He does so then sits down and waits for me to speak.

"Where do we know the last name Torino?"

Johnny thinks for a moment. "The name sounds familiar, but it's not coming to me. Do we have an issue?"

"I need you to look up Antonio Torino. He was Aria's boyfriend before she was taken. According to her friend, when Aria went missing, this Antonio kid told everyone she left on her own then he disappeared shortly after. Her friend said her stuff from her dorm was completely cleared out. Now that part could have been Weston, but why would her boyfriend say she left on her own?"

"Doesn't make sense. How long were they together?"

"I'm not sure, but when she tried to call him, his number was disconnected."

"All right. I'll find the kid. What do you want me to do once I find him?"

"Let me know. I want to personally handle this." I can't wait to see what this little punk says for himself.

"Got it. Anything else?"

I remember Aria's request to meet up with her friend. "Yeah, Aria needs to go to the city on Saturday. I'm going to have you take her with Caesar. We need to make sure she doesn't run and Weston doesn't get to her."

"Saturday is your meeting at the casino with Damian Briar."

"Shit. There's no point in taking two cars into the city. Let's take the SUV and I'll have you drop me off then take her to meet her friend. I'll take Rome with me. I want you to stay outside the coffee shop and have Caesar inside. We don't have any idea where

Hightower is. I don't want to take any chances, and while Aria seems to be playing nice, she can easily try to run."

"We'll handle it. One more thing…" I look down at my watch. It's only been a half hour since Aria laid down but I'm already antsy to get back to her. "You said you wanted to handle that stripper's loan yourself. She's behind again."

"All right, thanks. I'll pay her a visit soon."

After Johnny leaves, I attempt to get some work done. I check on various accounts to confirm payments are being made with the correct interest. I've never been in a situation where I've needed a loan, so I can't empathize with the people who come to me needing money, but I can't imagine being so desperate that I'm willing to sell my soul to the devil for money. Then again, the life I live, the family I'm a part of, I probably never had a soul to begin with.

While checking the books, I take note of the loans that aren't up to date, so I can have Franky and Carlos, my loan enforcers, handle them this week. I don't take lightly to people agreeing to pay a certain amount then not paying. It's just not good business. While writing down the names, I notice one of the names is Mayor Watkins. He's a huge gambler at the casino, so I note to let Nico know on Saturday while I'm there.

There's a knock on my door. "Come in," I say, too lazy to get up and answer the door. The door opens slowly and Aria's face peeks in.

"Am I bothering you?" she asks nervously.

"No, but did you manage to already get by Rome?"

She cocks her head to the side. "No, but he argued for damn near ten minutes before I finally convinced him to just walk with me over here. You can't make me stay in a room all day."

"I'll let Rome and the other guys know that as long as you don't try to run, you can go where you would like on the property as long as someone is with you. Even if you tried to run, we're on hundreds of acres. Unless you have a car, you aren't getting far anyway."

"Got it. Find a way to steal a car." Aria smirks, and I shake my head.

"How was your nap?"

She has a seat in the chair across from me. "It was good. I feel like I'm finally almost myself again. I'm still sore, but I'm not in pain. And I haven't had a panic attack all day."

"Good. Dr. Fox wants you to talk to someone. I've found a few people..."

Aria shakes her head vehemently. "No, the pills are working. You can get them for me, right?"

"I can, but you've been through a lot. You should talk to someone about it."

"There's nothing to talk about. My mom died, my stepfather went crazy and held me captive while abusing me. Now I'm being held here by you until you find another way to destroy Weston."

"Well, when you put it like that, it's not traumatizing at all," I say sarcastically. *When the hell did I become a smartass?*

"I wasn't a virgin when he took me. I'd had plenty of sex." Images of Aria naked and sweaty pop into my head and I quickly change the subject.

"You're a victim."

"Yeah, so? That doesn't mean I have to let what happened to me own me. He's a crazy asshole. Yes, he raped me, but I'm not going to let him take more from me. I'm broke and have no idea where I stand with school. I need to move forward. I need to get a job and get school figured out. Maybe I can even take online classes while I'm here if you aren't going to let me leave. I need to do something."

I love how strong this woman is. She has every right to place blame and cry and make excuses but instead she's picking up the pieces and handling business.

"All right. Money isn't an issue while you're here. Anything you need, I'll provide. As far as school goes, I'm sure we can figure something out. I get you want to be strong and I commend you for that, but I'd feel better if you would at least talk to someone...just once. If you don't feel it will help then you don't have to see her again, and keep in mind she's the one who will be prescribing your meds."

Aria huffs loudly, but I can see her giving in. "Fine, one time."

"Good girl. Now how about that movie? I'm sure we can get you some snacks from the kitchen and I might even be able to convince Maggie to make you a milk shake."

Aria smiles wide. "Only on one condition. You join me."

"I need to work."

"Take a break."

I know I'm going to regret giving into her. It's like watching two trains coming toward each other on the same track and not being able to stop either of them. I know the wreck will end tragically of epic proportions, but I can't help but watch. I want to look away, but I can't. I know being around Aria more than necessary will only end catastrophically, but I can't help but be drawn to her. The more I try to fight it, the more I want to be near her.

"Fine," I concede.

"Yay!" Aria grins, her nose scrunching up in the adorable way it always does.

Yep, I'm well and truly fucked.

Chapter Twelve

ARIA

IT'S BEEN ALMOST TWO WEEKS SINCE GIOVANNI SAVED me from Weston, although saving me might be a somewhat lenient term since in return, he's keeping me here at his mansion-slash-club under lock and key. I've quickly learned Giovanni has multiple sides to him. He can be cold and calculating when he needs to be, like when he confronted Weston or when he had to take a business call during our movie. Without so much as raising his voice, he made threats to whoever was on the other line, which weren't even aimed at me but still sent chills right up my spine. Giovanni is not a man I'd want to cross.

But then, when he hung up the phone, and we went back to watching our movie, Romeo and Juliet (Don't act like you didn't love the 1990s version with Leonardo DiCaprio and Claire Danes), and it got to the part where the families dueled, I jokingly asked him if that's how it works in the mob. He threw his head back in laughter and told me he could see his brothers as Mercutio and Tybalt. I had no idea he had brothers. It's obvious, Giovanni is an extremely private person.

When I grew tired and yawned several times, Giovanni grabbed a pillow and had me lay my head across his lap while he played with my hair. I fell asleep before the movie ended but woke up to him carrying me back to bed.

I've spent the majority of my time so far, cooped up in my room reading, aside from the movie night with Giovanni in the theater room. He said I have free reign of the place but also said it's best I don't spend time in the common room since that's where most of the members and escorts hang out. I plan to explore the outdoors soon, but I've been waiting for my ribs to heal all the way.

It's now Saturday, which means I'm going to see my best friend Amber today. I've spent the last nine months with my life on hold, so it'll be nice to see my friend and hopefully feel some sense of normalcy again.

"Good morning." Giovanni rolls over onto his back, yawning and stretching. I watch as he runs his fingers through his messy hair. His shirt rises and shows a bit of his happy trail. After everything that's happened to me, I shouldn't even want to look at another man again, and trust me, I have no intention of having sex any time soon, but I'd be blind not to notice how sexy Giovanni is. I'm a female with hormones, and while it makes me sick to think about what happened to me, I know sex can be enjoyable. I know what happened to me wasn't my fault. Plus, the therapist Giovanni made me see last week confirmed that.

I've agreed to keep seeing her once a week to talk to her. Her name is Dr. Weisberg and she's a really sweet woman in her fifties. She, just like Giovanni, said she thinks it's amazing how strong I am, but also said sometimes rape victims feel numb at first, and once it really hits them what's happened, they need a soft cushion to land on. She would like to be my cushion, and I agreed to let her.

I look at the man lying next to me and think of all the different personality hats he wears: serious, cold, and calculating when he's working, but then gentle, sweet, nurturing, and funny when it's just us. Unfortunately, it seems his life revolves around the former more often than the latter.

"Morning, Gio."

"Gio?" He smirks at me, his eyes still half-lidded from just waking up.

"Yeah, I've decided to call you Gio. Giovanni sounds too stuffy and serious, and I've seen you catch popcorn and jellybeans in your mouth. I know your whole 'I'm the boss' is just a front for the softy you really are."

Gio rolls to his side with his hand propping his head up. "I'm a businessman. I'm supposed to be stuffy and serious." He grabs my shirt and pulls me closer to him playfully. "And don't use the food catching against me. You made me do it."

I ignore the feeling stirring in my belly at our sudden closeness.

"Umm...yeah...after you made fun of me for crying during *Romeo and Juliet*. Plus, I like Gio better. You aren't stuffy...serious, maybe, but only when someone doesn't do as you say then you go all cold and mean. Like I said, it's a front." I shrug and get up to use the bathroom—needing some space.

"It's not a front. I'm a serious fucking guy, woman!" he calls out after me with laughter in his voice.

"Uh huh! Whatever you say! Want to watch another episode of *The Vampire Diaries*?"

"Don't tease me! I'm still pissed you insisted we wait to start season two! I need to know if Jeremy turns into a vampire."

"You'll have to wait until tonight! Now let me get ready. We need to leave soon."

Three nights ago, after staying up late and watching several romantic comedies despite Gio's whining, I had enough of him sleeping on the couch. I offered to sleep in another room but he wasn't having it, so I told him the only way I would sleep in his room was if he agreed to sleep in the bed with me. His jaw almost hit the floor.

"Will you just come lie down and watch TV?" I pat the bed next to me. Gio's bed is huge, like if there's a size bigger than a California king, that's the size of his bed.

"I'm fine right here. I can see the television."

"Not without straining your neck! Look, the bed is huge. I'll even draw an imaginary line across the middle."

"Nope."

"Fine." I throw the sheets back and climb out of bed.

"Where the hell are you going?"

"I'm not taking over your bed anymore while you sleep on the couch. I'll find somewhere else to sleep. This place is humongous. Surely, there's a room that's not occupied."

"All right. All right. Chill, woman. I'll lie down in the bed. Just don't try anything while I'm sleeping. I would hate to have to handcuff you back to the headboard."

I roll my eyes. "You wish."

Gio grunts. "What are we watching?"

"Vampire Diaries. Have you ever seen it?"

"Can't say that I have," he responds dryly.

"Ohh! I'll start it from the beginning. It's an awesome show. It's about this cheerleader, Elena. She falls in love with this guy, Stefan, but he's a vampire." Gio grumbles something about being too old to watch this shit, but I ignore him. Everyone knows The Vampire Diaries *is the shit.*

After showering and blow drying my hair, I throw a robe on and head back out to the bedroom. Gio's on his laptop, typing away with his cell phone attached to his ear and barking orders to whoever is on the other line.

"Okay, Nico. I will see you in a little bit. I know...I know I've been MIA. I'll explain over dinner tonight...okay...bye." After he hangs up, he looks up realizing I'm standing there.

"Everything okay?" I ask.

"Yeah. That was my brother, Nico. Why aren't you dressed?"

"Oh! I needed to grab the bags of clothes you had Johnny pick up. Thank you by the way. As much as I love wearing sweats all day, I'm dying to get back to dressing up to leave the house."

Gio scratches his stubble, looking a little uneasy. I don't know what the big deal is. He's seen me naked before, and I'm in a robe. "I'm going to use the guest bathroom to get ready. I'll meet you downstairs in thirty minutes so we can leave." He jumps out of the bed, practically running out of the door.

"Okay, sounds good," I say, but he's already shut the door behind him.

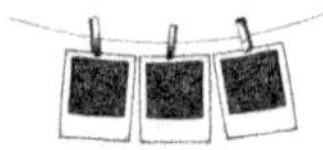

WE'RE IN THE BACK OF THE CAR ON OUR WAY TO DROP off Gio. Johnny is driving and Rome is in the front seat. Gio and I are sitting in the second row and Caesar is sitting in the third row. We pull up to a beautiful hotel and Gio turns to me and frowns. "Caesar and Johnny will be with you at the coffee shop. Please don't do anything stupid. We don't know where Weston is or if he's hired anyone to follow you. Stay with my men at all times. Even if it's to use the bathroom. After you're done meeting your friend, Johnny will drive you back to the club."

I want to make a sarcastic comment, but Gio is wearing his serious-business-mode hat, so I just say, "Okay."

"Good. I'll see you later tonight."

"Wait! Is that your hotel?"

He turns to look at what I'm seeing. Standing about ten floors high, the hotel in front of us isn't just a hotel. It's like an Italian paradise in Vegas. While most hotels here are sleek and modern, this hotel gives off a more enchanting, worldly feel. With large white pillars across the front, beautiful green plants and trees surrounding the area, and a breathtaking fountain in the center, this hotel screams class and wealth while still making you feel at home. The balconies facing the street are made up of white wrought iron railings and have planters hanging from each one. The roof is a beautiful royal blue, reminding me of the pictures I've seen of many places in Italy.

"Yes, one of them."

I stare at it for another few seconds. Giovanni and his family have taken the beautiful pieces of Italy and brought them to Vegas. "It's beautiful, Gio."

His face stays in business mode but his eyes smile at me. "I'll give you a tour one day. But right now, I have an important meeting to get to and you have a friend you haven't seen in almost a year."

With that, he's out the door, along with Rome. The ride to the coffee shop is quick and quiet. When we arrive, I spot Amber immediately and jump out of the car. Johnny calls my name, but I ignore him, too excited to see my friend. Amber sees me running, and just like in those movies where the guy and girl run toward each other in slow motion, we run at each other. Only when we meet and our arms go around each other, we topple to the ground laughing.

We hug each other on the ground, both of us in tears but grinning.

"I didn't think I would ever see you again," Amber says through her tears, holding me tight to her. I hold her back, just as strong. There's a throat clearing and we look up to see Johnny and Caesar standing over us, both of their eyebrows raised.

"Can we help you?" Amber's attitude is the same as it was nine months ago. I attempt to stand but my body, still sore from the abuse, doesn't work properly, and Caesar catches me. helping me onto my feet. Johnny puts his hand out to help Amber, but she ignores his gesture and stands on her own.

"Amber, this is Johnny and Caesar." Not knowing how to explain to Amber that they're my bodyguards who work for the man technically holding me captive, I just leave it at that. We go inside, both guys behind us, and order coffees and pastries, then sit down at the table together. Johnny and Caesar stay back, but it's obvious they're guarding me.

"Okay, Aria, spill."

"Gah! Okay, but it's not pretty." I sigh. "So, you know my mom died right after my birthday, but then a few weeks later, I was taken from my dorm."

"Like kidnapped?" Her hand flies to her mouth.

"Yeah. I don't know who took me, but I ended up in my basement. My step—Weston held me captive down there."

Amber's chair slides toward me until she's close enough to hold my hand. "I always knew something was wrong with that asshole. So what, he just let you out?"

"No, he had no intention of letting me go. I think he planned to hold me until my twenty-second birthday. This guy, Giovanni, found me and saved me."

"Holy shit! Aria, this doesn't make sense. When I went to your dorm to study for our finals, Antonio was there cleaning out your room. He told me you needed a break from it all to get through your mom's death. He said you left and didn't want to be found. I texted and called for days, but you wouldn't answer. I told him I wanted to go to the cops, but he told me not to. He showed me messages between you two. They all said you were leaving and to not look for you."

Amber's right. None of this makes any sense. "Maybe Weston used my phone and told Antonio all of this."

"Maybe. Have you spoken to Antonio since you got out?"

"No, his phone is disconnected, and I don't have a cell phone." Speaking of which, I need to talk to Gio about getting one. "Can you try to look him up on Facebook?" He was never into social media while we were together but maybe something has changed.

Amber takes her phone out and starts a search. Nothing comes up. Not wanting to waste our time focusing on Antonio, we spend the rest of our time gossiping about school, our friends, old boyfriends, Amber's crazy, strict parents, and the latest fashion styles. Amber's majoring in fashion design and marketing. I tell her I'm planning to go back to school as soon as I can and that I need to look for a job. When she asks about my living situation, I stick to details like the indoor pool, Jacuzzi, and beautiful gardens. I make it a point to leave out the parts about being held there against my will and that the place is filled with high class prostitutes-slash-escorts.

I have no idea how long we sit and talk but when a hand lands on my shoulder and Amber goes all googly-eyed, I jump and turn around, only to find Gio standing next to me.

"Holy shit!" My hand goes to my heart. "You scared me."

"Definitely not my intention, but I'm glad to see you're at least alert."

"What are you doing here? I thought you had a meeting."

"It ended quite a while ago, so I had Johnny come get me. You've been here for almost eight hours." I go to check the time and remember I have no watch or cell phone.

"I'm so sorry. Gio, this is Amber, my best friend." Gio nods once and gives her a reluctant half smile, if you can even call it that. Must he always be so serious?

"My mother has requested my presence at dinner. Since we're already in the city, it looks like you'll be coming with me." He frowns. Well. screw him. It's not like I want to go break bread with people who are probably just as stuffy and serious as Gio is.

"If you don't want me to go to dinner, I can go back to the house."

"The house?" He quirks up a brow and I roll my eyes.

"Yeah, the house where we live." His eyes dart to Amber, then he chuckles, finally catching on. For such a smart businessman, he really is dense sometimes.

"We came in one car, an oversight on my part."

"I can bring her home," Amber pipes up.

Gio's hand on my shoulder tenses, but his words come out smooth. "That's not necessary."

Amber and I hug goodbye with promises of seeing each other soon. Once back in the car, I explain everything to Gio about Antonio and the text messages, and he assures me he will look into it.

About ten minutes later, we arrive in a beautiful neighborhood in Summerlin. We pull up to a gorgeous house and as we are getting out of the car, a petite woman with light brown hair and perfect highlights comes walking out.

"Giovanni, *ciao, mio figlio.*" She wraps her arms around Gio and he hugs her back. I've learned a decent amount of Italian over the years since my dream is to study photography abroad. So, I recognize that she called him *her boy.* She must be his mother. It suddenly hits me—I'm about to meet Gio's family. The people who created him. Maybe they'll help shed some light on the man who's so hot and cold.

"Mamma, *mi hai appena visto un paio di settimane fa.*" *Mom, you just saw me a couple weeks ago.* His mom's about to argue when she spots me standing behind Gio. While she's dressed like she's attending a dinner party, in a blood red Prada dress with matching peep-toe heels, I'm in skinny jeans, ripped down the front, and a soft off-the-shoulder knitted black sweater—no bra since Gio still hasn't bought me any—complete with tall black Uggs, the ones with buttons that run up the sides.

I can feel her judging me and I'm thankful the clothes I'm wearing, while designed for comfort, are all name brand and currently in style. I didn't understand why Gio would order me such expensive clothes, but now it all makes sense. He comes from a family of wealth.

"And who is this?" his mother asks Gio, but her eyes stay trained on me.

"Mother, this is Aria. She's my guest for the time being."

Her head whips around to give me a better look and I cringe as she visually inspects me, her facial expression indicating she isn't thrilled with what she sees. Gio seems to ignore her look of scrutiny, continuing with introductions. "Aria, this is my mother, Claudia."

"It's nice to meet you." I bridge our gap and extend my hand to shake hers. She stares down at it for a moment and I'm almost positive she's not going to take my hand, but her manners win out at the last second and she delicately shakes my hand, offering me a reserved smile.

"Nice to meet you, dear." Then she turns to Gio. "I wasn't aware we would be having an additional guest. I'll have to have Beatrice set out another place setting."

She walks back inside and I catch Gio roll his eyes, which makes me giggle. "What?"

"You totally rolled your eyes behind your mom's back. It's like you're ten years younger, I'm telling you."

"Hush up. Not only am I older than you, I'm wise beyond my years. Let's go inside." Gio grabs my hand to pull me along behind him up the driveway. I notice Johnny, Rome, and Caesar take off. Apparently, they don't have to stay for dinner. Lucky them.

We enter the front door and step into the foyer. The home I grew up in was no shack, but this home makes my house look like one. To the right is a huge sitting room that looks like it's never been used. Between the expensive looking couches, the large fireplace, the liquor bar, and the perfectly matching décor, the room looks professionally staged, not like a family lives here. To the left is a dining room with a table that must seat fourteen people at least. Creams and browns seem to be the color scheme everywhere. It reminds me a lot of Gio's living area.

Gio steers me into the sitting room then leans down and whispers into my ear, "What would you like to drink?" I notice an older man eyeing us curiously from the far corner of the room but Gio doesn't acknowledge him or make any introductions.

"Water, please." I have no doubt I need to be sober to get through this dinner.

He leaves me to head over to the bar area to grab our drinks and I have a seat on the couch, unsure if it's allowed but needing to take some relief off my ribs. A gentleman who looks almost identical to Gio comes over to sit next to me. He has the same brown hair as Gio, but it's gelled to the side neatly. His eyes are brown but unlike

Gio's soft brown, his are darker, more menacing. He smirks at me when he notices I'm checking him out.

"See something you like?"

"You look like Gio," I blurt out as way of explanation.

His eyes lighten a bit as he laughs. "Gio? Does my older brother know you call him that?" This must be one of Gio's brothers. "I'm Nico, the younger, more handsome brother." He gives me a wink and I hear a growl. I look to my left and see Gio sit next to me while shooting daggers at his younger brother. He hands me my water and sets down his drink. It looks like some type of scotch.

Gio's hand goes to my thigh and I jump a little from his touch. It's been a while since I've had a man touch me possessively in a good way. Nico notices my actions and laughs harder. "*Gio*, what have you done to this woman? Making her jump like a scared little mouse."

Gio glares at his brother. "It's Giovanni, asshole. This is Aria."

Nico's eyebrows furrow like he's deep in thought, then his eyes go wide when he finally figures out whatever it is that had him stumped. "Wait! Aren't you the senator's daughter?"

My body grows stiff and Gio's hand on my thigh tightens. "She's his ex-stepdaughter. It's a long story. Leave it alone." Gio's voice is cold and menacing, leaving no room for argument. Nico nods his understanding and lets it go. We move into an awkward silence until the older man who was eyeing me a few minutes ago walks over with another older gentleman and introduces himself. "My name is Salvatore, Giovanni's father, and this is Stefan, my business partner."

Gio introduces me and I shake both their hands. The men talk business, but it's all extremely vague. By the topics of their conversations, they own a couple clubs, hotels, and casinos, which I already knew, and it seems they all work together. The entire time they converse, Gio keeps his hand on my knee—his thumb rubbing circles into my skin, and surprisingly, it comforts me, making me feel a tad bid more at ease in this awkward situation.

I hear a door open and shut and in walks Cecilia, the bitch from a couple weeks ago. I've seen her in passing, but she's made it a point to pretend I don't exist. *Works for me.* The doorman takes her coat and she's dressed just as beautifully as Gio's mom in a light pink chiffon dress that stops just above her knees. Gio and I let out a groan at the same time. I look over at him and giggle. He looks down and graces me with the most panty-melting smile, then leans into me and murmurs, "I had no idea she was coming. I'm sorry."

"You're going to owe me big, like another movie-slash-jelly bean-slash-popcorn night big." Gio groans again, only this time there's laughter mixed in.

"Jellybeans?" We both turn to Nico, who's smirking. "Did I hear you say jellybeans and popcorn? Did you get *Gio* to eat junk food and watch a movie?"

Before I can answer, Cecilia sits across from us, next to Stefan. She crosses her legs like the perfect lady she is, her back staying straight like she has a stick up her ass, and leans in for him to give her a kiss on her cheek. My eyebrows shoot up in curiosity and Gio leans toward me and whispers, "He's her dad." Damn, I thought maybe I would get to see some entertainment while here. Anything would help to liven up this gathering.

"What are we whispering about?" Cecilia asks, her tone still as snarky and stuck up as the last time we spoke.

"Well, *Gio*—" Nico begins, earning him a punch to his arm from behind me courtesy of Gio. "I'm sorry..." Nico cackles. "...big bro. I just didn't know Gio was an option."

"It's not, so drop it." Hmm...well, I'm going to keep calling him Gio.

"As I was saying, *Giovanni* has apparently been watching movies and eating junk food with Aria, here." Nico says it mockingly, and it doesn't surprise me that Gio doesn't usually do that sort of stuff. He's all business, and looking around at the way everyone is dressed and conversing, at the home décor, and the staff of butlers and servants, I can see this is all he knows.

"Is that so?" Gio's mom walks over and stands next to Cecilia, with her hand on her shoulder and a fake smile plastered across her face. Cecilia's dad is staring at me like I don't belong and Gio's dad is straight up glaring at me. I'm not sure why, but it seems as if some silent line has been drawn.

Chapter Thirteen

GIOVANNI

I SHOULD HAVE KNOWN BRINGING ARIA HERE WOULD BE a colossal mistake. On one side of the living room is my mom, Cecilia, Stefan, and my dad. On the other side is Aria, Nico, and me. I know when Aria feels the tension because her body stiffens, not for the first time tonight, and she tries to push my hand off her leg. I let her do it because I don't want to argue with her here.

This just reminds me how different Aria is from my family, from my life. She doesn't belong here. She's full of life and energy. These past couple weeks, watching Aria revert back to what I assume is her old self has been nothing short of amazing to watch, and I'm thinking this is only the beginning. She's carefree and fun and doesn't take much seriously.

She eats junk food at midnight and watches crap television. She steals my phone daily to snap pictures of everything that captures her attention. She wears what she wants and speaks her mind. Her being here in my parents' home for only a short time has already begun to diminish the beauty and aura which surrounds her. I need to find Weston and figure out what he has up his sleeve so I can take care of him and then set Aria free. It was selfish to ever think I could in some way keep this girl for myself.

"Mom, is dinner ready?" I break the silence, ignoring the comments about the movie and junk food.

"Yes, let's all go sit at the table."

Aria excuses herself to use the bathroom and when she gets to the table, Cecilia is sitting on one side of me and my mother is on the other side. When my mother told everyone where to sit, I didn't want to draw attention to Aria by suggesting she should sit next to me, but the look in her eyes—jealousy? Hurt? I don't know—has me wishing I would have taken a stand.

My mom has her sit next to Nico and across from Cecilia on the other side of the table. The meal goes smoothly for the most part. Aria eats quietly, and Nico engages her in some conversation. My dad asks her a few questions, but she sticks to polite responses. knowing my family is simply fishing for answers. After dessert, I announce we need to get going.

"Would you mind giving me a ride home?" Cecilia asks too sweetly. "When the guys returned, I had Rome give me a ride over since he said he was coming back to pick you up anyway. My car is acting up." Somehow, I doubt her new Mercedes is acting up, but I'm not up for arguing.

"Sure." I stand and give my parents a hug, Stefan a handshake, and slap Nico on the back before we head out. Aria quietly says goodbye and Cecilia goes around the room giving hugs and kisses to everyone.

The ride home is filled with Cecilia talking to me about La Stella business. Aria remains quiet, looking out the window, and my fingers twitch, wanting to pull her into my side and tell her not to take any of this personal, but knowing this is probably for the best. My life, my family, my business, none of it could ever fit in with the person Aria is.

When we arrive back at home, Aria quickly excuses herself. I let her go and head to my office to get some work done. While I'm checking on the books for the loans I have out, Johnny knocks and comes in.

"Boss, I have some info on Antonio Torino." I close out what I'm working on to give him my full attention.

"What did you find out?"

"Unless it's a coincidence, Antonio Torino is the son of Anthony Torino."

Shit, that's where I recognized the last name from. The Torino organization. "He has an organization in New York. And if I'm thinking of the same guy, he owns a real estate company over there, which is worth millions."

"Yep, that's the guy," Johnny says. "He doesn't seem to have any ties to the Lorenzo organization, but I'm going to keep digging."

What the fuck was Aria doing dating the son of a mob boss?

"All right, we need to confirm this is the same guy. Why the hell would he give Aria his real last name?"

"It might have been an oversight on his part or maybe he didn't have anything hide." I glare at Johnny because he knows better than that bullshit. "Yeah, I know. That sounded stupid as fuck. If he's the son of a mob boss, he's in deep."

"I'm going to talk to Aria. See if I can find out anything else. We need to get into that house and get inside those safes."

"You got it."

I walk Johnny out of my office and head upstairs to find Aria. When she isn't in our room—Jesus, I just referred to my room as ours—I start my search for her. I text Rome and Caesar and they both tell me they didn't know they were supposed to be watching her. When we got home, I didn't give them any instructions. I text them back to find her—fuck! It goes without saying they should always be watching her!

I search the first floor, kitchen, dining room, and living room, but don't find her. I move up to the second floor, and knocking on each door, ask if anyone has seen Aria. Nobody has seen her. Just as I'm about to lose my shit, Caesar texts me a photo of Aria out back, sitting on a bench in the gardens. Even in the photo, I can see her face is red and blotchy from crying. Instead of going to check on her, I tell him to keep an eye on her. Comforting her will only make shit more complicated.

I send a group text to my employees that I'm leaving and head out to the bar. I need to get laid. A warm body underneath me will surely knock the visions of Aria out of my head, and since fucking Cecilia anymore is out of the question, picking up a woman in the bar will have to do.

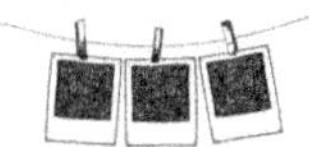

I'M SITTING AT THE BAR, TWO SCOTCHES IN, WITH A woman—with blonde hair as fake as her tits and tan—practically in my lap, and all I can think about is how real Aria looks in comparison. Her tits aren't half the size of this woman's but Aria's are perky and real. I imagine how my hands would fit around Aria's tits. I bet they would be a perfect handful. I look at this woman, who has her face covered in all types of makeup with her hair sleeked pin straight. Aria's brown hair is always up in a messy bun, and her face is always clean and makeup free. Aria blows this woman away in the looks department without even trying.

Her hand glides up my thigh, landing on my dick, and I will myself to block Aria out and focus on getting balls deep in this woman. Instead, Aria's face, blotchy and tearful, pops up and I push the fake and willing woman away. "I gotta go."

I throw a couple bills down and leave the bar on a mission. I can't stand the sight of Aria crying. I'm heading back to the mansion when an idea comes to me. I turn around and head into town. I stop at a store and have the associate guide me to everything I need.

I remember Aria mentioning she was majoring in photography. Hopefully, a camera will put a smile on her face. Several thousand dollars later, and I'm on my way home.

It's late and the main floor is quiet. By this time of night, members and escorts are either in private rooms, out for the night, or have gone home. I jog up the stairs, hoping Aria is in our room. I see Rome standing outside the room and nod to him. When I open the door, I find Aria curled up in bed asleep. Her iPad is still on and open to whatever book she was reading. I take it from her hands and turn it off. She stirs and her eyes flutter open.

"Hey, I must have fallen asleep reading." She sits up and stretches, her perky tits jutting out, reminding me of my earlier thoughts.

"I bought you something."

Aria eyes me curiously. "For what?"

"I guess...kind of an apology gift. My family...they..."

"Kind of suck," she finishes my sentence with a frown but quickly gives me a small smile. "Except Nico. He's super intense but also really sweet." The thought of Aria warming up to my brother causes something inside me to burn, but I push it aside.

"Anyway, here you go."

I hand her the bags, and she takes them from me. "You didn't have to do this. I was upset earlier, but it was stupid—" Her words are cut off when she sees what's inside the bags. "Oh. My. God! Gio!" Her eyes dart from the camera box and accessories to me and back again before she jumps up off the bed, wrapping her arms around me.

"Thank you so much! I'm going to use the hell out of this camera!"

"There's more." I nod toward the other bags as I sit on the bed, setting Aria back down next to me.

"A laptop? And printer! This must have cost you a fortune."

"The only thing that matters is that you like it. If any of it isn't what you would use, we can exchange it."

She looks at me like I'm crazy. "This is all perfect. Seriously, thank you." She opens the camera box and starts setting it up and plugging it in.

"We think we found Antonio today."

Her eyes go wide. "Really? Is he okay?"

Only Aria would be concerned about a guy that could easily put her six feet under without blinking an eye.

"Aria, if it's who we think it is. He's not a good guy. We're looking into it and will know more soon, but for now, don't try to find him anymore. We need you to stay under the radar until we get this all sorted."

"Okay. Oh, I was wondering if I can use your phone. I wanted to call Amber and I don't have a cell phone. I was hoping I could go over to the college and we could hang out."

Shit, I completely forgot I need to get her a cell phone. "How about you have her come here? You guys can go to the pool and hang out. I have an indoor pool and another outdoor one that's heated."

"And how would I explain to her that this is a sex house?"

I chuckle at that her description of the bordello. "Nobody is going to be fucking out in the open. Just hang out in the back or on the third floor, or in the kitchen where you usually are, eating your weight in food." I wink at her. Aria practically lives in the kitchen. She loves her food, especially the sweets. The last few weeks, I've had the pleasure of watching her body change from skin and bones to having some meat on her—and that meat on her looks damn good.

"Shut up!" She slaps my chest, but before she can pull her hand back, I grab her arm and pull her into me. "I'm not complaining. These new curves you have going on are sexy."

Aria swallows thickly, her eyes meeting mine. Her tongue darts out, wetting her bottom lip, her top teeth tugging on it, and without thinking, my lips crash into hers, needing to taste her. Without invitation, my tongue delves into her sweet mouth, her lips parting as she lets out a soft gasp of surprise as I suck her tongue into my mouth, craving more. In a blink of an eye, I'm grabbing her hips and pulling her up into my lap, her legs straddling me. My hands grab her ass, pulling her even closer, until our bodies are flush, her perky tits brushing up against my chest. Her hands come up to my hair, pulling on the ends, and her ass grinds down on my cock. A loud groan release into my mouth, telling me she feels exactly what she's doing to me.

There's a knock on the door and we both jump like we're teenagers who almost got caught. Aria almost falls to the floor, but I catch her and set her on her feet.

"Fuck," I mumble. "That shouldn't have happened."

She gives me a hurt look. "Wow, why don't you tell me how you really feel?"

"I didn't mean it like that." There's another knock. "Jesus, I'll be right there!" I bark out. "It's just that you're only twenty years old. You should be in college, hanging out with frat boys or some shit. I'm in the fucking mob. You met my family. I'm not good for you. You just went through a traumatizing event. You're wife material and I'm not looking for anything more than a good fuck."

Aria's hands go to her hips and if looks could kill, I might be a dead man. "I'm so freaking sick of people telling me what's good for me. I know what's good for me, and I'm perfectly capable of making my own decisions. You're just like my mom."

"Your mom?"

"Yeah, my mom. When I was little, I used to ask her about my real father, but she told me it was for the best that he wasn't in my life. She said he chose a dangerous life over us and he didn't want me to get hurt. I heard her and Weston arguing once about him being in the mob. It should have been my choice as to whether I saw him."

Her dad was in the mob? This is new and important information. "Do you know your dad's name?"

"No, she wouldn't tell me anything. I'm just so sick of everyone around me deciding what's best for me, and you're no different." Her chin tilts up in defiance, and fuck if it isn't adorable.

"Ever think maybe they're making those decisions because they love you and want to protect you? *This* life is a hard life, Aria. I was born into it and it's all I know. I'll never get married. I'll never bring a woman or kids into this shit."

"Whatever you say, *Giovanni*. Can I borrow your phone so I can call Amber?" It doesn't escape my attention that she didn't call me Gio like she usually does.

She holds her hand out, ending the conversation. What I want to do is grab her hand, pull her into me, and continue where we left off, but instead I let out a sigh, knowing it's for the best we were interrupted.

"Yeah." I hand her my phone, unlocking it so she can use it. "I'll get you an untraceable phone this week." She nods then turns her back on me to call her friend. I step outside to find Cecilia and Rome arguing. "What's going on?"

"She wanted to go inside and I told her you would come out."

"What were you in there doing with that *girl*?" Cecilia glowers at me.

"What I was doing isn't your concern. What do you need?"

"Mariah is moving to California so we're going to need to hire a new girl."

"Is everything okay?" Women coming and going in this business is normal. Some have been around for a while, but most work here to save up money, and once they meet their goal, move on. Many end up meeting a man and quit to start a life.

"Yes, just the usual. She wants to pursue an acting career." She rolls her eyes.

"Okay, well, go ahead and start looking for someone to replace her. Like always, I have final say." Cecilia gives me a mock salute before walking back down the stairs.

"Everything okay?" Rome tips his head toward the door.

"Why wouldn't it be?"

He simply shrugs then smirks. "You look a little"—his eyes peruse my body—"messy." I look down and see what he means. My shirt is tucked half in-half out. Several buttons are undone that I didn't realize Aria unbuttoned. I look like a man who was about to fuck.

"Fuck, Rome. I don't even know what I'm doing anymore." I scrub my hands over my face in frustration.

"You've smiled and laughed more around that woman than I've seen since I started working for you almost ten years ago."

"What are you saying? That I'm going soft?" I half joke.

"No, I'm saying happy looks good on you, Boss."

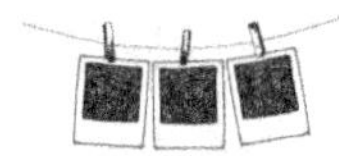

AFTER GRABBING A PINT OF ROCKY ROAD ICE CREAM from the freezer, popping a bag of popcorn and pouring half a bag of chocolate candies into it, and grabbing two sodas, I make my way back upstairs to the room. When I walk through the door, Aria glances over at me. Her face morphs from the scowl she was planning to give me into a tiny smile she's trying to hide.

"Truce?" I ask, showing her all the goods I've brought.

"You just want to see what happens next on *The Vampire Diaries*." She pulls the blanket down, welcoming me into the bed. She takes the ice cream, popcorn, and one of the sodas from my hands, and turns the television on.

"You're lucky I love Rocky Road." She takes a bite of the ice cream, her tongue darting out to lick a tiny bit that dripped down her lip.

I snatch the remote from her and click on the episode we left off on, willing *both* of my heads to ignore the gorgeous temptation sitting next to me.

Chapter Fourteen

ARIA

"GIRL, THIS POOL IS THE SHIT. THIS MANSION IS LIKE something out of an episode of cribs. Now spill." Amber and I are lounging out by the pool. She just finished with midterms, so today is the first day we have been able to hang out. It's been two weeks since Gio and I kissed and since then he's been more distant than usual. That night he came back up with junk food as his way of a truce, I thought maybe things would go back to the way they were, but I was wrong. He's grumpy to everyone including me and I'm over his shit. He's slept in the bed a few times but he doesn't usually come in until after I'm asleep and he's out of bed before I wake up. Some nights he'll sleep on the chaise lounge, and once I found him asleep at his desk.

"Gio is keeping me here because Weston has disappeared."

"And this mansion?" Her hands circle around.

"He owns an...escort service." I whisper the last two words. It's not like it's a secret since here in Vegas bordellos are legal, but I still feel weird admitting I live at a sex club.

"What?!" She sits up, her Bloody Mary sloshing onto her breasts. "Like a whorehouse?"

I don't know why but that word agitates me now even though I used the same term when I first found out. Maybe it's because the last several weeks I've been here, I've gotten to know the women and they might have sex with strangers, but they aren't whores...I mean, they are by the literal definition, but it just sounds so cold. There's more to these women, and they deserve more than to be labeled.

"No," I say, feeling the need to defend them, "escorts."

"Hey, I'm not judging." Her hands come up in a placating gesture. "To each their own."

"I'm going to take a dip in the pool." I pull my cover over my head and drop it onto the chair then walk toward the steps. Amber does the same.

There's a loud whistle and when we find the source, it's Nico, Gio's brother. "Well, well. It's not every day I come across not one but two sexy women."

I roll my eyes, but Amber giggles. "That entire house is filled with sexy women. Nice try."

"True, but they're off limits." He winks and Amber giggles louder. *Seriously? Do I sound like that around Gio?*

"Nico, Amber; Amber, Nico, Gio's brother," I say before I dive into the water and swim toward the deep end. When I come up for air, Nico and Amber are chatting. She's laughing at whatever he's saying—her hands hitting him against the chest—and he's eating that shit up.

Natalie and Sienna come walking out, suits on, and I wave to them. "Hey!" I had invited them when I made plans with Amber. They're both super sweet.

"Hey, Aria!" They both wave, throw their towels down, and join me in the pool. "This water feels so good! We don't use the accommodations offered here enough," Sienna admits.

"Seriously!" Natalie agrees.

We spend the next few hours in the pool hanging out. Nico gets his suit and joins us. He's a huge flirt with all of us, but he seems to focus most of his attention on Amber.

When my stomach starts to rumble, I swim to the stairs and get out. "I'm starving. Want to go grab something to eat?"

"How the hell do you eat so much and look like that?" Natalie appraises my body as she wraps her towel around her.

"I've been saying the same thing since we first met our freshman year in college," Amber adds.

"Oh, whatever. I lost a lot of weight this past year. I'm not usually this skinny." I laugh, but it comes out rough as I remember why I'm the skinniest I've ever been. We all make our way into the kitchen and I start going through the pantry to see what I can find to eat.

"I'm going to leave you ladies to it. I came here to find my brother and some women in sexy bikinis got me distracted." He winks at Amber and walks out of the kitchen with his towel strung over his neck. As he leaves, Maggie comes in and offers to make us sandwiches.

"So, if it's none of our business you can say as much, but what the heck happened this last year? Why are you living here?" Sienna questions.

I retell the same story I told Amber, leaving out most of the gory and horrific details, but telling them enough so they understand." I know Gio said I need to lay low and I am, but it feels good to talk to people other than him. It's not like these women are going to go running to the news channels.

"Are you planning to go back to school?" Natalie asks as she takes a bite of her sandwich and moans in approval. Everything Maggie makes is delicious. She's offered to give me some cooking lessons and I've taken her up on them. I can now successfully make lasagna, chicken parmigiana, and chicken fettucine alfredo.

"Yes...are you?" Cecilia walks into the kitchen, her nose stuck in the air as usual, butting into our conversation.

"I'm planning on it."

"And with whose money? Giovanni's?" Her question is meant to be rude, but I don't let it get to me. I'm here at Giovanni's insistence. He sought me out, not the other way around. I'm extremely appreciative of him getting me out of that basement, but I would never take advantage of him, and I sure as hell don't want to owe anybody anything.

"I haven't figured it out yet, but no, he has given me enough. I don't want to take advantage of him. I obviously need to make my own money but I'm stuck under this roof, which is making it difficult." I know if I asked Gio for the money to go to school, he'd give it to me in a heartbeat, but I don't want him to. I want to be independent. Show the world that what happened to me didn't break me. He's made it clear, he doesn't want anything to happen between us, so keeping our relationship on a friendship level means not taking anything more from him than necessary.

"If you don't want to rely on him, why don't you work here? You can do that right from under this roof."

"Cici!" Sienna yells.

"What? Mariah left and I'm hiring. If you're serious about needing a job, you can work here." She flips her hair behind her back as her head tilts slightly. Ugh! She's such a damn bitch.

"As an escort?" I clarify.

"I mean, unless it's beneath you." Her eyebrows raise in a challenge.

"No, it's not that. It's just..." I look around then sigh. "I haven't had sex since I was raped." I bite the side of my cheek hard, the metallic taste of the blood hitting my tongue.

"You wouldn't have to have sex," Natalie says.

"What do you mean?"

"We all have a profile. It lets the members know what we allow. Whether we allow sex and if we do, what our hard limits are. You could just put you don't allow sex."

Cecilia scoffs. "I'm not sure how many clients you'll get, but I guess if that's what you want." The thought of having sex with a stranger terrifies me, but the fact that I wouldn't have to until I'm ready settles my nerves, and who knows, maybe this'll be good for me while making money to pay for school.

"I'll think about it." This is a lot to consider. I can make money while living under this roof, but I'm not sure how I'll feel having to be close to men I don't know.

"Think about what?" Gio asks as walks into the kitchen and grabs a peach from the fruit bowl, with his brother following behind. All the women stop talking and stare at him. He's in his usual power suit—well most of it—his jacket and tie are missing—and his hair is messy like he's been running his fingers through it. The guy sheds clothes throughout the day like a dog sheds its hair. It's rather comical. He takes a bite out of the peach, a bit of juice coming out the sides, and suddenly I'm fantasizing about licking peach juice off Gio's lips.

"Aria was just saying she'll think about working here," Cecilia says.

Gio chokes on his peach, his hand coming up to his mouth as he coughs to get a piece that seems to be lodged in his throat. Once he's recovered, he shouts, "Like fucking hell!"

"Excuse me?" My hands go to my hips, preparing for a fight because who the hell does he think he is?

"I'm not hiring."

"Yes, we are," Cecilia jumps in, earning a glare from Gio.

"Cecilia, stay the fuck out of this," Gio barks, his eyes never leaving mine, his tone brokering no room for argument. She huffs and walks out, her heels clacking against the marble floor as she goes. "We can discuss this later. I have a business dinner I need to go to. I wanted to see if you'd like to join me. My brother has decided to take a date for once and is inviting your friend."

"Are you asking me to join you so you aren't the only one without a date?" I ask, just to give him a hard time because it's fun messing with Gio.

"What?" He runs his hands over his face in frustration. "No, that's not what I meant."

"Whatever, I guess I'll go." I shrug, but inside I'm giddy. A night out with Gio makes me feel all tingly inside.

"Great. Since it's last minute, can Aria borrow something from one of you?" he asks Sienna and Natalie.

"Absolutely! They both can." The girls grab Amber and me by our arms and rush us up to their room they share on the second floor. There's enough rooms in the club for each girl to have their own room but they choose to share.

After hours of pampering and primping—courtesy of Natalie and Sienna—Amber, Nico, Gio, and I are on our way to the function in a limo. Gio and Nico are both dressed to the nines in tuxes that fit them like they were designed just for them. Gio's hair is gelled similar to Nico's, making them look even more like the siblings they are. While I prefer his hair messy, his hair gelled like this makes him look like a sexy, powerful businessman.

"What?" He eyes me curiously.

"I like your hair gelled almost as much as I like it messy."

Gio grins devilishly at my compliment.

"So, what kind of dinner is this?" I ask.

"It's a charity function. The owners of the major resorts in the area get invited every year. I usually give a check and don't attend, but there's someone that's going to be there I want to see."

"A friend?"

"More like an acquaintance." Gio and Nico share a look that tells me whoever he's going to meet isn't one he would consider a friend in any way.

"What if someone recognizes me here?"

"Doesn't matter. Weston knows you're with me. You're staying with me so I can ensure your safety until we figure out what he's up to. Being seen in public only means he looks like an idiot when he says he's away looking for you." He shrugs. "Just don't leave my side. Rome and Caesar are already there and will be watching you."

We arrive to the event and I'm shocked as to how many people are here. It's being held in a hotel ballroom and is decorated for spring. It gives off a garden feel with colorful butterflies and flowers everywhere. The linens are cream with pastel lining. It's absolutely breathtaking and magical.

Nico and Amber take off in one direction while Gio pulls me in another. We're stopped several times by people who all seem to know Gio. They discuss hotel politics, ask how his mom is doing, some ask how his brother is doing in Italy, and a few men ask about La Stella's, the gentleman's club. I wonder how many of these men belong to the club and then I wonder if anyone will assume I'm one of the women who works for him.

Quite a few women stop Gio to talk as well. Several pretend like I'm not on his arm and flirt with him. He doesn't flirt back, though. He's polite and cordial, and his smile never falters, but from spending so much time with him, I know it's an act.

"Would you like a drink?" he asks when we get a moment to ourselves.

"Yes, please."

"What would you like?"

"Surprise me."

He nods and walks not even twenty feet away to get our drinks. I'm watching him stand at the bar ordering our drinks when I feel a hand run down my arm. I jump at the touch, backing up.

"I'm sorry. I didn't mean to scare you. I saw you from across the room and had to tell you that you're simply divine."

My eyes roll up to my forehead in my mind, but on the outside, I smile, not knowing if this man is a business associate of Gio's.

"Thank you."

"My name is Sebastian Lorenzo." He takes my hand and brings

it up to his lips for a kiss. It reminds me of when I met Caesar and he did the same thing, only where Caesar's approach was playful, this guy comes off as slimy. It takes everything in me not to pull my hand away and wipe his saliva off onto my dress.

"I'm Aria." I leave my last name off intentionally. Legally, it's Hightower-Sutton since my mom had it changed when she married Weston, but I'm planning to have it reverted to her maiden name, Sutton.

I notice Caesar walking toward us, his cell phone to his ear, but before he gets to us, Gio returns, giving Caesar a slight nod that one wouldn't notice if not aware of the situation. Caesar nods back and remains in eyesight but several yards back.

"Sebastian." Gio hands me my drink, then pulls me closer to his side, tucking me under his arm, either in a show of possessiveness or protectiveness. Either way, it's much appreciated.

"Giovanni. I was just acquainting myself with your date."

"Aria, I see Amber and Nico over there." He nods toward them. "Why don't you go say hello while I speak with Sebastian?" It's posed as a question, but it's clearly a command. I smile and agree, leaving the men to do...whatever it is they're going to do.

"Hey!" Amber gives me a one-armed hug, since her other hand is holding her drink. "Are you having fun?"

"Yeah, I guess. If you call watching Gio being hit on by every hot woman in a pair of Louboutin's, and me getting hit on by some seriously creepy guy."

"Who hit on you?" Nico asks, his voice laced with concern.

"That guy Gio's talking to."

Nico's gaze follows mine. "Sebastian Lorenzo. Make sure you stay away from him, both of you."

"Gladly," I assure him.

We stand by the bar, chatting for a while. I've finished off the sweet concoction Gio had gotten for me, downed another, and now I'm on my third when Gio makes his way over to us. He comes up next to me, his arm falling over my shoulders. He pulls me toward him and dips his head slightly to place a soft kiss to my temple, making my belly feel like it's being attacked by an onslaught of butterflies.

"Yeah?" Nico asks and Gio replies with a small nod. "You ladies ready to go?" Nico looks at Amber then to me for our answer.

"But we didn't get to dance." Amber pouts.

Nico laughs. "Well, we can't have that now, can we?" He takes her hand and pulls her onto the dance floor.

Gio's heated gaze meets mine. "Would you like to dance?"

"I would love to."

He pulls me around to face him, his hands going to my hips as mine wrap around his neck. We sway to Aerosmith's *Don't Want to Miss a Thing*, our bodies flush against one another. The lyrics hit me hard, reminding me how much I've missed these last several months and how I don't want to miss any more. I wonder how many people in this moment are making memories with someone they love.

Living their life to the fullest. Loving hard and without regrets.

My head goes to Gio's chest as we sway to the music. It's such a simple moment and to most it would be inconsequential, but to me, it's a moment of peace, a moment I almost wish would last forever. I haven't felt this kind of serenity in a long time, but here in Gio's arms, I feel content—like I'm finally ready to move forward with my life.

"You look exquisite tonight, Ari," Gio murmurs into my ear.

I glance up at him and the intensity in his eyes has my stomach twisting into knots.

"Are you giving me a nickname?" I ask, trying to keep the mood light.

He smirks. "I figured it was only fitting since you gave me one."

I laugh softly and rest my head back against his chest, enjoying the way our bodies move together—feeling the comfort of his heart beating against me.

"Thank you," I whisper, needing him to know how thankful I am for what he's done for me.

Gio squeezes me tight, his way of acknowledging that he knows I'm not just thanking him for a nickname, but for so much more.

Our time dancing ends too soon and before I know it, we're saying our goodbyes and heading back home. Nico insists the limo drops us all off at Gio's house, assuring us he'll get Amber home safely. I give her a silent look to make sure she's okay with that and she gives me one back that conveys she's more than okay with it.

When we get back to the house, Gio and I head to his room. I grab a pair of pajamas and go to the bathroom to change. When I come out, he's standing in his boxers, about to pull on his sweats. It might be the liquid courage in me, but without giving it a second thought, I bridge the gap between us, and stepping up behind him, I wrap my hands around his torso.

He freezes at my touch, then turns around. "Ari…"

"I want you," I say boldly, not wanting to think about or discuss this. I want to have this…have him. With all the craziness in my life, I just want something for me. I want to feel his touch and his warmth surrounding me.

Holding my gaze, he pushes a lock of hair behind my ear then studies me for a second. His eyes run over my face and down to my lips. He rubs the pad of his thumb across my bottom lip then his eyes flit back to mine, a sad smile gracing his face. "If we have sex, it'd be nothing more than that. Sex. You deserve more. You deserve shit I can't give you."

"I'm not asking for anything more than that."

He goes to turn away and I know it's because he can't handle the connection between us. I stop him, both of my hands holding onto his arms, needing him to understand. "I haven't had sex of my own free will in almost a year." I swallow thickly at my own words, holding back the tears threatening to well up.

"And it's still too soon. It's only been a little over a month since you got here. Since you miscarried your baby."

My hands fist at my sides at the rejection, but also at the fact that once again someone's telling me what I need and how I feel. "I'm aware of how long it's been," I grit out. "I know what I've lost. I was the one there."

"Then you know it's too soon," he murmurs.

"I know it's my body and my mind and it's definitely my heart and I get to decide that."

Gio rubs his hand over the scruff on his face, but I don't stop there. Reaching up, I frame his face with my hands, so he gives me his full attention. "When we kissed, I know you felt it too. How good we could be together."

"Of course, I did. But then what? We get married and have tons of babies and live happily ever fucking after? That's your future, not mine." He backs out of my hands and looks away. His words are cold, devoid of all emotion. They remind me of how he speaks when doing business.

"Don't speak to me like that," I snap. "Your parents are married." Regardless of how uptight they are, his mom and dad kissed and held hands while we were there. He doesn't come from a broken home so I don't get why he's so anti-relationship.

"My mom was a whore!" He takes a deep breath, trying to calm himself. "She was a whore in one of the bordellos in Italy. She worked for my father. He took her out of that life and saved her. Sure, her life is better now in many ways, but she also lives with guards around her. Her life is put at risk every day. My grandmother was killed in

Italy in a shooting. Is that what you want? To live in fear of being killed every day?" Gio shouts the last question, his temper getting the best of him.

And now it all makes sense. Him not wanting anything more. But it doesn't stop me from wanting him. When you've been through what I have, you come to realize life's too short and can end too quickly to live in fear.

"I think it should be my goddamned choice!" I shout back. "It's my life! You don't want me? Fine! But I need to move forward. I need to get a job and earn a living. I need to go back to college! I want my life back!"

"I can give you whatever you want, Aria!"

"Except you." It isn't a question.

"Except me," he confirms.

"I want to work here."

"Fuck no! That's off the table, so get it out of your head."

He pulls his sweatpants up his legs, throws on his shirt, and leaves the room, slamming the door behind him. I'm so livid, my hands are shaking. It's been a long time since I've had a panic attack, but I can feel one coming on. I grab my prescription and swallow a pill. Then I get dressed, needing to get the hell out of here.

I grab my new cell phone Gio bought me the other day and jog down the steps. The place is ghostly quiet and nobody stops me. I keep going out the front door and make my way to the side of the house, to the garage. One of the doors is open and I spot a box hanging on the wall full of keys. I grab a set and click the remote. A beautiful sporty-looking car beeps and I go to it. The car is keyless, so I hold down the brake and press the button to start the car. Looking around the vehicle, I find the garage clicker and press it. The door slides up and I back out, as my phone vibrates in the cup holder.

I exit down the driveway and through the gate, shocked I haven't been stopped yet. Once I hit the open road, I press down on the gas pedal, leaving everything behind me. I have no idea where I'm going, but I don't care. I just drive, turning at random stops, with the music blaring through the speakers. For the first time in a long time, I feel free. Putting the windows down, I enjoy the fresh air, the wind whipping around my hair.

As I drive, lost in the music and beautiful night, I think about everything that's happened. My life before getting kidnapped. How naïve I was. All the signs were there. I was just too trusting to put it all together. Weston's temper, my mom's willingness to obey his every command. How happy she was when I asked to stay in the dorms even though we didn't live far from the school campus.

My mind goes to my relationship with Antonio. It could just be me overthinking things because of the situations as of late, but looking back, I can remember his cryptic text messages and phone calls. I never knew where he lived, never met his family. Sure, we weren't serious. Most college students aren't. But we hung out quite a bit and the sex was decent, I think. But I must be missing something for him to think I left willingly...unless maybe he was working for Weston. I shake those thoughts out of my head. It's all not adding up.

My thoughts move to Gio. Him saving me and bringing me to his house. My life has changed so much. I've been forced to grow up and now I see things in a whole new light. My priorities have changed. I feel all over the place like I'm lost in the dark, my mind and heart running around and bumping up against the walls, trying to find their way.

I go back to Gio. The way he laughs when it's just the two of us but is so serious around everyone else. I find myself smiling when I picture him lying in bed, laughing to whatever television show I'm forcing him to watch. Our relationship is different than the one I had with Antonio. It's comfortable and natural. He says he can't give me , but doesn't he realize he already has? He's already let me in.

I have no idea how long I've been driving or where I'm at, but when blue and red sirens show in my rearview mirror, I have a sinking feeling my freedom is quickly coming to an end. In more ways than one.

Chapter Fifteen

GIOVANNI

I STORM OUT OF THE ROOM, PISSED. PISSED AT ARIA FOR wanting me. Pissed at myself for wanting her. Pissed at the world, knowing we could never work. Even more pissed at Cecilia for putting it in Aria's head that she should work here. I slam my office door behind me and slouch into my chair. I stare at the computer screen for several minutes, not focusing on anything, when there's a knock on my door.

"I'm busy!" I growl. The door opens and Johnny walks in. "I said I'm fucking busy."

"Too busy to hear that Aria has been pulled over by the police?" Did I just hear him correctly?

"What the fuck did you just say?" I'm already grabbing my wallet and cell phone and heading out the door.

"They pulled her over for speeding."

I turn around when I hear a hint of laughter in his voice. "And why is this funny?"

"She was driving your Lambo. Doing over a hundred." He has the sense to hide his grin. "They pulled up your plate and called me immediately, wanting to let you know. They're holding her at the station until you can get there."

"Jesus fucking Christ!" I get to my garage and sure enough my goddamned Lamborghini is missing. While the car isn't my most expensive, it's sure as fuck my favorite. Of course, that's the car she would steal. I grab the keys to the BMW and jump in as Johnny gets in on the passenger side.

We ride in silence for the first few minutes until Johnny says, "Cici told me Aria might be working here."

"Over my dead body." It feels like I've said that same sentence a dozen damn times in the past twenty-four hours.

"What do you care?" he challenges. "You've said for years you don't want to settle down. Have you changed your mind?"

"She's better than this shit." I see Johnny shake his head out of the corner of my eye. "What?"

"You've never been ashamed of this life."

"And I'm not. But it's not a life for her. She's good. She's been through too much." And that's the goddamned truth. Getting to know Aria, there's so much more to her. She's the bright in a world full of dark. She sees the good in everything. She's been through more shit than anyone I know, but it doesn't bring her down. A weaker person would be in the corner licking her wounds. But not Aria, she chooses to see the roses in a pasture filled with shit. Chooses to stand tall and face the world head on. It'd be so easy for her to play the woe-is-me card, but she doesn't. She takes what life has thrown at her and moves forward.

"Speaking of which, before I got the call from the cops, I was coming to tell you we got into the safes. They were exactly where she said they would be. A bunch of papers and contracts. But you won't believe this. Her birth certificate...The name listed under father: Angelo Moretti."

My head jerks toward Johnny, the car jerking as well, but I straighten it out quickly. "The real estate conglomerate from New York?" And then it hits me. "Holy shit."

"You thinking what I'm thinking?"

"I sure as fuck hope we're both wrong."

"That Aria's boyfriend being related to the man who was business partners with her alleged father isn't a coincidence?"

"How long ago was Angelo killed?"

"I looked it up. Only eight months before Aria's mom was killed in the car accident."

"If Angelo was Aria's dad, that would make her his heir if he recognized her as his daughter, which he clearly did according to her birth certificate. She would be worth millions. So where the fuck is all the money?"

Johnny shrugs. "And that's the million-dollar question, my friend." Literally.

We pull into the police station where I see my two-million-dollar limited edition Lamborghini sitting in a parking spot. Johnny chuckles under his breath as we get out.

We walk inside and Dan Mills, the chief of police—who is also a member at my club—gratis, of course—greets us and walks us back. "Dan, thank you for calling me before taking any legal action. I can handle it from here."

"Sounds good, Giovanni. She's lucky one of my guys pulled her over, otherwise she'd be behind bars right now for driving reckless, and your car would be impounded. She was clocked at doing one-oh-five in a fifty."

"I can assure you this won't happen again."

We shake hands and Dan opens the door to the small interrogation room where Aria is sitting with her arms crossed over her chest. Even being faced with reckless driving, she sits there tough as nails, ready to take on the world.

"Hey Johnny, can you drive the Lambo home? I'll drive Aria back with me."

He agrees and heads back up to the front with Dan. I stand in the doorway for a few seconds watching Aria without saying anything and thinking about my conversation with Johnny in the car on our way over here. Have I changed my mind about wanting to settle down? No. Not until I look at Aria that is, and then as clear as day, I can see an entire future with this woman. Her light shining down on my dark, illuminating my world. But am I going to act on those feelings? No. Aria will never understand this life, and just like her dad stayed away because of the dangers, that's what I'll do as well. Locked up in my house, it's easy to create a bubble for us. But outside those walls is reality, and bringing Aria into my life...my reality, isn't what's best for her.

"Did you have a nice drive?" I ask, stepping into the room.

"You have a fast car." She looks up at me, her eyes filled with unshed tears.

"No shit. It better be for what it cost. Where were you going in such a rush?"

Aria shrugs, a solemn tear falling down her cheek. "Trying to run, I guess."

I sit across from her. "From what?"

"My life."

"Is it that bad living with me?"

"No. I just..." She swipes her tears away and stares at the ceiling, trying to keep herself from letting any more fall. She shakes her head back and forth, then looks at me, her eyes filled to the brim. "I just want...fuck! Gio..." She swipes another fallen tear and takes a deep breath. "I just want, for once, to make my own decisions. My entire life has been based on everyone else. I didn't know my dad by his choice. I didn't know about him by my mom's choice. I went to the school Weston insisted on because he was paying. I even had to lie about my major because photography wasn't an acceptable career goal. My mom made me change my last name. She moved Weston in without asking me."

"What do you want, Aria?" I hold my breath, wondering if she'll say me, unsure if I'll be able to resist her if she does.

She stares at me for a few moments before she closes her eyes, takes another measured breath and swallows thickly, then reopens them, looking determined. "To be independent. I want to work at La Stella's."

There's a fork in the road. I can go left and tell her no. Tell her I want her and want to try to settle down. Or, I can go right. Tell her okay and lose her before I've even had her. My heart says to go left, but my head says to go right. Her working for me will mean she's off limits. It'll mean she's safe from the life I live and I know it's the choice I have to make. "Okay. If you want to work at La Stella's, I won't stop you."

She doesn't smile. She doesn't say a word. She simply nods once then stands and walks out the door, and fuck if my heart doesn't feel like I just made the wrong choice. Like she's not just walking out of this room but out of my life.

We ride home in silence and once we get up to the room, she begins to pack her stuff.

"What are you doing?" I ask, beginning to panic. There's no way she's leaving.

"Escorts sleep on the second floor."

"So what? You sleep in here." I snatch her clothes out of her hands, not wanting to come to terms with the fact I've pushed her away. That I've made my bed and now I have to lie in it…alone.

She takes her clothes back and sets them on the bed. "I'm going to be staying on the second floor, Giovanni. Sienna and Natalie said I can room with them."

I watch as she continues to pack. She's only moving one floor down, but it feels like she's moving across the fucking continent. I don't help her. She comes in and out of the room several times, taking all her stuff, while I sit here, frozen in my spot, unsure of how to fix this. When she's finally done, she closes the door behind her and I sit in my same spot, staring at nothing, my heart feeling like it's been ripped from my fucking chest, knowing this is the way it needs to be.

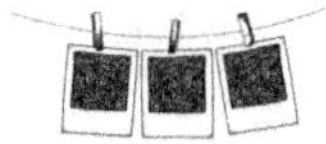

FOR THE NEXT SEVERAL DAYS I DROWN MYSELF IN WORK and getting information on Aria's biological father. Most nights I sleep on my office couch, not wanting to go back to my room—not wanting to accept that Aria is gone.

I stay away from the main area. Cecilia updated me that Aria is being trained, but I told her I don't want to know anything. She doesn't update me on the other girls, so there's no reason to update me on Aria.

My phone rings and it's a New York area code. "Hello."

"Giovanni Valentino?"

"Yes, who's this?"

"This is Anthony Torino. My assistant has told me you've called looking for me. What can I do for you?"

"I think it's best we meet in person." That way I can look him in the eye when I threaten him.

"Okay, I'm assuming since you want this meeting you'll be flying out to New York." Smart guy...he wants the home court advantage, but a true player knows it's not where you play but how you play, and I'll win at this game no matter where we are. *Game on, fucker.*

I check my calendar. "I can be there the day after tomorrow." We confirm the time and location before hanging up.

"Are you going to tell Aria?" Johnny asks, sitting across from me.

"I'm going to bring her with me."

Chapter Sixteen

ARIA

IT'S APRIL IN NEVADA. THE SUN IS SHINING AND IT'S humid as hell, but the flowers in the garden are blooming. I snap a couple pictures of each beautiful flower. Today is April twenty-ninth—also known as my twenty-first birthday. I'll be spending it out to dinner with Benjamin Fields. He's good-looking, with brown hair and brown eyes, looks to be in his mid-twenties, and is originally from New York, but travels all over opening up night clubs.

He doesn't know it's my birthday and it wouldn't really matter. While Benjamin seems like a decent guy—at least based on the one date we went on—I'm paid to focus on him. He said he joined La Stella's Gentleman's Club to try it out because he enjoys the company and it can be difficult to find a companion who isn't looking for strings. At first, I thought he'd try to hit on me, thinking I'd give him more, but at the end of the date, with a kiss to my cheek, he said good night.

I've gone on a few other dates with other guys similar to Benjamin—men simply looking for a woman to have dinner with, or attend a function with. I'm not sure why they waste their money to spend the evening with me, when they could get more from another woman, but I'm making money, and based on how much I get paid per date, a few more guys like Benjamin and I should have enough to sign up for a couple online classes. Gio was right. He does pay his escorts well...*very well.*

I snap a few more photos of the gardens before heading back inside to get ready. When I turn around, I'm met with a hard chest. "Jesus, Gio! Ever hear of personal space?"

Gio looks down at me and chuckles. "Are you getting annoyed because you weren't watching where you were going and ran into me?"

"What do you need?" I ask, trying to get to the point. Gio has been making it a point to avoid me, so for him to be here in my space must mean he needs something.

"I just wanted to wish you a Happy Birthday." He holds out a small box wrapped in silver and pink shiny paper, and I feel a crack in my carefully guarded heart, reminding me I need to keep this man at arm's length. He made it clear how he feels and now I need to move forward. Letting him in will only hurt me in the long run and I've been hurt enough.

"You remembered." I reluctantly take the gift from him.

"Of course, I did. You're officially of drinking age." Gio gives me his signature panty-melting wink. "You don't have to open it now."

"Oh, well, I want to." I rip open the paper and inside the small box is a shiny silver key. "A key?"

"It's to a dark room. I know you like digital prints, but I remember you saying you loved using the college's darkroom." I told him this one night while we were watching an old black and white movie, that I love and appreciate the new technology but sometimes it's nice to go at it old school.

"You built me a darkroom?"

Gio just shrugs, like turning an entire room into a darkroom is no big deal, when it is, in fact, a big deal. Most of my life I've been given gifts that people expect me to want. Clothes, jewelry, a car. Materialistic possessions wealthy people should want. When I was younger, before my mom met Weston, she was different. She would buy me personal gifts like scrapbooks for my pictures. But the longer she was with him, the further apart we grew.

But sometimes, my real mom, the one who knew me, would shine through. One time she bought me a polaroid camera. Weston would bitch every time I would drag it along with me everywhere we went, snapping pictures. The camera would make a loud scraping sound as it would develop, the photo printing right there. I would pull it out and shake the picture as it magically appeared.

I look down at the key sitting heavy in my hand. "Thank you. I can't wait to use it. There's nothing like the feel and smell of real photos."

"You're welcome. Do you have any plans tonight?"

"I'm working."

Gio frowns. "Okay. Well, Maggie made you a cake. It's in the kitchen. Make sure you find time to eat a piece."

"I will. Thank you." The awkwardness that surrounds us is palpable, so I make the first move to walk away, but before I do, Gio stops me, his hand touching my arm and sending a bolt of electricity through me.

"I have some info on your ex-boyfriend. We have a meeting in New York we need to go to. It'll be a same day trip, so you'll need the day after tomorrow off."

I have so many questions to ask but hold them in for now. "Okay, I'll let Cecilia know. Thank you, Gio."

He gives me a curt nod before stalking away.

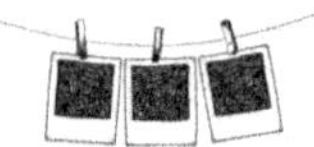

"I HAVE A CLUB OPENING IN TWO DAYS. I KNOW IT'S SHORT notice, but I'll let Cecilia know I'm willing to pay double for the inconvenience." Benjamin and I are sitting at the dinner table. Caesar is only about ten feet away guarding me. You wouldn't know it unless you knew him. He never looks my way, but I know I'm safe no matter where I am because he's always close. I've spent the last two hours pretending Benjamin and I are at this fancy Japanese restaurant for my birthday but when the waiters came out to sing Happy Birthday and they stopped at the table next to us, it hit me that while I wanted this, to work and be independent, I'm not any happier than I was before. While I might be going through the motions of life, I'm not actually living.

"I can't. I have a meeting in New York and I don't know what time I'll be back." Benjamin's mouth turns downward into a frown. "I'm sorry."

"Aria, what's going on?"

"Nothing. It's just a last-minute meeting."

"Not the meeting. Tonight, you seem down. You haven't spoken more than a handful of sentences the entire night."

"I'm sorry," I say again.

"Stop apologizing and tell me what's going on." Benjamin takes my hands in his and for a second, I think about what it would feel like to be on a real date with Benjamin instead of getting paid to escort him to dinner.

"Today's my birthday," I blurt out.

His eyebrows raise in shock. "Why didn't you say something?"

"Because I don't get paid to celebrate my birthday." I pull my hand out of his. "I'm twenty-one today and my life is nothing like I pictured it would be."

"How did you picture it?"

"In college, majoring in photography. Maybe traveling to Italy for the summer. Dating and hanging out with friends. Visiting art museums and taking tons of pictures to commemorate each new chapter of my life." I'm not sure why I'm telling Benjamin all this.

Maybe because he's an outsider and I don't have any feelings one way or another for him.

"I went through some stuff recently and I'm finally ready to move forward with my life. Start living again. But it feels like I'm hitting one obstacle after the next."

"Then you should start living," he says. "Life's too short to not live it how you want to."

Those are my thoughts exactly, so why haven't I started living my life with that mindset?

We finish our dinner and Benjamin pays the check. A twenty-minute ride in silence later and he drops me off at the front door. He leans in close, his lips grazing my cheek softly. "Good night, Aria. Good luck on living your life." He steps back, and with a wink, walks back toward his vehicle. He didn't say it, but I can tell by finality in his words, I won't be seeing him again.

I walk inside and find Cecilia sitting at the bar. I sit next to her and ask Emilio for a Jack and Coke.

"Aren't you a little young to be drinking such an adult drink?" God, this woman is such a bitch.

"I'm twenty-one today." I take my drink Emilio placed in front of me and lift it up, giving Cecilia a fake *cheers* before I down half the glass. I set it on the bar top and glance at her. "I want to change my profile. I want to add an option to it."

"Oh yeah? And what would you like to add?"

"Sex. I'm willing to have sex."

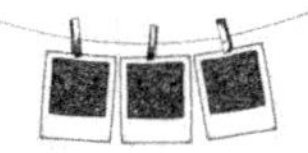

THE PLANE RIDE TO NEW YORK IS FIVE HOURS. GIO AND I are sitting next to each other in first class and for the first four hours, I read my book while he works on his laptop. Exactly one hour before the plane is scheduled to land, he puts it away and turns to me. "Before we arrive, I need to explain to you what I found out and my theories. You need to know what's going on before we walk through those doors."

I click off my iPad and close the case slowly. "Okay, you have my attention."

"Antonio Torino, your ex-boyfriend, is the son of Anthony Torino. His father is a well-known *leader*." He says leader, but I know what he means. He's a mob boss for another organization.

"Okay." Gio pulls out a piece of paper and hands it to me. "My birth certificate?"

"Take a look at who's listed under your father."

"Angelo Moretti. I've never seen this before. Is this my dad?" All this time, my father's identity has been written in black and white on my birth certificate. No wonder my mom never gave it to me.

"It would make sense. You said your mom insisted your dad's life was too dangerous. Angelo Moretti was huge in the mob."

"Was?"

"He was killed eight months before your mom died." My heart tightens and hot tears burn my lids, not necessarily for a man I never knew but for a man I would never know.

"Anthony and Angelo were business partners. Your father was worth millions, possibly even billions, before he died. When did you start dating Antonio?" I think back to when I met him. It was about a month into my Sophomore year. My mom died the first week of May...Eight months before that would be...I gasp loudly, causing someone in the row next to us to glare. "September. He showed up in September, eight months before my mom died. But why?"

"My theory is your dad had shares in the company, and when he died, they had to go to somebody or Anthony would get the entire company. My guess is they went to you, only you didn't know. We also found an envelope with attorney information on it. He's based in New York. I placed a call to him and I'm waiting to hear back."

"But why would Antonio date me? It doesn't make sense. He never once asked me anything regarding my dad. To be honest, we weren't even that serious."

"I'm not sure, Ari. But hopefully we'll get some answers today."

A thirty-minute cab ride later, and we arrive at a building that reads *Torino Real Estate.*

"Let me do the talking, okay?" Gio says.

I nod in agreement, while glancing around. It feels like I'm being watched, but I'm not sure why...

"Rome and Caesar are here," Gio whispers, answering my silent question, and I feel my shoulders sag in relief.

When we get to the top floor, Gio lets the secretary know we're here to see Mr. Torino. She escorts us to the room and when I walk in, I come face-to-face with Antonio Torino. I gasp for the second time today louder than planned. Gio takes my hand and gives it a comforting squeeze.

"Gentlemen. I don't believe we need to make introductions. After all, Aria dated Antonio, for what, eight months?" Gio has slipped into business mode. His voice is cold and calculating, his face devoid of all emotion. It'll never cease to amaze me how he can so easily switch from hot to cold.

He sets his briefcase down and pops open the locks, taking some papers out. "Anthony, before I begin to share with you my theory, would you care to explain anything?"

"Giovanni, why don't we have a seat?" Anthony gestures to the conference table which seats probably twenty people easily.

"We could, but I don't expect to be here long enough to waste my time getting comfortable. Why don't we just cut to the chase? You have shares of Aria's that belong to her. Either you give them back or I'm going to dismantle your entire life piece by piece, starting with your organization and ending with this business." Gio waves his arm in the air to emphasize his point.

"You motherfucker!" Antonio seethes. His father holds him back and Gio laughs, only it comes out dark and sinister, sending a chill up my spine.

"Looks like I hit the nail on the head." Gio turns to me. "Before we proceed, Aria, do you want to be a part of this business? Does real estate interest you?" He knows it doesn't, but I go along with his question.

"No, I don't want any part of this business."

"Very well. Mr. Torino, I have put a call into Angelo Moretti's attorney. He'll be getting back to me with the specifics of the will and when he does, I'll know exactly how many shares Aria owns."

"She signed them over to me!" Anthony booms, his fist slamming down on the table.

"No, she didn't. Weston did. What I want to know is why? There's a couple pieces to the puzzle I'm missing. Maybe you would care to fill me in?" When Anthony doesn't speak, Gio adds, "Keep in mind, your company and organization are at stake here. Now is not the time to stay tight-lipped."

And with that, Anthony sings like a canary. "I built this goddamned company from the ground up! And what did Angelo do? He left his half to his daughter! A daughter he didn't even know. They should have been left to me."

"So, you what, had her kidnapped and forced her to sign?"

"No, that was all Hightower. When I approached him after finding out about the will, I offered him a finder's fee if he could get his wife to sign over the shares. Five months later she died, and a month after that, Aria signed over her rights."

"Where does your son fit into all of this?"

"He was keeping tabs on her...until her mom died. Then he took her and delivered her to the senator in exchange for her signature."

My eyes go to Antonio. "You're the one who kidnapped me?" My voice raises several octaves with each word I spit out.

"You didn't really think I was in love with you or some shit, did you? You were nothing more than a decent fuck to pass the time with until we got the business of the shares handled." No, I didn't think he was in love with me. I sure as hell wasn't in love with him, but damn, how did I misjudge his character so badly?

Gio stalks toward Antonio and grabs him by his shirt. He shoves him up against a wall and punches him straight in the jaw. Antonio's face jerks to the side, his lip gushing out blood. Anthony's guards, as well as Caesar and Rome, run into the room, prepared to defend their bosses.

"Let that be a fucking warning to you. Don't speak about Aria. Don't speak *to* Aria. Hell, don't even look at her. I have the means and motive to destroy you, and I won't hesitate to do so."

"Giovanni, please. He is nothing more than a child." Anthony tries to calm Gio, but he couldn't care less. He keeps a hold of Antonio's shirt for a few more seconds before he finally lets it go.

"If he's in this business, he's not a fucking child, and the moment he plotted against Aria and took her, handing her over to Weston, you brought him into this business, so teach your son how this business works before he gets himself killed. Now get him the fuck out of here while we discuss these shares."

Anthony sends Antonio out, but the guards remain in the back. We sit at the table to discuss the selling of my shares, but if

I'm honest, I'm not sure what is said. Numbers are flown out every which way, Gio threatens to call his attorney, Anthony tells him that won't be necessary, and about an hour later they're shaking hands and Gio's telling Anthony he expects a contract to be sent over in the next forty-eight hours.

When we got done with the meeting, Gio tells me we have a few hours before we have to be back at the airport and pulls my camera out from his bag. "How about some sightseeing?"

I jump up and down and pull him into a hug, ecstatic that I'll get to see some of New York. "Thank you! Thank you!" I clap my hands before grabbing my camera from him. "What should we see first?"

We spend the afternoon sightseeing. Gio takes me through Central Park where I snap pictures of the Shakespearean Theatre from the Belvedere Castle. From there we go to the Empire State building. I insist we take a selfie at the top and Gio reluctantly agrees. We have a late dinner in Times Square, and before heading back to the airport, we stop by the nine-eleven memorial pools. I take the most heartbreaking photo of the names that are engraved around the edges, of the people who lost their life on that horrific day. One name hits me hard because directly underneath, it reads, "And unborn baby."

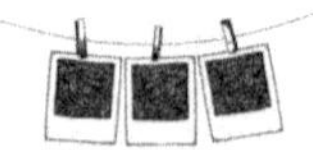

WE'RE BACK ON THE PLANE AND HEADING TO LAS VEGAS.

I'm exhausted on so many levels but at the same time I've had such a wonderful afternoon, it felt like it counteracted all the bad shit. "Thank you for today."

"No problem. Once the contract arrives, we'll go over it before you sign anything."

"No, I mean, yes, thank you for that, but also thank you for the sightseeing. One day I'll travel all over the world capturing places like New York."

"You most definitely will, Aria." He leans over and gives me a chaste kiss on my temple before settling down to work.

Chapter Seventeen

GIOVANNI

IT'S BEEN ALMOST A WEEK SINCE ARIA'S AND MY TRIP TO New York. I received the contract in the mail within forty-eight hours, but I wanted to speak with the attorney before making any final decisions. Aria offered to get her own attorney since she's on her *I'm Miss independent* kick, but I explained the less who know about this the better and my attorney knows how to deal with situations such as this. She then offered to pay, but I refused to let her. At first, Angelo's attorney was reluctant to speak with me, but once I explained who I was and Aria's situation, he agreed to meet with us. He was in Texas for a business meeting, so he said he'd fly over to meet with us in person.

"Boss, there's a Mr. Cohen here to see you," Edgardo announces.

"Thank you, you can see him back and can you let Aria know to come back as well?"

"You got it."

Mark Cohen steps into my office first. We shake hands and have a seat. A few minutes later, Aria comes back. She's dressed beautifully. In a pale pink wrap around dress and nude heels. Her makeup and hair are both done. She must be going somewhere, maybe on a date with a member. The thought is like a punch to my chest.

"Aria, please have a seat," I choke out. "This is Mr. Cohen. He was your father's attorney."

"It's nice to meet you, Mr. Cohen." She smiles softly and shakes his hand before having a seat next to him.

"Please call me Mark. I knew your father for many years. I'm so sorry for what has happened. When he passed away, I contacted your mom and she assured me she would go through the specifics of his will with you. When she passed away, your stepfather contacted me. He told me he was taking care of you and asked for the trust to be released to you early. I explained to him that I couldn't do that.

"Had I known Mr. Hightower had ill-intentions, I would have contacted you myself. When your dad contacted your mom years ago, she felt twenty-two would be a good age for you to receive your inheritance God forbid something happen to him before then, and I explained that to Mr. Hightower. He wasn't pleased but had no choice but to agree."

"My mom spoke with my dad?" Her words come out broken and who can blame her? She's an only child with two deceased parents. Both were only children, leaving Aria with no family.

"They spoke on occasion to make sure you were taken care of."

Mark pulls out a stack of papers and sets them on the desk. "Aside from the shares he left you—which Giovanni tells me you went over with Anthony—your father left you a substantial trust fund that will go to you once you turn twenty-two."

"Twenty-two," Aria whispers and looks at me. "This is why he was holding me in the basement."

"He was in need of money and must have found out about your trust." All the pieces to the puzzle are finally coming together, but the picture isn't pretty.

Mark hands Aria the papers and she reads the first page, her button nose scrunching up like she always does when she's confused. "I'm sorry. I don't understand any of this." She sighs. "I told Gio I should hire an attorney."

"That's okay. Unless you're in the business, it can be confusing, and I'm an attorney so I can help you. What it says in a nutshell is that when you turn twenty-two you are to be given your trust of five hundred million dollars. If your mom passes away, I am to hold on to it until then. Your mom was made guardian of the shares of Angelo's company, but it seems she signed them over to Weston, who signed them over to Antonio."

"I'm handling that," I assure Mark.

"I-I'm sorry. Did you just say five hundred million dollars?" Aria's eyes go wide in shock.

"Yes, ma'am. Five hundred million on your twenty-second birthday."

"Hol-y shit."

Chapter Eighteen

ARIA

"ARE YOU READY FOR YOUR BIG DATE?" SIENNA, NATALIE, and Holly—another woman who works here that I've grown close to—all lay across our beds as I fix my hair one last time. I'm trying so hard to focus on my date tonight. I'm not sure how, but the day I changed my profile to allow sex, Benjamin scheduled a private room. My guess is Cecilia told him—I wouldn't put it past her.

Benjamin was out of town but returns today and has booked me for dinner and then the private room afterward. When I changed my profile, I thought I knew why I was doing it. I want to have sex by choice. I want to have sex with a nice guy who'll treat me good and it won't involve me being held down or raped. I spoke with my therapist about all of this and while she doesn't agree with the escort business, she didn't judge. She said only I can decide the right way to handle it. Then she asked me to close my eyes and picture myself lying in bed and about to have sex...

"Who's the first guy that popped into your head, Aria?" she asked.

I didn't want to tell her it was Gio. Fantasizing about him is pointless. So instead I said, "Benjamin." She smiled and said, "Well then, there you go. Maybe he is the one."

Which means, since Benjamin wasn't the man who popped into my head, he isn't the one.

"Earth to Aria!"

I shake myself out of my thoughts. "Sorry, yes, I'm ready."

I check myself out one last time and after saying goodbye to the girls, head downstairs for my date.

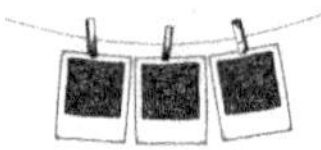

GIOVANNI

"DO YOU THINK SHE'LL GO THROUGH WITH IT?"

"I'm not sure. She's been through so much. I get why she's doing it, though."

"I agree, but I think she should have waited to have sex with a guy she cares about."

I walk into the kitchen to find Sienna, Holly, and Natalie sitting around the island snacking on Maggie's freshly baked cookies. Grabbing one, I pop a piece into my mouth and the girls stop talking.

"Don't stop gossiping on my account. Do we not work anymore?"

The three women glare at me. "Our dates don't arrive until later."

"Who were you guys talking about? Is one of the girls in over her head? You know Cecilia can help." The women all roll their eyes and turn back to their cookies. "What's going on?" My tone gets more serious.

"Cecilia is the reason for this. She won't be of any help," Natalie says.

"Seriously! Ugh! You know damn well she called Benjamin herself to let him know," Holly adds.

"You guys are going to have to explain a little better." I try to hold down my temper, but I'm starting to get irritated.

Natalie huffs. "Fine, Aria changed her profile. Her hard limits no longer include sex, and Benjamin, the guy she's escorted a couple times, found out and scheduled the private room."

The cookie in my hand crumbles as my fist clenches, and I drop the crumbs on the counter. This is my fault. She wanted to have sex of her own free will and instead of being there for her, I pushed her away. But I'm still in the same spot I was in months ago. If I have sex with her, I still can't offer her anything more. My life hasn't changed. I'm still in the organization. My family and business are still dangerous. But she said she was okay with that. She said to let her make her own choices. Fuck! "Which room?"

The three girls look at me, stunned. "Which room?" I repeat.

"Umm...I think room two," Sienna says. Without waiting for her to be sure, I bolt out of the kitchen and head to the rooms. When I get to the second room, I turn the nob and it opens. It's not locked.

Nobody is in the room.

"Edgardo, what room is Aria in?"

He pulls his iPad out. "Room two."

"So, where is she?"

"They might be done with the room, Boss. It was scheduled for a couple hours ago."

I thank Edgardo and head upstairs to my room. When I get to the second floor, without giving it a second thought, I stop at Aria's room. I knock once and wait.

"Come in."

I open the door and see Aria lying across her bed. "You're in here."

Her eyebrows furrow in confusion. "Where else would I be?"

"The girls mentioned you had a private room scheduled for tonight."

Aria stands from the bed, her hand going to her hip. "You're checking up on my schedule? Do you do that for all the girls?"

I step toward her. She's in those adorable fucking sweatpants she always wears. The ones where I don't even have to look to know they have some cheesy writing across her ass. Her face is makeup free and her hair is up in her signature messy bun. Out of all the different looks Aria has, the way she looks right now is hands-down the most beautiful version of this woman.

Grabbing the hair tie in her hair, I pull on it a few times until her hair comes free, falling down her shoulders. "No, I don't keep track of all the women. Just the one that means something to me. Did you have sex with him, Aria?" I hold my breath as I wait for her answer, but I know deep down, her answer won't change how I feel. I want her, every part of her.

"Let's not play this game, Giovanni." Her eyes dart around the room to avoid making eye contact with me.

Grabbing her chin between my thumb and forefinger, I force her to look at me. "This isn't a game."

"Then what is it?"

"I don't fucking know. I just know I want you and no matter how much I try to stop the way I feel, I can't tame down these feelings."

"I didn't have sex with him."

Everything in me relaxes but tenses at the same time for completely different reasons. My hands go to her ass and I lift her up, her legs wrapping around my waist. I carry her out of her room and up the stairs to mine, slamming the door behind us and locking it. The entire time she's quiet, staring at me, her fingers running through my hair.

Laying her on the bed, I climb up her body, trapping her in the circle of my arms, and take a second to memorize her in this position. Her hair is splayed out across my pillow, her deep green eyes shining, and her lips, fuck, those lips, so naturally plump and ready for me. Her breathing is accelerated and I know she's just as overcome with lust as I am.

Not so gently, I bring my lips to hers, claiming her, my tongue slipping inside her mouth as I taste her. Aria moans into my mouth, her hips bucking up and rubbing against my already hard cock, spurring me on.

My lips move to her neck as I trail kisses downward to her collarbone. She shivers in response. Her breathy moans, the only noise in an otherwise quiet room. I pull her shirt up and she finishes pulling it the rest of the way off her for me, leaving her naked from the waist up. Her tits are even more gorgeous than before. Her eating has filled her out in all the right places. Luscious and full and perky as fuck, her nipples are hard.

Taking a nipple into my mouth, I suck on the hardened tip. Aria's back arches as she lets out a loud gasp then a sigh. I take the other one between my lips and suck on it the same way. Then grabbing both tits in my hands, I bring them together, both nipples going into my mouth as I lick and suck and nibble on the rosy buds.

Aria's body starts to wiggle and her hand goes to my shirt, wanting me to remove it. Reluctantly letting go of her tits, I sit up and pull my shirt off my body. My mouth goes right back to where it was, placing kisses all over her.

"Gio..."

I look up when she whispers my name and notice her eyes darting all over the place, like she's nervous. "What's wrong, *cuore mio?* You want me to stop?" The thought that I just called her *my heart* doesn't go unnoticed, but I push it aside for now.

"No, but..." She swallows thickly.

"Talk to me. What do you need?"

"I want to be in control."

Her words have my dick pressing against my zipper.

"You got it. What do you want?" I sit up and wait for her to tell me what she wants from me.

"I want you to give me an orgasm, but I was thinking maybe we can do it at the same time." She sure as fuck doesn't have to tell me twice.

"Whatever you want, baby. Come here."

She crawls over and begins unbuttoning my pants. I help her out and push them, along with my boxers, off, throwing them onto the floor. Her hand goes straight for my cock, and she strokes it a few times before leaning down and putting it into her mouth. Her tongue swirls over the tip of my head before she takes me all the way in—her hot wet mouth deep throating damn near my entire length. I pull back a bit, and her mouth makes a popping sound as my dick leaves her beautiful lips.

"Aria, lie down," I tell her gently, guiding her onto her side. Once she's in position, my cock goes right back into her mouth, while I strip her of her pants and underwear.

With the way we're situated, her sweet cunt is directly in my face, glistening and ready for me. Grabbing her legs with both my hands, I tug her to me, my mouth and tongue delving right in between her pussy folds. I lick up the middle, landing on her clit and giving it extra attention. She tastes like the perfect fucking addiction, and I already know I'll never get enough of her.

Her muffled moans vibrate around my cock, telling me she likes what I'm doing. Her mouth goes lower, taking each of my balls into her mouth, sucking and licking, giving them her undivided attention. Then she runs her tongue back up my shaft before taking me all the way back down her throat once again, making me almost come like a damn teenager.

I need to step up my game before I come in her mouth. Pulling her up and on top of me so she's sitting directly above my face, I push two fingers deep into her and begin fingering her tight pussy. My tongue massages her clit until she's squirming in pleasure, her mouth fucking my cock with such force, I know she's ready to explode. And a few seconds later, she does just that. She lets out a throaty moan, her mouth bobbing on my dick even harder and faster as she comes all over my tongue and fingers.

When I know she's come down from her orgasm, I pull her off me and push her flat on her back. She looks confused as fuck, but I don't explain. Kneeling above her chest, I stroke my dick above her. She catches on quickly as to what I want and takes over.

"Come on me, Gio. Come all over my breasts." She licks her swollen lips in anticipation and it tips me over the edge. My cock throbs and two pumps later, cum is jetting out all over her luscious tits, coating them with my seed. Before I can pull away, Aria raises her head and delicately takes my cock into her mouth, cleaning the head off with her tongue. Then, with her finger, she swipes a string of cum from her tits and brings it up to her mouth, slowly sucking on it, her tongue swirling around the tip of her finger as she tastes my cum.

And I might have come all over again had I not just released everything in me.

Chapter Nineteen

ARIA

GIO AND I ARE LAYING IN HIS BED. AFTER WE BOTH GOT cleaned up, he pulled me into the bed with him, refusing to let me get dressed, and we've been lying here together, neither of us saying a word. My head is on his chest as he runs his fingers up and down my back, shivers tickling their way down my spine. Every time my body reacts, Gio laughs softly.

"You called me your heart." It's not a question. I know he did.

"You know Italian."

"I do. I told you I want to travel there one day."

"You did,"

"What is this?" I ask, and Gio's hand stills.

"This is you quitting your job."

I roll my eyes. "I'm serious."

"So am I." His fingers go back to trailing a line of goose bumps up my spine. After a few minutes, he lets out a soft sigh, his chest rising and falling under me. "I'm going to suck at this, Aria. I'm going to fuck it up at every damn turn. You're going to be in danger every day we are together."

"We can take things slow."

"I can't promise you anything."

"Okay." A lot of people would be upset at what he says, but when you've lived a life like mine, having had shit kept from me and have been lied to most of my life, I respect his raw honesty. I may not like his truth, but I still appreciate it.

"I'm leaving next week to go to the Bahamas. Come with me." A little balloon inside me inflates at the thought of spending some time on the beach with Gio and at the fact he wants to spend time with me, too. Until he adds, "My family will be there, but we'll have plenty of alone time."

And just like that, my balloon pops. "Your family hates me."

"Nico mentioned bringing Amber. Her finals are over and he wants her to go. Apparently, they're getting serious." It doesn't go over my head that he doesn't argue about his family hating me, but I focus on the part about Amber's finals almost being over.

"What's the date?"

"May fifteenth, why?"

A huge ball of emotion clogs my throat. "My mom died today. How could I forget?"

"Baby," Gio says softly, his strong, comforting arms caging me in. "You have a lot going on. You've been through some crazy shit this year. Did she have a burial?"

"No, asshole Weston said she wanted to be cremated. I know he just didn't want to spend the money on a funeral. He wouldn't even give me her ashes."

"I'll have Johnny find them for you. If they're in that house, we'll get them. I promise you."

We lie in silence for a few minutes before I remember what we were talking about.

"Why do they hate me, Gio?"

He frowns then kisses my forehead. "Who?"

"Your parents."

"They want Cecilia and I to marry," he says on a sigh. "I'm the oldest and one day I'll take over the organization. Stefan and my dad are best friends, practically brothers. If we marry, it would make us family by marriage, and if we had children, we would become family by blood."

"Will she be there?"

"I can try to get her to stay here, but she usually goes. Whether she goes or not won't matter, though. My time will be spent with you."

I give him a kiss on his chest. "Okay, I'll go."

Gio and I fall asleep together, but when I wake up, he's gone. I go back to my room, shower and get dressed. Then I go downstairs to let Cecilia know I won't be working here anymore, but when I approach her, her attitude and brush off tells me she's already been informed.

"Can you at least stay on for another couple weeks? Gio and I are going on vacation to the Bahamas and I'll need to look for your replacement once I return."

"I would, except I'll also be on that vacation with Gio." I shrug my shoulders in nonchalance and walk away, leaving her with her jaw halfway to the ground.

I grab my camera and ask Rome if he'll take me to the strip to take some pictures. Natalie overhears and insists on coming. "We can do some shopping while we're there!"

Normally I would say no because I'm usually broke, but after the attorney left the other day, Gio informed me the sale of the shares went through and I'm several million dollars richer. He gave me my credit card and account info and with a laugh, told me not to spend it all in one place.

Not having heard from Amber the last few days, I give her a call. She screams through the phone how excited she is to be going to the Bahamas with Nico, and even more excited to know I'm going as well. Then agrees to join us on our little outing.

Holly and Sienna are both working, so it's just Natalie, Amber, and me walking from shop to shop. They're spending money and I'm snapping pictures of the crazy tourists and attractions. My mom never let me come down here growing up, so it's cool to finally experience the city I've lived in most of my life.

"Hey! Isn't this the guys' hotel?" Amber points to the exquisite hotel in front of us. I recognize it from the day Johnny dropped off Gio for a business meeting.

"It is."

"Let's go in and see if the guys are here!" She grabs my hand, pulling me inside before I can protest. Natalie just shrugs and follows behind. The gentleman at the door asks for our identification to confirm we're all over twenty-one since there's a casino here.

"We're here to see Giovanni or Nico Valentino," I tell the concierge, who in return frowns at me, just as the gentleman from the night at the charity ball walks up to me, a devious smirk plastering on his face. Something about this man rubs me the wrong way. "Miss..."

"Aria," I say, still refusing to give him my last name.

"Aria, I was just about to go up and see Mr. Valentino. Why don't you join me?" He ignores Amber and Natalie, taking my arm in his. I look behind me to make sure the girls are following. They both give me a *what the fuck* look, but none of us say anything.

When we get to the elevator, Mr. Lorenzo—I can't, for the life of me, remember his first name—tells the guard we're going up to see Mr. Valentino. The guard scans his license before patting each of us down. I'm still not sure which brother we're going to see, but I keep my mouth shut.

When the elevator dings on the top floor, the four of us get out. Johnny's standing there and when he sees me, his eyes visibly widen for a half a second. "Mr. Lorenzo, Giovanni and Nico are waiting for you, but I don't believe they were expecting guests."

Mr. Lorenzo laughs and glances around him. "I was on my way up and found these beautiful women looking for Mr. Valentino. I thought I would do him the favor and bring them on up."

"I'll let them know you're here." Johnny walks to the desk behind him and picks up the phone. He speaks in a hushed toned for a few seconds before setting the phone back down. "Giovanni is on his way." Not even thirty seconds later, Gio comes barreling down the hallway. If it were possible, smoke would be steaming from his ears. His body is visibly tense and his jaw is ticking. His eyes are trained right on me and Mr. Lorenzo, where our arms are entwined. *Shit!*

"Sebastian, I suggest you get your hands off her if you want to keep your limbs intact." *That's his name! Sebastian!*

Sebastian removes his arm from mine and puts his hands up in a placating motion, his body shaking with laughter. "No need to make such violent threats, Giovanni."

"Johnny, take Sebastian back to the conference room while I speak to Aria." As he says this, Nico comes down another hallway, and once he takes in the scene in front of him, curses under his breath.

"This way," Johnny commands, but before Sebastian lets him guide him down the hallway, he turns to me, and taking my hand in his, lays a wet kiss on the top of my knuckles.

"Until we meet again." He gives me a smarmy wink and a shutter rips through my body. When he turns to follow Johnny, I wipe my hand down my jeans, trying to get his grossness off me.

"What the fuck were you thinking coming here?" Gio barks as he stalks over to me, getting in my face.

My defenses go up, ready for a fight. "Whoa there, buddy. Back the hell up." My hands come out and I push him slightly back. "We came to say hello. I didn't know your hotel was off limits." I spent months being treated like garbage and I'll never allow that to happen again.

Thankfully, he visibly calms before he speaks his next words. "You can't be doing shit like this."

"What my brother is trying to say," Nico takes over, "is that as much as we love seeing you pretty ladies here, this is business only. It's not safe to be seen around here." Nico wraps Amber up in his arms and gives her a kiss, and she melts into his arms, smiling up at him. "Next time, call me first. Okay, babe?" Amber nods and kisses him back.

Natalie rolls her eyes. "I'm just along for the ride. I didn't even want to see either of you."

"I'm sorry, Gio. We'll go." I turn to leave, the feeling of rejection hitting deep, but he grabs my hand and pulls me toward him, until my back is flush against his front. Natalie smirks as I screech at his assault.

"I need to keep you safe, *cuore mio*. I'm sorry for yelling." His cool breath hits my ear, sending a completely different kind of shiver down my spine than the one Sebastian sent. "I'll see you at home tonight..." His lips press against the sensitive skin behind my ear. "I want you back in *our* room." My lips part in protest, but he murmurs, "Don't argue. Second floor is for employees. I want you in our bed."

I nod in agreement, and tilting my head to the side, Gio gives me a soft kiss on my lips, his tongue sliding in quickly before he lets me go. "I'll call you guys a car."

"We're shopping on the strip."

Gio smirks and turns me around to face him. "Anything for me?" He waggles his eyebrows.

"What would you want?"

"Anything you buy for yourself is technically for me. You should pick up a few items for our trip."

I give him a quick kiss and Nico shows us out.

"I've never seen Giovanni act like that!" Natalie laughs once we are out of the hotel and walking back down the strip. I look behind me and see Rome following us. He must have been following us earlier, yet he didn't warn Gio. I turn and give him a soft smile and he nods once. I'm not one hundred percent sure, but if I had to guess I would say he didn't warn Gio because his job is to protect me, not rat on me.

"Like what?" I ask, turning my attention back to Natalie.

"He's always so serious, but you didn't even have to do anything and he calmed down and was so...sexy and playful. I should have recorded it to show the other girls. Cecilia would've a heart attack. She's always trying to worm her way into Giovanni's arms, but he always rejects her."

That makes we wonder if Cecilia and Gio have had sex. I know he's had sex with plenty of women. We all have pasts and it's ridiculous to expect someone to not have one, but I want to know if her stuck up bitchy self is part of Gio's past. Instead of asking Natalie, I decide to wait and ask Gio himself.

Chapter Twenty

GIOVANNI

INSTEAD OF TAKING A COMMERCIAL FLIGHT TO THE Bahamas, my family has decided to charter a private jet. We have to take two flights. One to Fort Lauderdale and then get on the charter plane that will take us to Fowl Cay. Mario, our brother in Italy, flew in last night and is flying over with us. He has brought his girlfriend of five months and they seem to be very cozy. Nico and Amber are sharing a couch and my parents are sitting together with Stefan and Cecilia.

I tried to stop Cecilia from coming on this trip but she wasn't having it. She found out Aria was going and lost her shit. I told her Aria and I aren't her business and she and I are over in every way. I reminded her that I haven't fucked her since before Aria moved in but that didn't stop her from trying to convince me she's the better choice. I shot her down until she finally gave up.

Aria and I are currently sitting on the couch across from Nico and Amber. Aria's head is in my lap and she's snoring softly. Any time this woman is near me, my body is calm. She has this aura that surrounds her and I can't help but feed off it. I lean down and give her temple a kiss, needing to feel her skin on my lips.

Nico shoots me a knowing smirk and I shake my head. When I look away from him, my eyes lock with my parents. My mom is frowning, but she looks more curious than upset. My dad on the other hand is glaring. When I told them Aria and I were seeing each other and she would be coming with us, they freaked out. My mom cried that Cecilia wouldn't be a part of the family and my dad threw out some bullshit about being the first born and having responsibilities. I told them both I'm not going to change my mind and to let it go. Thankfully, they did.

The last several days, Aria has been sleeping in our room. The night after she came to visit me at the hotel, she asked about Cecilia. I told her the truth, that we've fucked for years but it's not and never will be more than that.

We've spent every night making out and going down on each other, but we haven't had sex. She begs and pleads and one night threw a fit saying I'm taking her choices away. I threw it back at her saying she's taking away mine. She glared and I laughed. Any other woman and I'd already be balls deep in her, but Aria is different. She means more. She's been through more, and fuck if she doesn't deserve more.

The pilot announces we're landing and I gently shake Aria to wake her. She stretches, her perfect tits jutting out, causing my cock to stir.

"Hey," she says groggily.

"Hey," I answer back as I pull her in for a kiss. I nibble her bottom lip before slanting my mouth to kiss both her lips. Aria deepens the kiss, her tongue plunging into my mouth, and I suck on it for a few seconds before I hear a throat clearing behind us. It's so easy to get lost in this woman. Reluctantly I let her go, remembering we aren't alone. "Later," I mouth, and she grants me the most adorable, shy smile.

Once we deplane, we make our way to the next flight, which takes about forty minutes, and then take a boat directly to the island and resort. When my mom found out her sons were all bringing women, she was forced to call the resort and make last minute changes. Mario, Nico, and I are staying in one villa with three bedrooms while my mom, dad, Stefan, and Cecilia are staying in another.

My mom checks us all in and we're given our keys. Nico announces he and Amber are going to the pool. Mario says he's starving and he's taking his girlfriend, Rachel, to eat. Realizing Aria and I will have the place to ourselves, we head straight to the villa.

"Gio! This place is gorgeous!" Aria is staring out the back slider at the ocean. "Can we go swimming?"

I come up behind her and, without wasting any time, my hands go down into her shorts, landing on her mound. "We can...but I was thinking we could get a little dirty first, then wash off in the water."

She giggles and nods. Pulling my hands out of her shorts, I lift her shirt up then unlatch her bra, both items hitting the floor. She stays facing the slider as I place small kisses along her shoulders. Her hair is up, giving me access to the back of her sexy, slim neck. I trail more kisses down her spine until I get to the small of her back. She has two indents just above her ass and I kiss them both.

"Put your hands on the slider," I command. When I hear her hands hit the glass, I remove her shorts and underwear, helping her step out of them.

I continue kissing where I left off, right above her ass, and when I get to her ass cheeks, I give each one a hard bite. Aria playfully wiggles her hips and I slap her cheek, eliciting a moan from her.

"Spread your legs, baby." She obliges, parting her thighs. "More." She moves them apart until they're spread enough that my hand can slide easily between her legs. I insert one digit into her and find she's already slick with want. I insert another and another until her pussy is filled with my fingers. I give her another kiss on her ass cheek as I fingerfuck her wet cunt.

Her legs spread a little wider, welcoming my touch and I hear her forehead hit the glass as she moans out in pleasure. "Fuck, fuck, fuck!" she cries out, her body pulsing in pleasure. Her mantra continues as my fingers go deeper and harder, working her into a frenzy. Her breathing becomes erratic as my fingers hit her G-spot. Her legs go tense, and I give the back of her thighs soft kisses. Her pussy clenches around my fingers, but I keep going, hitting the spot repeatedly. I can feel when her body has had enough and finally lets go. Her body shakes uncontrollably, her juices dripping down my fingers and hand as she screams out her orgasm.

I pull my pants and briefs down just enough so my cock springs out, then turn Aria around and lift her up. Her back hits the glass as my cock enters her tight cunt. Her hands grab ahold of my hair while mine grip her ass, and I fuck her like a goddamned animal up against the slider.

Her head goes back in pleasure as she chants my name, along with praises to God. Her tits bounce up and down, begging for me to take one in my mouth. I grip her ass tighter to make sure I won't drop her, causing her back to hit the glass harder as my lips wrap around and pull on her perfect pink nipple.

"Fuck! Gio! Fuck me harder." Letting go of her nipple from my mouth, I nestle my face into the crook of her neck as she wraps her arms around mine. I thrust in and out of her. Harder. Deeper. The sweat from our bodies making a slapping sound. I fuck her with everything in me until my balls feel like they're going to explode.

"Oh my God, I'm going to come again. Right fucking there!" she shouts. I keep hitting the spot over and over again, trying to ignore the ache in my balls begging me to release.

Aria lets out a loud, "Fuuuuuckkkk," and I take that as my cue to release my seed into her. Her body goes limp as she gives me a satiated look. Even though I don't want to, I pull out of her and her feet fall to the floor.

"Best. Vacation. Ever." She giggles as she walks past me toward the bathroom, her naked ass swaying from side to side. But before she makes it out of my reach, I swat her ass. She squeals and runs quicker to the bathroom, grabbing her bathing suit along the way.

"The vacation hasn't even started yet!" I yell out to her. Her head pops out of the bathroom door and she gives me a playful wink. "Well, if that's just the beginning, I can't wait to experience the rest." Then she slams the door shut.

Chapter Twenty-One

ARIA

FOR THE MOST PART, OUR TIME IN THE BAHAMAS HAS been nothing short of amazing. We've spent our days lounging by the beach and pool, our nights going to dinner, and in between we've had spa days and couples massages. Gio's mom hasn't welcomed me into the family yet, but I think she's starting to warm up to me. Cecilia has pretty much been doing her own thing and only joins us all for family dinners, during which time she spends the entire meal glaring at me.

We're coming up to our last day here and the guys have rented a boat for the day. Rachel was shy at first, but once Amber's loud ass got ahold of her, the three of us hit it off.

After getting the keys, the guys load up the huge boat with our cooler full of food and drinks and then Gio helps each of us women onto the deck. Mario and Rachel sit in the front seats and Nico and Amber sit toward the back, leaving Gio to drive.

"Can you drive this thing?" I ask.

Gio laughs. "I own one of these things. C'mon." He pulls me in front of him, sandwiching my body between his front and the steering wheel, and turns the ignition, starting the boat. I have no idea what he does, but after pressing a few buttons and pulling a lever down, the boat moves forward. We wade away from the docks slowly, but once we get into the open water, Gio's breath hits my ear. "Hold on, baby, it's about to get rough."

Pulling hard on the lever, the boat smoothly increases in speed. The wind is slapping Rachel and Mario in their faces, but Gio and I are protected by the glass. The water comes up around us as the boat hits each wave. We continue to increase in speed, the ocean breeze whirring around us, when I feel Gio's fingers enter my bikini bottoms. Nobody can see us because of the dashboard, but I still dart my eyes around to make sure.

"Hold the wheel, baby," he croons, and I do as he says, my hands holding the steering wheel steady so we keep going straight. The speed evens out, but we're still going fast enough that the wind is loud to our ears. His hand taps my thigh and I separate my legs slightly, giving him access.

His fingers push into me and he pumps them in and out a few times until I'm slick with arousal. I feel his fingers move to my clit and he spreads my juices, massaging my sensitive nub. My head goes back slightly, my eyes rolling back in pleasure, and I feel Gio softly laughing at me. "Baby you're holding the steering wheel. You need to open your eyes." My eyes flutter back open, my mind trying to focus on keeping us straight, but it's almost impossible with his fingers gently massaging my clit. He knows exactly what he's doing and it feels so good.

His mouth comes down onto my neck, sucking lightly along the sensitive skin under my ear as his fingers and thumb pinch my clit. I gasp and he does it again. "Come for me, Ari. Come on, baby." His assault on my clit and neck has me whimpering and begging for release as I pray my legs don't give out and I don't get us into an accident.

His fingers aren't gentle. They're rough and desperate and I can feel my orgasm building higher and higher until my body finally detonates, waves of pleasure pouring through me. My eyes roll back as everything goes black for a moment.

I open my eyes and look at Gio just in time to see him pull his hand out of my suit bottoms and bring them up to my mouth. "Taste yourself, baby." I willingly part my lips, but instead of pushing his fingers inside my mouth, he brings them up to his mouth, sucking my juices off—a soft groan resonating from his chest. Then he brings them back to my lips and pushes them into my mouth. My tongue swirls around his fingers as I suck my juices and his saliva off his flesh. "Fuck, woman." He pulls the digits from my lips and replaces them with his mouth and tongue, devouring me.

"Gio!" someone yells, but I'm so lost in this man, I don't pay any attention. "Fucking Asshole! We aren't moving." I recognize the voice as Nico's. *Oh shit! The boat!* I push Gio's mouth off mine and look around, realizing the boat has come to a complete stop right in the middle of the ocean. Gio chuckles softly, licking his lips. "You taste damn good." He leans down one more time, kissing the side of my throat before he turns me back around and pulls the lever again, the boat lurching forward right along with my heart.

Chapter Twenty-Two

ARIA

"HOW LONG WILL YOU BE GONE FOR?" WE'VE BEEN BACK from the Bahamas for over a month, during which time I've been looking into reenrolling in college for the fall and finding out which classes I'll have to make up. Gio asked that I stay living here until the Weston situation gets dealt with. He's concerned he's waiting for me to slip up so he can take me again.

I made it clear to him that I wouldn't be going anywhere unless he made me. I love spending my days with the girls here at the mansion and my nights wrapped up in Gio. We've gone on several double dates with Nico and Amber and if I didn't know better, I would think Gio's been in several relationships. He's that good at it.

"I'll only be gone for the weekend. Stay here and behave, please." He picks up his suitcase and gives me a kiss. It ends too quickly, so I grab his neck and pull him back down into a more passionate kiss, our tongues exploring each other's mouths. I suck on his lips and when we finally separate, I'm panting unabashedly, needing more.

I look in Gio's eyes and see my entire future standing right here in front of me, and the words escape before I can reign them in. "I love you."

Gio stills, but his eyes soften and he pulls me into another punishing kiss. Only he doesn't stop there. His luggage hits the ground and when he releases me, my lips feel bruised and puffy when I run my tongue along them. He pulls his jacket and shirt off, his pants next. I follow his lead and rid myself of my clothes.

Picking me up by my ass, he throws me onto the bed. "Flip over and get on your knees, baby." I do as he says, my ass lifting in the air, waiting for his next command. Crawling up behind me, he leans down and places a kiss on each cheek. Then he continues upward, pressing soft, wet kisses along my spine. When he reaches my shoulders, he dusts my hair to the side and trails dozens of kisses along my shoulders and up my neck.

He nudges my legs open, and I can feel the head of his cock seeking entrance as his weight comes back down on me. Tilting my head to the side, my mouth searches for his as he pushes into me slowly from behind, a low moan escaping me. His lips find mine and our kiss deepens. We stay like this for several beats, until I wiggle my ass, needing him to move in me.

Releasing my mouth, his thrusts pick up. His hands palm my breasts, his fingers pinching my nipples as he fucks me deep. My back arches in pleasure, pushing back and meeting him thrust for thrust. He pulls back and angles my ass higher, allowing him to go deeper so he's hitting that perfect spot in me. My body begins to shake as my orgasm overtakes me, and Gio follows shortly after.

Leaning back down, still inside of me, Gio whispers, "I love you too, Aria." He pulls out of me and I immediately miss the warmth he elicits within me. I turn over onto my back, needing to take a calming breath before I get up to clean myself. Only before I do, Gio returns with a warm washcloth. He spreads my legs and cleans me up. Throwing the washcloth to the side, he crawls up my body and gives me a soft kiss. First on my lips, then on my throat. He works his way down, giving each breast a kiss, then trails dozens of kisses down along my torso until he reaches my sex. He places a soft, wet kiss on the top of my mound then looks up at me, granting me with a playful lopsided grin before he works his way back up my body ending where he started, with my lips. Not wanting our connection to break, I wrap my arms around his neck and my ankles around his waist.

"I'm late." He chuckles, then pulls back, peeling himself off me.

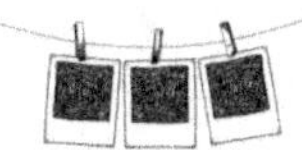

IT'S DAY TWO WITHOUT GIO AND I'M MISSING HIM LIKE crazy. We text throughout day when he's not busy and last night we video chatted. He even convinced me to participate in some kinky phone sex. While that was hot, I can't wait for him to return.

I'm hanging out in the kitchen with Natalie and Holly when

Cecilia walks in. "Veronica, the new girl, had to go home for an emergency. Can either of you take over her date tonight?" Both girls shake their heads.

"Great!" She taps away on her phone for a few minutes, then says, "I spoke with Giovanni and he asked if you could do him the favor and meet with the new member tonight."

"Gio would never ask that." I look at Cecilia incredulously. She turns her phone around so I can read her texts, and my stomach feels like lead.

Giovanni: Stanley is an important member. Ask Aria to do it. Tell her I'm asking her as a personal favor.

My heart breaks that Gio would even consider me an option. He hasn't said it since the day he left, but when he told me he loved me, I thought it meant something to him. To ask me to work for him, to be with another man, this can't be right.

"He wants me to have sex with him?"

Cecilia rolls her eyes. "Of course not. It's just a meet and greet. He's booked the private room, but it's only for companionship."

"I'll call him and ask him myself." I grab my phone from my back pocket, but it rings once and goes to voicemail. I try again and it does it again. "Fine. If that's what he wants, then I'll do it." I leave the kitchen to go get ready and send Gio numerous texts, asking him why he would do this, but he doesn't answer a single one.

Once I'm dressed and ready to go, I try to call Gio one last time, getting the same voicemail. "Hey Gio, it's me. I'm about to entertain a new guest for you. Cecilia said you asked me to do it as a favor, but I don't get it. I know we haven't made anything official, but you asked me to quit working here. I just don't understand. Okay, well, call me when you get this, please."

I tuck my phone into my pocket in case Gio calls or texts and head downstairs to greet Stanley. Normally Edgardo tells us where to go, but when I get down there, Cecilia is waiting. "Room one, Aria." She gives me a tight-lipped smile and I nod and head down the hallway.

I knock once before opening the door. At first, I don't see anyone, so I walk farther into the room. The door slams closed behind me and when I turn around, I'm face-to-face with the man who has haunted me every night in my sleep.

"Help!" I scream out, hoping somebody will hear me. "Heeeellllpppp!" I scream again. Before I can scream for a third time, Weston's hand comes down and hits me across my face. I try to run—where? I'm not sure—but he catches me and throws me onto the ground like I'm a ragdoll. The back of my head hits the marble floor and the room begins to spin. I will myself to fight. I kick and punch and at one point, I feel myself bite him, the metallic taste of his blood coating my tongue and lips. But he fights back harder. His hands grab mine, pinning them above my head, and I take the opportunity to scream again as loud as possible until Weston shoves a piece of material into my mouth, gagging me.

"Shut the fuck up, you slutty piece of trash."

I try to kick, but his heavy legs are pinning mine down. His hand comes down to my breast and he violently grabs it, tweaking my nipple until I silently scream out. My vision goes blurry as my eyes bleed with pain. His hand goes to my silk shorts and he shoves his fingers into my panties.

Just as his fingers find my sex, light fills the room. The door swings open and Weston flies off me and into the wall. I scramble back, removing the material from my mouth and watching as Edgardo beats Weston into a bloody pulp. He punches him repeatedly in the face, never letting up. At some point, Rome and Caesar run in and pull Edgardo off Weston. He's not even moving anymore. If Weston isn't dead, he's damn close to it.

"Come on, Aria. Let's get you up to your room." Rome lifts me into his arms, bridal style, and carries me into my room, laying me on the bed. I don't let go of him, not wanting to be alone. My body is freezing and I'm pretty sure I'm going into shock. "I don't know what happened, but I promise you we will get to the bottom of this." Rome sits on the bed next to me, petting my hair gently. My eyes begin to close, the adrenaline wearing down, but they pop back open when images of Weston attacking me come to the front.

Once they start, I can't stop them. My mind plays like a song on repeat. Him hitting me, attacking me, silencing me, grabbing me, trying to rape me. I don't know how long these images run on repeat or for how long I'm crying, but suddenly I'm being picked up. I scream, scared I'm being attacked again, but Gio's soothing voice calms me.

"It's okay, Ari. It's me. I got you, baby. I'm so sorry." He holds me close to his chest, rocking me as one would do a baby. I feel him push a single pill past my lips and I swallow it dry, and in the comfort of Gio's arms, I allow my body some peace, closing my eyes and letting it all slip away.

Chapter Twenty-Three

GIOVANNI

I WAS ON A FLIGHT FROM NEW JERSEY TO LAS VEGAS with my phone turned off when the texts and phone calls must have started. I was so aggravated from dealing with Sebastian and his bullshit all day, I didn't text or call Aria once. Sebastian thought he'd be slick and intercept a shipment coming in, thinking we were all on the other side of the country, but what he wasn't prepared for was me being there to intercept him.

Normally the shipments come in and our hired men unload them and reload them for delivery. When one of my guys put a call in to let me know Sebastian pushed my guys out, I knew I had to jump on a plane and handle that bullshit myself. He declared war and he was about to lose. The joke was on me, though. Because while I was handling the shipment, my girlfriend was being attacked by the fucking senator.

If you asked me a couple months ago if it's possible the senator could be working with several mob families, I would have laughed in your face. Nobody, not even Senator Weston Hightower, would be that stupid. But I was wrong. After I finished overseeing the shipment, which went off without a hitch, I went into the city to find Sebastian. Words were spoken, threats were made, and I quickly learned once I had Sebastian against the wall that the senator made promises to the Lorenzo organization he can't keep, in order to get them to work against me.

Unfortunately, it was too late and while I was sitting on a flight, sipping on my scotch, Aria was fighting off that asshole. The minute the plane landed and my phone was turned back on, a slew of messages blew up my phone. They ranged from Aria asking why I would request for her to entertain a member, her clearly upset and confused, to Rome letting me know Aria had been attacked.

The ride home was the longest forty minutes of my life. I tried to call Rome and Caesar but neither answered. I called Cecilia several times but she didn't pick up. I had left Johnny in New Jersey to investigate further into the Lorenzo organization's relationship with the senator. So as I sat in the backseat of the car while the hired driver took me to my house, I prayed to whatever God is up there that Aria is okay. I promised him that if she's alive and safe I would do everything in my power to ensure she stays that way.

The driver dropped me off and when I walked inside, the place was ghostly quiet. Edgardo wasn't standing guard by the door. Emilio wasn't manning the bar. The women and members were nowhere to be seen. I dropped my bag by the door and ran up the stairs to the third floor. I swung open my door to find Rome sitting on my bed, and in his arms, was Aria. She was awake and crying. Her eyes were open, but she wasn't lucid. Tears raced down her cheeks as she silently lost it—my girl finally reaching her breaking point.

Rome gave me a nod and moved off the bed. I picked her up and cradled her to my chest, rocking her until she finally fell asleep in my arms. When her breathing evened out and I knew she would be asleep for a while, I texted Rome and Caesar and told them to meet me up here.

"Boss," Rome says as he and Caesar enter my room. I keep Aria in my arms, afraid if I put her down, she'll wake up. Afraid if I leave her alone, whatever she went through will haunt her in her sleep... more than it already does.

"What happened?" I ask, keeping my voice low so she won't wake up, when what I want to do is scream and shout and throw shit.

Rome answers. "Cecilia was working with the senator. She has text messages between them, but to hide it, she had him in her contacts as you. She told Aria you needed her to entertain a member and when Aria went to go meet him, it was the senator waiting for her. Edgardo happened to be passing by, checking to make sure another room was clean, when he heard Aria screaming. He thought maybe it was coming from another room, but when he checked the video camera to make sure none of the girls were being pushed past their limits, he saw Aria on the ground with Weston over her."

"Did he…" I start, unable to finish the question.

"No," Caesar answers. "Edgardo got to him before he could. He roughed her up, but he didn't get a chance to rape her. According to Cecilia, he wasn't supposed to attack her. He was just supposed to take her and bring her back home."

"What?" I bark out. Aria stirs and I soothe her so she stays asleep.

"The senator approached her and made it seem like Aria was using you for your money. A young girl lashing out at her dead mom's husband and seeking attention. She agreed to help him take her home. She swears she didn't know he was going to hurt her."

"She's gone. She's fired effective immediately and I want her and all of her shit out of this place tonight."

"You got it."

"Sebastian was working with the senator," I inform them.

"Fuck," Rome spits out. "Wait…was?"

"Was. I'm going to kill Weston, therefore, their alliance is in the past tense."

"Edgardo just about killed him. He ran in and saw him on Aria and nearly beat him to death."

"But he's still alive, right?" I'm going to make damn sure I'll be the one to end this asshole's life.

"Yeah, he's down in holding. Should I contact Louie?"

"Yeah, let him know I'll have a body for him to handle in a few hours. Let Edgardo know I appreciate what he did for Aria tonight. I'll thank him myself once I make it back out there. I gave Aria a sedative so she should be out for the night, but just in case, send Natalie up to stay with her. We'll open back up tomorrow, business as usual. I'm going to have my mom come here and run things until I find a replacement for Cecilia."

"All right."

"Thank you. I don't even want to imagine what would've happened to Aria had you guys not been here tonight."

"We got your back, Boss. Always."

I lie with Aria for a little while longer, stroking her hair and watching her chest rise and fall until Natalie comes up to stay with her while I go down and pay the soon-to-be former senator a visit.

"What do you need?" Caesar asks as we walk down the hall toward the holding room. I shake my head because I don't need a fucking thing to end this man's life. Just like he put his hands on my woman, I'm going to put my hands on him. I swing the door open, Rome closing it behind me, and Weston's eyes widen as he tries to edge closer to the wall like it's going to camouflage him.

"Take the cuffs off him," I demand. Caesar unlocks the handcuffs and removes them from Weston's hands. "Get up, motherfucker, now!" Hightower scoots back and up the wall, barely able to stand. Rome wasn't kidding when he said Edgardo did a number on him. His face is barely recognizable and judging by the way his eyes are dilated, he probably sustained some sort of head injury. Soon though, it won't matter because his life is over.

"You think you're any better than I am?" Weston spits out.

Knowing his life is about to end apparently gives him some brass balls. "You think you and that tease are going to ride off into the sunset? You're just as fucked up as the rest of us. You whore women out for Christ's sake!"

My initial plan was to draw this out, create a blood bath, make him hurt the way he hurt Aria repeatedly, but listening to him spew this shit—words that are hitting too close to home—has me stalking over to him, wrapping my hand around his throat and pushing down on his windpipe.

Anything to shut him the fuck up.

The back of his head hits the wall and I press harder and harder against the carotid artery watching as his breaths become labored and his body begins to convulse. "You will never hurt Aria again," I tell him, staring into his eyes as they slowly dim. Within minutes, his body is no longer fighting and shortly after, it goes limp beneath my touch. I keep my hand pressed tightly for several more minutes to make sure he's dead. When I let go of his throat, he falls to the floor like a sack of potatoes. Leaning down, I place my hand over his heart to confirm there's no longer a heartbeat.

His words run on repeat in my head. *You're just as fucked up as the rest of us.* He didn't tell me anything I didn't already know, but the words being said aloud make them feel more real.

Aria deserves so much more than the life I can give her. I know killing Weston Hightower was the only option. But the question that runs through my head is, *did I just pull Aria into a life just as fucked up as the one I saved her from?*

Chapter Twenty-Four

ARIA

I WAKE UP AND, FOR A SECOND, I FORGET ABOUT THE events that took place last night. That is until I look over at Gio and see him lying next to me, his beautiful lips curved downward. His thumb gently grazes my cheek and it stings. When I flinch, his frown deepens. I don't need to ask him if he was part of what Weston did to me last night. I know he would never put me in harm's way. I also don't need to ask if Cecilia was a part of it. I know she was. Why a woman would stick an abusive rapist on another woman is incomprehensible to me.

"I didn't know," he says, his voice gravelly.

"I know."

"He's dead. I can't give you the specifics, but he'll never hurt you again."

I would never wish death on anyone, but knowing he can never get to me again gives me a sense of peace I desperately long for.

"And Cecilia?"

"She's gone."

My eyes widen. Surely, he wouldn't...

"Not dead," he says, answering my silent question. "She's just gone from here. I fired her."

Gio stares at me for a few minutes, with a mixture of sadness and something else marring his features. It causes a weird feeling in my gut to stir, like there's more but he doesn't want to say it.

"Can we get out of here?" I ask. "Let's go away. Anywhere but here. Just the two of us."

His frown deepens. "I can't. There are too many fires to put out and I need to do damage control." He gets up from the bed and goes to the bathroom and that feeling in my gut intensifies. He didn't kiss me and he hasn't touched me. I could be overthinking this but something in me is screaming that I'm about to lose Gio.

I hear the shower running, so I throw the covers off me and, ignoring the pain radiating from my body, strip my shirt and panties off. Gio's shower is different from most. It's a huge rectangular shape, tiled throughout but instead of having a shower door, it's completely open, with two entrances you can step down and walk through. There are five shower heads that spray down and there's a bench that runs along the entire back wall.

I step into the shower and, coming up behind him, wrap my arms around his middle. He stills for a second then turns around. "Aria, you should be resting. You were attacked last night."

"Nothing happened." I know I'm downplaying it, but I don't want him to push me away.

"You might not have been raped but you were still assaulted. Please go lie down."

Standing on my tiptoes, I wrap my arms around his neck, but he reaches around and removes them, stepping back. "I need to get ready for work. Go rest." His voice is no longer soothing but cold, devoid of any emotion.

"Don't do this, Gio. Talk to me, please." Stepping toward him, I put my hands on his chest, but once again, he removes them.

"There's nothing to talk about, Aria. You were attacked last night and you should be resting. I'm not going to fuck you right here in the shower mere hours after you were almost raped." I flinch at the way he's speaking to me. He's never spoken to me like this before. Before he can see my tears, I turn and get out of the shower, grabbing a towel to wrap myself up in.

I pull the top outfit out of my drawer and throw it on. Snatching my cell phone from the nightstand, I push it into my back pocket and run downstairs and out the door, needing some air.

"Need to go somewhere?" I look over at Rome standing behind me. "I figured I would ask before you steal another vehicle."

"I can drive, you know. And now that Weston is dead, I don't need to stay here under lock and key."

"That's true, but you don't have a car."

"Maybe I'll go buy one today," I challenge.

He chuckles and shakes his head. "Would you like a ride to buy a car, Aria?"

I sigh, having no idea what the hell I'm doing, then sit on the curb on the side of the house. "I think Gio needs some space. Would you mind taking me over to Amber's place?" I pull my phone out and dial her number. She answers on the second ring. "Aria? Nico just told me what happened last night! Are you okay?"

"I am, but I need to get away from here for a little bit. Can I come stay with you?" There's a pregnant pause and then Amber shocks the hell out of me when she says, "Well, I'm actually living with Nico. A few of my roommates graduated this year so we had to give up the apartment."

"You're living with Nico? How did I not know this?"

"It literally just happened. I was so busy moving everything, I haven't had time to tell you. Why don't you come here? Nico won't mind. Plus, he's out of town until the end of the week. We can do a girls' night."

"Are you sure? I don't want to cause any issues with you two."

"Oh my God, stop! Get over here and let's hang out."

"Okay, I'll be over shortly."

After hanging up, I head back up to the room. Gio isn't there anymore, so I grab a suitcase and fill it with some clothes and toiletries. Then I go back to the first floor to his office. He's not in there either so I write him a note to let him know I went to stay with Amber for a few days.

Rome is outside waiting for me when I walk out. He grabs my suitcase from me and throws it into the trunk. "Where am I taking you?"

"To Nico's place, please. Amber is living there now."

The ride to wherever he lives is quiet and I use this time to do a mini-evaluation of my life. Everything has changed so much this last year and a half. I went from being a college student, to being kidnapped, to being saved by Gio. I told a man for the first time I love him only to have lost him because I was attacked. I thought I was finally in a good place. Even after Weston attacked me, I woke up this morning and wasn't going to let it bring me down. I can't control what others do, but I can control what I do, what I say, and how I choose to handle what life throws at me. I wish Gio would tell me what's on his mind so we can work through it.

"Aria, we're here." The hotel comes into view that Gio encouraged me to stay away from.

"He lives in this hotel?"

"Yep. Just go to the east elevator and type in this code." He hands me a sheet of paper. "It will take you right up to his suite." He gets out with me and hands me back my luggage.

I thank him and say goodbye, then head through the front door and to the east elevator. The code works as Rome said and a minute later, I'm face-to-face with a guard standing outside the only door on the floor. "Is Amber here?" He nods and knocks on the door for me. "Thank you." Another nod. *Okay then...*

Amber swings the door open and pulls me in for a hug. "Eeeeek! Get in here!" She slams the door shut behind us and grabs my luggage, throwing it to the side.

"You didn't tell me Nico lives here, and what's up with the mute guy standing outside your door?"

"I didn't know! The night of the charity function we went for a drive and after that we spent time at my place. I didn't know he lived here until he asked me to move in, and that guard is a requirement. Nico said it's to be on the safe side." Amber parks her ass on the couch and I plop down next to her. "So, what's going on, Aria?"

"If that isn't a loaded question."

I explain to her how good things have been between me and Gio recently, about our shared confessions of love, and how everything finally felt good. Then I tell her about last night, about Cecilia being fired, and how cold and distant Gio was to me this morning.

"Maybe he feels responsible. You just might be overthinking this, chica."

"Maybe, but it all felt off—I had to get out of there and give him some space. He yelled at me like he does to his employees when he's mad. He was so cold and distant. I want to put what happened to me behind us, but he wouldn't even talk to me about what's wrong."

Amber bounces in her seat. "You know what we should do? We should go clubbing!"

"And how will that help fix my Gio situation?"

"Oh, it won't, but we'll have a blast! We're both finally over twenty-one. Weston is out of the picture and we need to have some fun. We can call Holly and Natalie and Sienna! Oh, and I can call our friend Vicki!"

"I don't know…"

"C'mon! Some drinking and dancing. It will be a fun girls' night."

"Gah! Okay! Fine."

Amber jumps from her seat, grabbing me in a hug and pulling me up so we're dancing around the house. "Call the girls at the club and I'll call Vicki. Tell them to meet us here and we can all go get manis and pedis!"

We spend the day hanging out. We go to the nail salon, to lunch, and then everyone comes back to the hotel to get dressed and ready for tonight. All of us are dressed similar, tight dresses in various styles and colors with high heels. Throughout the day, I kept checking my phone in hope that Gio would text or call but he hasn't. It makes me sad that after everything, this is how it will end.

Since we'll be drinking, we're having one of Amber's guards, Mack, drive us to the club. She said Nico promised her she wouldn't be guarded around the clock, but since he's out of town she'll be with a guard until he gets back.

When we get out of the car, I eye the name of the club and immediately recognize it as one of the clubs Benjamin mentioned owning. "Maybe we should go somewhere else."

"What? Why?" Vicki whines. "This is the hottest new club."

I don't mention I escorted the guy who owns it, instead following her lead as she walks up to the bouncer and flirts her way in.

"What are we drinking to?" Amber shouts over the music, after shots of tequila are brought to the table. We all look around at each other and laugh when not one of us can think of a single damn thing to drink to.

"To each other?" I shout back. Everybody nods in agreement and shouts, "To each other." We down the shots, then make our way to the dance floor. Forming our own little circle, we dance our asses off as each song flows into the next and we get lost in the music.

Rialto
Rialto

Chapter Twenty-Five

GIOVANNI

I WAS RUDE TO ARIA THIS MORNING. SHE WAS CONFUSED and needed me to tell her everything is going to be okay, but I couldn't do it. Not when I have all these thoughts swirling around in my head telling me that maybe she would be better off without me. I woke up this morning feeling all types of guilt: for her being sexually assaulted under my roof, for not being here when it happened, for not seeing what Cecilia, Sebastian, and the senator were plotting—I still don't even know why Sebastian is mixed up in all this. But most of all, for feeling like maybe this happened for a reason, like it's fate's or God's or whoever's way of intervening and reminding me of where I come from. Not even two days ago, I told Aria I loved her. I've never spoken those words to anybody besides my family, and now I'm reminded of the type of life I live. The type of life where the woman who feels scorned doesn't simply key the guy's car but instead helps a rapist plot a way to kidnap his victim.

I'm not excusing Cecilia for what she did, but she was raised in this life like I was, and to her, you do what you have to do to get what you want. She sure as fuck did what she had to do, but she isn't getting what she wants. I'm at my parents' house where my dad has called a family meeting. Nico, who was supposed to be out of town until the end of the week, has flown in, and we've all congregated in the living room. I'm standing against the wall while Cecilia sits on the couch, pouting like she's been scorned.

"Giovanni, Cecilia has come to me upset. She's out of a job and for what? Because your girlfriend is upset with her?"

At my father's words, I slam my fist into the drywall, a picture falling and hitting the ground with a loud crash. Stalking over to Cecilia, I grab her chin. "Is that what you fucking said? You want to lie some more, you fucking bitch?"

"Giovanni!" my mom cries out.

"Son, that's enough. What the hell is going on?" my father demands.

"What's going on, is she was jealous of my relationship with Aria, so she got the bright idea to help the damn senator kidnap her!"

"I didn't know!" Cecilia sobs.

"It wasn't your fucking concern! You knew damn well she was taken from her home by me. You knew she came to my house bruised and broken! You fucking knew."

"He told me she was lying. He said she was acting out because her mom died."

"Then you should have come to me. This isn't fucking business. This is my goddamned life. It's the life of a twenty-one-year-old woman!"

My dad comes over and places his hand on my shoulder. "Giovanni, you need to calm down, Son. I understand this girl is important to you, but she isn't family. Explain to me what happened."

"He had raped her repeatedly when I found her. She was locked in the basement, drugged and passed around."

Cecilia cries harder. "I didn't know!" *A little too late to fucking care, bitch.*

"Why didn't you tell us all this?" Dad says. "I knew she was the senator's stepdaughter, but you should have made me aware of what was going on."

"I got her help. I was keeping it all under wraps because Weston Hightower disappeared. Aria was staying with me so he couldn't get to her, and what does Cecilia do? She hands her over to him. Edgardo ended up almost beating him to death in order to stop him from raping and taking her."

"Almost?" Dad questions at the same time Stefan says, "Did you handle it?"

Walking away from Cecilia and toward my dad and Stefan, I say, "Yeah, I killed that fucker with my bare hands and Louie made it look like a hunting accident. When they find him, he will have been destroyed by animals."

"Cecilia didn't know. None of us knew because you kept it from all of us. You can't fire her because of this," Dad says matter-of-factly. "And what were you thinking killing the goddamned senator? You know we're trying to lay low right now with Lorenzo causing all types of problems."

"Bull-fucking-shit, I can't. She's not stepping foot in the bordello as long as Aria is under that roof and as far as killing the senator, I don't give a fuck. He got what was coming to him."

"Cecilia is part of this family," Mom points out. "She didn't know the man was going to hurt her. She made a mistake. If Aria and Cecilia can't be under the same roof, maybe it's time for Aria to leave."

"I don't give a damn what Cecilia thought. Have her go work at one of the clubs or restaurants or the damn casino! I don't care. But she isn't coming back into the bordello and Aria isn't going anywhere."

"Who's going to take care of the women?" Mom asks.

"I was hoping you could help me train another woman."

Cecilia huffs loudly and lets out a sob. "Gio, please. I'm sorry."

I turn around and walk back over to her. She's now standing like everyone else. "Don't you ever call me Gio. You want to play the innocent act? Fine. But as far as I'm concerned, you and I are no longer family." I look around the room, four sets of eyes staring at me in shock. "And if any of you have a problem with me being with Aria, you come to me. Don't you dare say a fucking word to her."

"Is she even aware of the risks?" Dad questions, accusingly.

"What about Nico? He's living with his girlfriend! Are you asking him if she's aware of the risks?"

"Bro, don't bring me into this shit. I run a casino and hotel. I'm not being prepped to take over the Valentino organization."

"It's still dangerous."

"And Amber knows she has to have a guard with her everywhere she goes."

"Aria knows it as well."

I look at my mom and see she's frowning. "If she is who you want, I will respect it, Giovanni. I just hope you know what you are doing because mark my words, whether you mean for it to happen or not, you will destroy that girl." She walks out of the room shaking her head with Cecilia trailing behind her.

"Your mother is right, Son. This life isn't for everyone. Hell, it's not for most. Now, you haven't debriefed me on what happened in New Jersey. Let's discuss this is in my office where I can have a cigar without Claudia bitching about the smoke."

We spend the rest of the morning discussing possible theories regarding Sebastian and the Lorenzo organization. Around three o'clock, my mom brings us all a late lunch and we spend the rest of the afternoon going over numbers. It's been awhile since we've had a meeting like this so there's a lot of shit to discuss. When my mom asks if we're staying for dinner, I realize I haven't spoken to Aria all day. I tell her I need to check in with Aria first and then take a moment to check my phone. There's nothing from her, so I shoot Rome and Caesar a text asking if she's okay, because while I'm perfectly comfortable destroying a man like Sebastian, I'm a damn pussy when it comes to texting my girlfriend after I gave her the cold shoulder this morning and pissed her off. When Rome texts back that she left to Amber's place with a suitcase, I shoot a glare to Nico.

"What?"

"Did you know Aria is staying with you?" I show him the text from Rome.

"No, but Amber thinks I'm gone until the end of the week. I didn't tell her I'm back since I'm planning to surprise her." He waggles his eyebrows and I roll my eyes.

"You said she has a guard, right? Text him and see if Aria's still there."

He sends him a text. "He said the girls were out all day with their friends and they're on their way to dinner and then to a club to go dancing." He holds his phone out to show me a picture of the backs of all the women walking into the restaurant. I recognize Aria right away. She's wearing a peach colored skintight dress with black fuck-me heels, and her hair is in waves down her back.

"Which club?"

Nico laughs. "Great minds." He shows me the next text: **Lush.**

Is she serious? She went out with Benjamin a couple times, and he owns that club. That better be a fucking coincidence. I have no problem with Benjamin, but he better not be anywhere near my woman.

We go to the kitchen and let our mom know we won't be able to stay for dinner.

"I'm going to run home and change. I'll meet you at the club," I tell Nico.

"Sounds good."

I run by the house and change my clothes, then check on the girls and let them know my mom will be by tomorrow. Caesar, Rome, and Edgardo are all here and know to look after the place until Johnny returns.

I arrive at Lush, and after giving my name to the bouncer, I'm let through immediately. The music is thumping and the lights are dimmed down low. I search for the women in several areas but don't see them anywhere. Just when I'm about to send a text to Nico to see where he is, a blur of peach catches my attention.

On the dance floor, shaking her ass like it's 1999, is Aria. She's surrounded by her friends and they're all dancing, but my eyes are locked on her. Her arms are in the air and her head is thrown back as she laughs. Her body is swaying to the music, and in this moment, she looks so young, carefree, the way a woman of her age should look.

Instead of going to her, I stand on the sidelines and observe her. I watch as she lights up the darkened floor with her natural brightness. The other women gravitate toward her, feeding off her energy. And I wonder if I have ever really seen her smile like that. Was my mom, right? Would being with Aria mean destroying her? She was supposed to be safe at La Stella's and look what happened. What if the next time my guys can't get to her in time?

Before I can give it any more thought, Aria's eyes land on mine. Her smile falters slightly, and it hits me dead in my gut, I want to be the one to bring her smile back, which raises the question: what if that means having to let her go? I push the thought down and give her a small wave. She tilts her head slightly and crooks her finger in a come-hither motion, granting me with a gorgeous smile.

Bridging the gap between us, I take her into my arms—noticing her face has more makeup than usual to cover the bruises Weston left on her—and even though the song booming through the club is a fast, pulsating number, I pull her body close to mine as she dances seductively against me. My knee parts her thighs and she grinds against my leg, giving me access to feel her heat against me. Leaning down, I whisper into her ear, "I'm sorry."

She looks at me and nods, her arms coming around my neck as she pulls me down to her, her lips brushing mine. The kiss starts off tentative, but quickly becomes more fervent—hungry. It isn't until her tongue finds its way in, that I taste the alcohol on her breath.

Looks like I'll be apologizing again once she's sober.

Chapter Twenty-Six

ARIA

AFTER I ACCEPT GIO'S APOLOGY—THOUGH, WE'LL definitely be talking more later—we spend the rest of the night dancing and drinking until the club closes. As we're walking out, Benjamin stops us to say hello, welcoming us back any time and mentioning he'll be opening a club in LA next month, if we're ever in the area, we should stop by.

"Come home with me, baby. Please," Gio says, once we're outside. He pushes me against the side of his vehicle and his hand goes to the curve of my hip, descending past the hem of my dress and landing on my bare skin, as he peppers kisses along my hot flesh, down my collarbone, and over my shoulder. When he licks my earlobe, I visibly shiver, making him chuckle.

"We need to talk," I say, trying to stay focused. His kisses are an aphrodisiac, each and every one of them going straight to my core.

"Come back home and we'll talk. I promise." Rests his arms

above my head, he cages me in and plants a kiss on the corner of my mouth. His lips move to my throat, then to my neck.

"What happened this morning?" I ask. "Was it because Weston touched me?"

Gio's body freezes. His thumb and index finger go to my chin and he raises my face so I'm looking at him. "Ari, I can't keep my hands off of you. Nothing he's ever done to you could change how I feel about you. How much I want you. How much I love you." His lips come down on mine for a kiss.

"Then what was it?" I murmur against his lips.

Gio lets out a sigh and backs up, taking his warmth with him. "I didn't keep you safe."

"You couldn't have known Cecilia would work with him."

"I should have been more on top of it. It happened under my roof. The life I live is dangerous. Cecilia has lived that life right alongside me. She's watched people get killed, get beaten to death. She's watched threats get made and those same threats be followed through."

"I could get into an accident driving and be killed. You can't predict the future."

"No, but I can keep you from being put in harm's way. My biggest fear is that by loving me, you're signing your death wish."

"So, what do we do?"

Gio's head drops and he lets out a defeated sigh. "We keep living our life. We see where things go. I love you so much, but, Aria, if you're ever put in harm's way again because of me—"

"Don't finish that sentence," I plead, grabbing him around his neck and pulling him to me. "Don't say that. Take me home, please. Take me home and make love to me. Nothing is going to happen to me."

Gio doesn't take us home. Instead, he takes us to his hotel. He checks us into a room, and once we get inside, he hands me a robe. "We don't have any clothes here so put this on so you can be more comfortable." He takes his shoes and socks off then strips out of his pants and shirt.

Taking the robe from him, I go to the bathroom to freshen up. I fix my makeup the best I can, using the soap on the sink to wipe the black smudges from under my eyes, and run my fingers through my hair. Then I remove my dress and heels. I debate whether I should leave my undergarments on and decide against it. Once I have the robe secure, I walk back into the room.

Gio isn't there, but I see the slider open so I head out to the balcony. When I get out there, I notice each balcony has a privacy wall. Gio is sitting out there with a tray from room service. When he hears me approach, he turns around, grinning at me.

"I ordered some dessert. It'll help absorb some of that tequila in your system." He shoots me a wink, and I roll my eyes but go to the tray to see what he's ordered. Under the lid is a large slice of chocolate cake drizzled with hot fudge. With my index finger, I swipe a bit of the fudge off the top and lick it off my finger until its clean. Gio groans, so I swipe up some more, this time making a production out of licking my finger.

Grasping the side of my robe, he pulls me to him so I'm straddling his lap. He grabs my finger, sticks it in his mouth, and sucks hard. When I try to pull my finger back, he bites down on it.

"Hey! You know I love my cake. Get your own."

"This cake is for us to share." He sits up higher and adjusts us, then he grabs the plate with the delicious cake on it along with a fork. When he breaks off a piece, I lean forward to take a bite, but he smirks and takes the bite himself.

"Not cool, Valentino." I pout and he laughs, the sound sending butterflies to my belly. He takes another forkful and this time brings it to my mouth. I part my lips and he gives me the bite. The cake practically melts in my mouth and I can't help the moan that slips out.

"I think I need another bite of this cake," Gio murmurs, his gaze burning into mine. This time when he breaks off a forkful, he pulls down the top of my robe and spreads the cake along my collarbone, crumbs falling all over us. Before I can make a smartass comment, his mouth is on my body, sucking and nibbling the cake off my skin. He swipes a piece of frosting with his finger, and moving my robe down farther so my breasts are completely exposed, he rubs the frosting across one of my nipples.

"Now, this is my kind of dessert." He lifts a brow and gives me a devilishly handsome grin before grabbing my breast in his hand and bringing my nipple to his mouth.

He sucks on the hardened peak almost to the point of pain. The sensation hits at the apex of my thighs and I clench my legs together in need of some kind of relief. Gio takes another bit of frosting and rubs it onto my other nipple, licking and sucking it, making me squirm in his lap.

When he goes to swipe another piece, I grab his hand. "You aren't sharing," I tease.

Guiding his finger to his chest, I rub the frosting over the tattoo he has above his heart, and leaning down, I lick my way across his flesh. I can feel the raised skin from his tattoo and I make a mental note to ask him what it means to him. I've seen it a million times but keep forgetting to ask him about it.

I take more frosting off the top of the cake and wipe it across his neck. I run my tongue downward, licking the chocolatey goodness off him. Just as I'm licking the last of the chocolate off, Gio grabs my ass and pulls me closer to him so my pussy is grinding against his hard cock through his boxers. I let out a throaty moan and he groans. His hands go to my breasts as he eagerly takes a nipple into his mouth, licking then sucking on it.

I lean back—his mouth making a popping sound as my nipple gets plucked from his mouth—and grab hold of his shaft, rubbing it through his boxers. I can feel the precum leaking through the material and I need to have it in my mouth. Sliding down the lounge chair, I pull Gio's boxers down and his dick springs free. Taking his shaft in my hand, I stroke it up and down, getting it harder. Once it's standing at full attention, I hover over his dick, give him a small smile, then holding my tits together, glide down and around his dick.

"Jesus, baby. Fuck me with those tits." He lets out a guttural groan as I glide my breasts up and down, fucking him. The head of his cock is glistening with precum and every time his dick comes up, it enters my wet mouth, my lips wrapping around the head, sucking and tasting the saltiness.

Gio's hips begin to buck, his movements growing more frantic. "I need to be inside you." He grabs me by my arms and pulls me up. With his dick in his hand, he guides himself into me. I lower myself onto his entire length and once I'm completely seated, let out a heady moan.

"Holy shit. You're so deep." I start moving my hips up and down, as Gio groans out, his head going back in pleasure. My arms come up and hold onto his shoulders, my breasts rubbing up against his chest as I ride him. He brings his head down and presses hard kisses all over my breasts before pulling a nipple into his mouth.

"Suck on it harder," I cry out, needing more, "and pull the other one." Clamping my nipple down with his teeth, he sucks hard on one nipple while pinching and pulling the other one. Sparks shoot down to my core. My movements get wilder, my vaginal muscles tightening. Gio lets go of my breasts and pulls me into a rough kiss, taking possession of my mouth. His tongue thrusts inside, swirling around mine, as his fingers stroke my clit, the sensations sending volts of pleasure through my body. I can't get enough of him, and I'm not sure if I ever will.

"Aria, come for me, baby." His fingers continue to massage my clit as my pussy clenches around his dick. My orgasm builds higher and higher, about to spill over. When Gio's thrusts into me from below, hitting me deliciously deep, I let go, waves of ecstasy rolling through me like a tidal wave as he follows right behind me.

I let out a satisfied sigh and my head drops to Gio's shoulder as we both sit quietly, catching our breaths. "I love you," he whispers into my ear.

"I love you, too." I pull back and give him a slow kiss, my lips lingering on his, not wanting our connection to end. Finally, he pulls back slightly.

"Let's go take a shower. Then we can finish this dessert." He gives me his signature panty-dropping wink and lifts me, setting me down so he can stand up. Once he's righted himself, he swoops me up over his shoulder and slaps my ass hard, making me squeal as he carries me to the shower where we both get cleaned off, only to get dirty several more times throughout the night.

I wake up to the sound of someone knocking on the door. With one eye still closed, I peek out of the sheets to see Gio taking a bag from Johnny. He closes the door, but opens it again when there's another knock. This time, it's room service. He wheels the cart in and tips the guy before closing the door once more.

I sit up in the bed, pulling the sheet up as I go. "I'm starving. What do you have there?"

"Since I have plans for us today, I figured we would go with something less messy." He lifts the lid up, showcasing the croissants, coffee, and fruit. He brings the tray over to the bed, setting it down in between us, and hands me my coffee. I set it on the nightstand.

"There's a lot we could do with that fruit," I say as I pull the sheets down, exposing my breasts. "Like this strawberry..." I take a bite out of it, chewing slowly, then place the other half onto my nipple, rubbing the juice all around the hardened peak.

Gio lets out a rough growl then pounces on me, his mouth going straight to my nipple as he laps and licks the dripping juice. The tray of food goes flying when he grabs the sheets and rips them from my body, the cold air hitting my nipples and making them even harder.

He grabs my hips and pulls my body down, my head hitting the pillow, and then he grips my thighs and spreads them open. His body climbs back over mine, and his fingers thread through my own, pinning them over my head as he thrusts into me in one fluid motion, the head of his dick hitting the spot deep down in me that will have me coming in minutes.

I let out a moan as he fucks me hard and deep, pumping into me mercilessly over and over again. With my hands pinned above my head, my back arches, my chest rising. Gio rains kisses along my neck then all over my breasts as he fucks me senseless. Our bodies are rubbing against each other, while he's thrusting into me, heat spreading throughout my body, my clit being stimulated.

I scream out in pleasure as my climax hits me hard, my body bowing off the bed. My pussy clenches around his dick as he empties himself into me.

"Jesus, Aria." His hands are still in mine as his head drops. He glance back up at me and I grace him with a lazy, sated smile.

"What? It's not my fault you ordered strawberries." I shrug and he chuckles lightly, shaking his head.

"Let's go, woman. We have shit to do today. We need to shower and eat." He gets off me and I get out of the bed, running to the shower. He reaches out and slaps my ass again like he did last night.

"Keep that up and we're never going to leave this room," I yell as I slam the bathroom door behind me. Of course, Gio follows me into the bathroom and by the time we are dressed in the clothes Gio had Johnny bring us, fed, and ready to go, it's almost lunch time.

Chapter Twenty-Seven

GIOVANNI

"WHAT ARE WE DOING TODAY?" ARIA ASKS FOR THE millionth time since I made the mistake of using the word surprise. We're riding down to the second floor in the elevator, and for the millionth time I tell her she has to wait and see. The elevator dings, letting us off and Aria lets out a loud gasp. "Wow! Gio, is this your casino?" I nod and take her hand, leading her to the entrance.

Last night, I decided to take Aria to the hotel instead of going home. I felt like we needed a night away from everything and since we're here, I figured she would enjoy experiencing a casino for the first time. Since she was living with me when she turned twenty-one back in April, there was a good chance she hasn't experienced being at a real casino before.

The guard who checks IDs recognizes me immediately and lets us through.

"Have you ever gambled before?"

"Nope," she says, looking around and taking it all in.

"Let me give you a tour." Holding her hand and guiding her around the casino, I show her all the different areas, ranging from the penny machines, to the blackjack tables, to the poker tables, and ending at the roulette tables.

"I want to play this one," she says.

"Roulette? You know how to play?"

"No, but I like how the ball rolls around the spinner thingy."

I chuckle at her innocence. "Okay, sit here." I point to the chair and sit on the one to the right of her, pull out several bills and setting them down in front of us. The dealer scoops up the money and gives us a stack of chips. I attempt to explain how the game works but when she gives me her adorable look of confusion, I go with the easy version. "Take your chips and place them on the numbers you think the ball will land on." I place a couple chips on a few different numbers and Aria follows my lead.

"What's this?" She points to the outside betting area.

"You can place a bet on whether you think it will land on red or black."

"Oh! That would mean I have a fifty percent chance of winning!" She takes two chips and places them on red. The dealer calls last chance and then spins the wheel. The ball lands on a red twenty-three and Aria squeals that it's on red. The guy sitting next to her laughs at her enthusiasm.

"Do I take my money?" She reaches for the chips.

"They're chips, and no, the dealer will distribute your winnings." She watches with wide eyes as the dealer takes the chips and distributes them back out to those who won.

"I got like double the amount I started with!"

I find myself grinning at how animated she is. I've learned quickly that Aria finds pleasure in everything she does. Whether it's learning to cook and bake with Maggie, taking photos and developing them in her darkroom, or playing a game of roulette here at the casino, she approaches everything with equal excitement and enthusiasm.

The dealer starts the process all over again and everyone picks their numbers. This time Aria loses everything she won plus a few extra chips, making her pout. When a waitress comes over and asks us for our order, Aria orders a coke and I order a Macallan neat. She plays several more rounds, losing more often than not. I keep giving her more of my chips until she's down to her last few.

"Where did all the chips go?" She looks around us like I'm hiding the chips from her. She grabs my hand and searches in my lap.

The gentleman next to her cracks up laughing. "You lost them all. That's what the casino does to you, sweetheart. It's a mindfuck. You start off winning so you gain confidence. The more you win, the more you think you're invincible. Then, little by little, the house takes from you in such small increments you don't even realize you're being robbed with your eyes wide open, until you're sitting in this chair, thousands of dollars poorer." He gives Aria a small wink and if he didn't look to be in his eighties, I'd probably have decked him for flirting with her, but seeing as he's old enough to be her great grandfather, I simply chuckle.

"Wait! What do you mean thousands?" Aria turns to me. "How much did we lose?"

"We?" I laugh. "You lost all our money." She bites on her lower lip nervously looking around like the money will reappear. Running my thumb over her lip, I pull it out from her teeth. "Did you have fun?" She nods. "Then that's all that matters. What do you want to play next?"

We grab our drinks and she says bye to the guy sitting next to her.

"How much did I lose?"

"It doesn't matter. It's my casino. I get it all back regardless."

She rolls her eyes. "Okay, but just tell me. If it wasn't your casino, how much would I have lost?"

"Two grand." I shrug.

Aria splutters out her drink. "Two thousand dollars?"

"Baby, that's child's play. The man next to you put out and lost probably triple that."

"I think we should go play the penny machines," she says seriously, and I can't help but laugh at her. She has millions of dollars in the bank from the sale of the shares and in less than a year she'll be five hundred million dollars richer, and the woman wants to play the penny slots.

"Well then, let's go play those penny slots."

Aria and I spend the day gambling. She tries out damn near every table and machine in this place. She cheers when she wins and pouts when she loses, and I feel like my face should be in pain from all the goddamn smiling I'm doing watching her every reaction.

When it's close to dinner time I get a text from Nico letting me know he's aware we've been down here all day and we better meet him and Amber for dinner. I text him back that we'll meet them at one of the restaurants in the hotel.

"Let's go up so we can shower and change for dinner. We're meeting Nico and Amber." Aria agrees and throws the couple chips she has left into her pocket.

"What are you doing? We have to go cash them in."

"I only have a couple. I want to keep them." Her face heats up, turning a faint pink shade.

"Why are you blushing?" I pull her into my side while we wait for the elevator to go up to our room.

"I like to keep mementos. It's similar to taking a picture." She shrugs. "This was my first time in a casino and it was with you. I want to keep the chips to remember this day."

We enter the room and I strip my shirt off as I walk toward the bathroom to jump in the shower, stopping at the door. "You coming?"

Aria giggles. "Hell yes." It takes me a second before I put it together. My girl has jokes.

"You're a bad girl."

"I blame you! You've turned me into this."

"Into what? A beautiful woman? I'm pretty sure you were just as beautiful the day I took you. A bit skinnier, but still just as beautiful."

"What I meant was, you've turned me into a horny sex maniac! But now I'm stuck on the fact that you just called me fat."

Grabbing Aria's shirt, I lift it over her head then reach around and unclasp her bra, pulling it off her. Her hands go to her soft stomach and I ignore it while I undo her jeans and pull them, along with her underwear, down to her ankles.

I turn the water on so it can heat up, then set her on the counter, separating her legs and stepping in between them. "You see these beautiful, perfect tits?" I don't give her a chance to answer. "When you moved in with me, they were still gorgeous, but the last several months they've become full. When you wear those tiny little tank tops, they spill out and it takes everything in me not to spend my days and nights sucking on them." I take one hardened nipple into my mouth and suck on it before letting go of it and sucking on the other one, earning me a breathy moan from Aria.

I release her nipple and, pushing her back against the mirror, kiss a trail down the center of her tits straight to her stomach. "When you came to me, you were beautiful but too skinny." Bending down, I kiss a line across her stomach from one hip bone to the other. Then I stand up and pull her hips toward me, her hot cunt hitting my cock. "I had nothing to hold on to." I push my pants and boxers down, stroking my dick a few times before I guide myself into Aria, holding onto her hips while I push in and out of her slowly. "You're fucking perfect." I thrust into her, my entire shaft bottoming out before I pull back slightly and then thrust back in.

"Play with those beautiful nipples, *tesoro mio*." *My treasure.* Aria brings her hands to her breasts and palms them at first, then, with her index and forefinger, she pinches both of her nipples, her eyes never leaving mine. "There's nothing wrong with a skinny woman." I grip her hips harder as my movements get rougher, her tight cunt quickly bringing me to the brink. "But fuck if a man doesn't love his woman with meat on her. Tits to suck on, hips to grip on to." Grabbing her thighs, I start to pump in and out of her deeper, harder. "Fucking thighs to grab ahold of." I can feel her pussy clenching around me, growing even tighter as I pick up the pace, fucking her hard. "You're fucking perfect and you're mine. Say it, Aria. You're perfect and mine."

My thrusts turn savage as I push into her, her tits bouncing as she pinches her nipples. Her eyes still trained on mine. "Say it, Aria! Say it and then come all over my fucking cock."

Aria's eyes briefly close. "I-I'm perfect," she moans out.

"And?"

"And I'm yours!" She screams out the last word as her orgasm rips through her. Her pussy chokes my cock like a goddamned vice grip and I'm coming so fucking hard I almost black out.

"Fuck, yes, you are," I rasp. Pulling out of her, I grip those perfect hips of hers and pull her up to me so her face is only inches from mine. I seal my lips over hers, my tongue running over the seam of her lips before I pick her up and move us into the shower, setting her down under the stream of hot water.

Ripping the loofah out of the package, I pour some soap onto it and wash Aria's body, focusing on all my favorite parts of her. When I'm done, she takes it from me and does the same thing.

"What does this mean?" she asks, stopping the loofah on the tattoo over my heart. I'm surprised she hasn't asked me sooner.

"*Dalla nascita. Per sangue. Famiglia.*" I say the words without having to look at them.

"I know they say something about birth and family. I don't know the middle word, though."

"By birth. By blood. Family. It's the family motto. Every son has gotten this tattoo the day he was officially brought into the organization."

"How old were you?"

"Eighteen, but I grew up in the organization. While kids were out riding their bikes, I was learning about money laundering. When my friends were hanging out playing video games, I was helping my dad count shipments of various illegal paraphernalia. Hell, I lost my virginity to an escort when I was fifteen when he was teaching me about the ins and outs of the bordello. It's all I've ever known."

Chapter Twenty-Eight

ARIA

"IT'S ALL I'VE EVER KNOWN."

I frown at Gio's words. Not at his obvious fierce loyalty toward his family and the organization but at the fact that I know I could never compete with either one. I'm not his family or his blood. I'm just a woman he saved and is sleeping with. Sure, he's called me his girlfriend, but I also saw the way his mom and dad looked at me, like an outsider, which is crazy because at first, everyone you meet is an outsider. Technically, at one time Cecilia was an outsider. I wonder if it'll always be this way. If his family will ever give me a chance to become a part of their circle or if I'll always remain on the outside looking in. The thought is mildly depressing.

"Hey." Gio lifts my chin. "What's wrong?"

I push my negative thoughts aside and ask a question I've been wondering for a while. "Will you one day take over the organization?"

"Yes, I'm the eldest of the three of us. Nico loves working at the hotel and casino and while Mario has talked about moving back here on several occasions, he's never taken the initiative to actually move. I've known I would take over since I was little."

"If you could do anything, what would you do?"

Gio looks at me with confusion. "What do you mean?"

"If you weren't in the organization and you could have any career you wanted, what would you want to spend your life doing?"

His lips curve into a puzzled frown as he considers my question. "Probably running a restaurant." He smiles, and it shocks me he didn't say he would want to be doing exactly what he's doing. "When I was growing up, my parents owned—still own—a few restaurants. I used to love hanging out in the kitchen with the chef and learning about all the foods. When my dad would hold meetings at the restaurants, I would constantly get yelled at for wanting to help in the kitchen instead of attending the meetings and learning about the business."

Gio's lips turn upward into a soft smile, most likely remembering a fond memory, and it tugs at my heart that I've never seen him smile so carefree as he is right now while discussing the restaurant. When he discusses the business and organization, he's always cold, completely void of all emotions. He never smiles, especially not like the one he's sporting right now. When you love something, when it's your passion, it makes you happy. His reaction tells me the organization isn't his passion, but instead an obligation, and that makes me feel sad for him. I couldn't imagine spending my life doing something I don't love and feel passionately about.

Gio reaches over and turns the water off then grabs us both a towel. I wrap mine around my body and he does the same. "So, you can cook?" I ask, wanting to know more about this passion of his.

"I can, but I'd want to take it a step further. I'd want to go to culinary school and learn how to do it all the right way."

"Well, now you're going to have to cook for me sometime." I give him a playful shove with my hip as I walk passed him to get dressed.

"If it'll end the same way it did with the cake and strawberries, I'll gladly cook for you any time."

Chapter Twenty-Nine

ARIA

AFTER OUR BRIEF DETOUR FROM REALITY, WE'RE BACK home and Gio is back to work. If you would have asked me a year ago if I could ever consider a mansion where women prostitute themselves out to men to be my home, I would have laughed in your face, but now I can't imagine living anywhere else. I've grown to love the women here. The problem is, while Cecilia is gone, Claudia is now here training Natalie to take over and she isn't exactly fond of me.

The last few days I've been roaming the expansive property taking pictures. Then an idea came to me. I could take pictures to go in the women's profiles. Gio could include a couple photos of the women, so the members could see a good image of who they're picking. Right now, there's a simple head shot of each girl in their portfolio, which isn't flattering at all. At first, Gio said no, but when I started following him around, bored out of my mind, taking pictures of him, he said whatever I wanted to do is fine.

So, I had each girl let me know when they're dressed up and would like her picture taken. I did mini photo shoots for each of them and now that I'm in the darkroom developing their photos, I'm in love. I've always been more of a landscape photographer, but seeing how these photos turned out, I think I've found what I want to do: professional shoots. From boudoir to family shoots, I want to capture the special moments people want to remember.

As I'm hanging up the last of Holly's photos from her shoot to dry, there's a knock at the door. Gio put a lock on the door so when I'm developing, people can't just barge in and ruin the photos. I rinse and dry my hands and step outside to find Claudia standing against the wall with her arms crossed. She's dressed similar to the way all the women dress around here, in an expensive formfitting dress and tall heels. Her makeup is done to perfection and if I didn't know she has a thirty-two-year-old son, I would think she was no older than forty years old.

"Claudia," I say, giving her my best smile. She's made it a point to ignore me the last week so I can't imagine why she wants to speak to me now, but I know it's probably best to be pleasant if she's ever going to give me a chance.

"Aria, I was hoping we could speak." She hits me with a smile just as big as the one I gave her and something tells me hers is fake as well.

"Absolutely." I follow her out to the back patio near the pool.

She asks Darla, one of the servers, to bring us some sweet tea then gestures for me to have a seat.

"I thought since Giovanni is out on business for the day we could talk. He's made it a point to keep me away from you all week but there are a few things I need to say." I'm stunned to learn that Giovanni has kept her away from me. I thought this whole time she was simply avoiding me, but to learn it was his doing has me extremely curious as to why. Without waiting for my response, Claudia continues. "I wanted to apologize for Cecilia's part in what happened regarding Senator Weston Hightower."

She's apologizing for something Cecilia did? "No, please, I can't let you take the blame or apologize for something you had no control over."

"Please let me finish, dear." She places her hands into her lap and sits up straighter, her shoulders jutting back. "As I was saying, I am sorry for her part. She did what she felt was best for this family but she should have come to me first because I would've told her it was a waste of her time. You're twenty-one years old and while I'm sure your pussy is fresh and tight, just how my son likes it—since he is his father's son after all—you have no future with Giovanni."

My drink splutters out of my mouth as I take in her words. This woman has no intention of apologizing. Gio kept her from me because he knew how she felt. My only hope is to explain to her how I feel about Gio.

"Claudia, I know Cecilia is close to your family."

"No, she *is* family." Her left eyebrow quirks up, daring me to argue, and I take a sip of my tea to fill my mouth before I say something I can't take back.

"Okay, she is family. But I love Gio and I didn't force him to be with me. He chose to be with me and he loves me as well."

Claudia scoffs. "Has he told you that?"

"Yes."

Her eyebrows furrow in shock, but she quickly recollects herself. "It doesn't really matter. Cecilia and Giovanni were meant to be together. Stefan has been part of our family his entire life. Giovanni will one day take over for his father and he needs a strong woman by his side. My dear, you just aren't fit to be in this life."

"Mother!" Gio's voice roars from behind us and we both turn to look at him. He stalks over to the table and stands next to my chair. "I made it clear you are not to speak to Aria unless you're willing to give her a chance." He turns to me. "Aria, please give my mother and me a few minutes. I came out here to tell you we're flying out this afternoon. Go on up and pack, and I'll be up in a few minutes. Make sure you pack a nice dress and heels." Gio places a small kiss on my forehead, silently dismissing me.

Before I walk inside, I turn to Claudia. "I'm sorry if you feel I'm coming between your family. I understand I'm not who you want for your son—for your family—but I love him and until he sends me away, I'm not going anywhere."

I walk inside, closing the doors behind me to give them their privacy and head upstairs to pack. I have no idea where Gio and I are going but maybe getting away is a good idea. I would never be disrespectful to Gio's mom, but it hurts to have your relationship belittled by someone who isn't part of the equation. I understand she's his mom and therefore family, but she doesn't understand how deep my feelings run for her son. She doesn't get how my heart feels complete when he touches me. How, when he smiles at me, my chest tightens and the butterflies my mom used to tell me about show up, fluttering all around my belly. She isn't there at night when we're sleeping and Gio subconsciously reaches for me, needing to hold me close to him, needing my body against his. She doesn't hear the conviction in his words every time he tells me he loves me.

I grab a suitcase and pack a couple outfits, including a dress and heels like Gio requested. Then I throw in some lingerie and my toiletries and my camera. By the time I'm done packing, Gio's swinging open the door, his fingers running through his hair in frustration.

"You ready?" His voice is gruff and I stop what I'm doing.

"You want to try that again?"

He scrubs his hands over his face. "Fuck!" His fingers go back to his hair, pulling on the ends. I bridge the gap between us and, removing his fingers, bring them down, entwining our hands together.

"Hey, please calm down." I stand on my tiptoes and give Gio a gentle kiss, my lips lingering on his but my tongue never seeking entrance. His body visibly relaxes. "Where are we going? Are we running away?" I give him a wink and he cracks a smile.

"It's a surprise."

Five hours later and we're walking out of the Miami International Airport to wait for the car service. Johnny is with us but keeps his distance. The air in Miami is a lot like the air in Vegas: hot and humid and sticky as hell. It's almost ten o'clock at night in Miami, but it still feels like it's a hundred degrees outside. July in Florida is no joke. The sweat instantly beads above my brow and I wipe it away.

Thankfully, the car service pulls up only minutes after we step outside, and after taking our bags, we take off to the hotel. Johnny sits in the front with the driver, Gio sitting in the back with me. He makes several phone calls and sends numerous messages on the way while I stare out at the view of the Miami bay. It's pitch black but the twinkling lights of the city reflect off the water. I pull out my camera and hit the button to roll down my window and snap some pictures. If the hot air whipping through the car bothers Gio, he doesn't say anything.

We pull up to a luxurious hotel and, without grabbing our bags, Gio takes hold of my hand and walks inside to check in. While he's speaking to the woman at the desk, I spot a sign near the front door and damn near have a heart attack.

Miami Photography Art Exhibit

The date for the exhibit is this weekend and it's featuring several artists I would die to meet. If this isn't the reason we're here, I'm going to have to convince Gio to go with me if we can still get tickets. He finishes checking in and I point to the sign. "Please tell me we're going."

He follows my line of vision to the sign and tries hard to stifle his smile, but I catch it before he can contain it.

"Yes! Yes! Yes!" I jump up into his arms—his strong hands catching me—and bring my hands to either side of his face, pulling him in for a passionate kiss. "Thank you! I can't believe this. Francis Ricci, Cheri Vitelli, and Valerie Malone are all here!"

"I'm assuming they're photographers..."

I gasp at Gio's ignorance. "Not just photographers. The *best* photographers."

He chuckles and drops his hands from under my ass, my body dragging down the front of his as he slowly brings me to my feet.

"And what would you do for these tickets to see the best photographers, *amore mio?*" he asks, waggling his eyebrows playfully. I press my body up against his, bringing my knee up slightly to rub against his crotch, feeling him grow harder as I rub.

"I think we should go up to our room and I'll show you *exactly* what I'm willing to do for the tickets." I rub my knee one last time before backing away and sauntering toward the elevator, making it a point of putting a little extra sway in my step.

Chapter Thirty

GIOVANNI

ARIA IS DRESSED IN A ONE-OF-A-KIND VALENTINO BLACK off the shoulder floor length gown. On one side, there's a slit that goes all the way up her thigh almost to her hip bone. It's the perfect mix of classy and sexy. Her brown locks are hanging down her back in loose waves and she's almost to my chin in her five-inch fuck-me heels. Her face looks flawless with the little bit of makeup she's put on, and she's pacing the living room of our hotel while I'm texting on my phone. I've felt the heat of her stare on me for the last ten minutes but I've ignored her.

It's true that we're here for Aria to meet her favorite photographers and see the , but there's something else we're here for, something that will make her night even more memorable. I'm waiting for the exhibit coordinator to text me and let me know when we can head down to the convention center where the exhibit is being held.

My phone buzzes in my hand with the message I've been waiting for. Standing, I throw on my tuxedo jacket since it's a black-tie affair, and tie my tie. When Aria sees this, she lets out a loud huff. "Finally! You would think with the way you screamed my name during that blow job I gave you last night, you would've let us go down there early!"

My cock twitches remembering Aria's warm wet mouth wrapped around my cock, the way she slurped and sucked and showed me over and over again how badly she wanted the tickets. "Keep talking like that and we'll be late." I reach over and pull her into me, kissing the corner of her mouth so I don't ruin her lipstick. "You look absolutely stunning."

Her mouth twitches as her beautifully lined lips pull up into a soft smile. "Thank you. Now can we please go?"

I nod and open the door for her. When we get to the exhibit, I hand the doorman our tickets and we walk in. Holding Aria's hand is what I would compare to holding a child's hand who's walking into Disney. She's shaking with excitement, and with our fingers entwined, she's trying to drag me along faster.

"Slow down, *cuore mio*," I murmur. She grants me an eye roll in response and I chuckle.

We haven't even walked fifteen feet in the door when Aria is squeezing my hand and gasping.

"That's Cheri Vitelli," she whispers, nodding toward an older woman, probably in her fifties, wearing a multicolored dress with...

is that fruit? all over it. Her hair is up in a messy bun similar to the one Aria wears when she isn't forced to actually do her hair.

"Let's go say hi." I pull her with me toward the woman and introduce myself. "My name is Giovanni Valentino and this is Aria Sutton. She's a huge fan of your work."

Cheri smiles and gives Aria a kiss on each cheek. "Oh, my sweet girl, I know exactly who you are." Her words are heavily accented, English most likely not her first language.

Aria nervously laughs. "I'm pretty sure you have me confused with someone else, but your photos are amazing. The emotion that seeps through them is so heart wrenching and beautiful."

Cheri gives Aria a confused look. "*Grazie*, but I could have sworn I saw..."

"You have the right woman," I point out to Cheri. We're just heading that way now." I give her a knowing wink and she quickly catches on.

"Please, Aria, if you are ever in Florence, you must come and visit me." Aria nods emphatically in complete shock as Cheri moves on to greet another fan.

"That was really weird, right?" Aria questions as we make our way toward the back. We stop several more times as Aria meets the photographers she looks up to. She's completely enamored with every one of them. They all mention they know her, but I stop them each time before they can say too much. They each invite her to visit them and Aria is on cloud nine.

When we finally make our way to the exhibit she knows nothing about, I walk her through the narrow hallway and watch her as she gasps in shock, her hands coming to her mouth, as tears spill over the sides of her eyes and trickle down her cheeks.

"Gio! What did you do?"

Chapter Thirty-One

ARIA

AS I LIVED OUT A DREAM COME TRUE, WHICH HAD ME mentally pinching myself to make sure this was in fact real life and not literally a dream, I felt like I was an outsider, like there was a secret everyone I came in contact with was a part of, one I wasn't privy to know anything about.

That is, until Gio walked me down a hallway which lead us to a circular room, and as I looked around at the blown-up images surrounding me, all the comments suddenly made sense. Because surrounding me were my images. Shots of the hills where my mom and I used to hike, the beautiful boudoir shots of Holly and Natalie, images of the gardens in the back of the house. Some in color, some in black and white, all mine.

I walk into the room and twirl slowly, taking it all in. These are my photos. We aren't the only people in the room. Several others are in here, all pointing at and discussing my photos. In the corner is a photo of me with a plaque, like the other photographers have, that reads: **meet the artist.**

"You did this, not me." Gio's arms go wide, pointing to the room around us. The hot tears falling down my face can't be stopped as he pulls me into his arms. "You did all this, baby."

"I don't understand. How did you get my photos into this exhibit?"

"I might have snuck into your darkroom and stole a couple of your photos. I sent them to a few different galleries, and Blake, the exhibit coordinator, called me a couple days ago saying it was last minute but he would love to have your work featured as an up and coming artist."

My heart feels so full at what this man has done for me. It's easy to tell someone you support them, but it's another thing entirely to go above and beyond—to take action. The last person who supported my art was my mom until she sided with Weston, saying it shouldn't be anything more than a hobby, insisting I major in something with a future in college. I know my mom loved me—at one time she was my best friend—but she was sucked in by the false glamour of the world of politics. She lived for the sense of power that came with being a senator's wife. She stopped supporting me to support him and I never realized until this moment how much I needed to feel supported.

"This is simply amazing. Thank you." I close the distance between us and give Gio a kiss I can only hope conveys how much all of this means to me.

We spend the rest of the evening mingling with other photographers and guests. When I run into some of my favorites for the second time, I thank them for their encouraging words and invitations. They laugh when they find out I had no idea my work was on display here, and congratulate Gio for pulling off such a thoughtful surprise.

When we get back to the hotel it's late and I'm shocked to see Gio's father, Salvatore, sitting in the living room, only a single light illuminating the room.

"We need to talk, Son." Salvatore completely disregards my presence but Gio doesn't.

"Aria, do me a favor and head to our room for a few minutes while I speak with my father." He gives me a soft kiss and I do as he says, closing the door behind me. I slip out of my dress and heels and take a quick shower to rinse off my body and face before putting on a shirt and comfortable sweats.

I know I shouldn't, but I open the door slightly to see if Gio and his dad are still talking. I see they've moved to the kitchen and are both drinking what looks like scotch.

"By killing the senator over *that* girl, you've practically pinned a bullseye on our foreheads!" Salvatore booms.

"I don't give a shit. I did what needed to be done. I'll deal with Sebastian just as I've been doing for the last year."

"I don't trust your judgement, Giovanni. You have continuously chosen her over your own family, your flesh and blood. It's time to let her go." Salvatore throws back what's left of his drink and slams the glass on the counter.

"And what? Marry Cecilia? You can't be serious!"

"It's her or your family."

Giovanni goes silent and my heart shatters. Gio's life is his family and his dad making him choose has me wanting to attack him, to knock some sense into the man who has no idea what he's doing to my heart, but I don't. I do, however, slide on my flip-flops and slip out the front door without waiting to hear what Gio's answer is. Needing some space and a bit of fresh air, I take the elevator down to the lobby and head out the back to go for a walk along the beach.

I kick off my flip-flops and toe the water. It's warm to the touch from the summer heat beating down on it all day. After walking for what seems like miles, I sit in the sand and stare out into the Atlantic, the moon's reflection hitting the soft waves as they come up and just barely hit my feet before rolling back. I think about Gio's father's ultimatum: me or his family. I would like to believe in Gio's eyes and heart, they are one in the same—I know in mine they are. But it doesn't matter how Gio or I feel because his father doesn't share the same feelings we do.

I wasn't able to see Gio's face when his dad gave him the ultimatum, but I could feel it, deep in my gut, that those five words broke him. I think about how Weston came into my life and slowly destroyed mine and my mom's relationship. For some reason, he was jealous of how close my mom and I were from the beginning. He wedged a rift between us that grew and grew until we were so far on opposite ends of the spectrum there was no healing the damage he created. I can't do that to Gio. I can't come between him and his family. I love him with every ounce of my being but the cliché quote I've read so many times comes to mind: *sometimes you have to love someone enough to let them go.*

I have the money to move. I have the means to start over, no matter how bad it'll hurt. I can walk away and not make Gio choose. I can put him first, the same way he's put me first every day since the day he saved me from that basement, from that nightmare that would still be my reality if it weren't for him. The same way he believed in me enough to make my dreams a reality.

I've only just made the decision and my heart already feels like it's been ripped out of my chest, but I stand and take in a deep cleansing breath, set on returning to the hotel room, having one last night with Gio, then putting him first and walking away. I wipe the sand from the back of my thighs and start the trek back to the hotel room.

I don't see it coming.

I don't hear the footsteps.

But I feel the hand cover my mouth.

I feel the needle prick the side of my neck.

I smell the masculine cologne engulf my senses as my eyes, against my will, close.

Chapter Thirty-Two

GIOVANNI

"IT'S TIME FOR YOU TO GO. IF YOU'RE MAKING ME CHOOSE between Aria and this organization then I'm choosing her."

My dad gives me a stunned look for a brief second before anger takes over his features. "This is not the son I raised. Letting a piece of pussy dictate your future. If you choose that girl over your family, you will regret it. *She* will regret it."

I shove my dad up against the wall, my hand wrapping around his throat in the same way I did to the senator. "You want to threaten me? Go for it! But don't you ever fucking threaten Aria. You got me?" My dad's breathing begins to go erratic, his face turning a slight shade of red before I let him go. He bends at the waist to catch his breath.

"You aren't thinking straight. I'm going to give you twenty-four hours to come to your senses." He grabs the front of my shirt and yanks it to the side, exposing my tattoo. "*Dalla nascita. Per sangue.*

Famiglia. Ricorda da dove proviene prima che sia troppo tardi." Remember *where you come from before it's too late.* He walks down the hall and out the door, slamming it behind him.

"Aria!" I shout her name, needing her in my arms. When she doesn't answer, I go into the room but she's not here. The bathroom is still fogged up from her shower but the room is empty. I check the other room, the living room, the terrace. No Aria. I pull my cell phone out and hit her name under my recent history. Her phone buzzes on the nightstand. I pick it up and type in her passcode. No calls or texts. I dial Johnny and after the second ring, he answers. "Where are you?"

"I'm down at the bar. Your dad asked me to give you guys some time alone."

"Is Aria with you?"

"No...she was with you up in the room."

"She's gone. Her fucking phone is still here and she's gone." My heart begins to go crazy—something is wrong. "She might have run away again. My dad and I were arguing over her. If she overheard it, it might have upset her."

"I'm heading to the security room now to check the footage."

Johnny and I hang up and I check the hotel room one more time before calling my dad.

"Son, have you already come to your senses?"

"If you did something to her, I'll kill you."

"To who? Aria? I haven't touched her." I can hear the truth in his words. He doesn't have her.

"She's gone. Fuck!" I bark, hanging up on my dad.

My phone rings and it's Johnny. "Any news?"

"I pulled up the feed. She walked through the lobby about thirty minutes ago toward the back, leading to the beach." I hear his fingers furiously typing on a keyboard. "The camera ends at the beach. She headed north along the water."

I hang up and run out the door, taking the stairs to the lobby, and head out back. When I get to the beach, it's dark, only the moon shining over the water. I make a left and start jogging up the quiet beach. I come across a few couples taking a stroll and stop to ask if they've seen a brown-haired woman walking alone down the beach. Nobody has seen her. I jog for what seems like miles until I hit a restaurant. It's closed down, but I walk up to it, looking for her. She's nowhere. It's like she's disappeared.

I turn around and walk slower back toward the hotel. As I'm pulling my phone out of my pocket to check back in with Johnny, I spot bright pink flip-flops in the sand. *Aria's.* I would recognize these anywhere. They match the sweatpants with the writing on her ass. I pick them up and look around. There's no way she would have gone into the water. I look behind me and see a wooden walkway, so I head that way. Once I get to the end of it, there's a small park with some restrooms and a parking lot. It's after two in the morning so the place is deserted. I walk into both restrooms to see if she's in there, but she's not.

I dial Johnny's number. "I found her flip-flops about a mile down. I've checked everywhere, Johnny. She's not here." Even I can hear the sheer panic in my voice conveying the thoughts I don't want to speak out loud.

"All right, Boss. Meet me back here and we'll regroup and make some calls. We'll find her."

I don't respond, but the words are said in my silence. *But what if it's too late?*

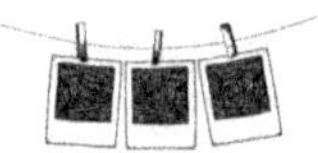

IT'S BEEN TWENTY-FOUR HOURS SINCE ARIA HAS disappeared. The thing about having money and connections is that when you need strings to be pulled, they get pulled. I have law enforcement checking into the cameras near the park. Rome and Caesar have flown out and are making calls. I'm calling in every favor owed to me.

"We found her!" Johnny pulls an image up on the computer. "Miami PD was able to confirm with facial recognition, this is Aria." I lean in closer to the zoomed-in photo and see her. She's being carried by a man, her head hanging back like she's passed out, her bare feet dangling.

"Who the fuck is carrying her?"

"He's wearing a mask."

"Zoom in here." I point to his forearm, which is wrapped around Aria's thigh as he carries her bridal style down the sidewalk toward the parking lot. Johnny hits a few buttons and the picture, blurry as fuck, appears closer. The word is in black against his white skin: *Lorenzo.*

"Fuck, Boss."

"Sebastian has her." I pick up my phone and call the one man who can help me get her back. "Dad, I need you. Sebastian Lorenzo has Aria."

"We'll get her back, Son. But once we do…"

He doesn't need to finish the sentence. *I let her go.*

"Yeah, I got it."

Chapter Thirty-Three

ARIA

THE ONLY DRUG I'VE TAKEN IN THE LAST SIX MONTHS HAS been my anti-anxiety meds, and even those, thanks to my psychiatrist, have been lowered to a mild dose and are only taken when needed. Sebastian Lorenzo has shot me up with enough heroin in the time he's had me, that I'm not even sure if I'm awake or asleep, alive or dead, but I'm not complaining because as I lie in the bed he has me tied to, as he spreads my legs for the fifth maybe sixth time since I woke up here, I'm grateful that the drugs are running through my system to numb the pain. I can feel the tears running down the sides of my face, hitting my ears.

"Open your fucking eyes, bitch!" A slap against my sex has me jumping up slightly and opening my eyes. With the two black eyes he's given me, his face is blurry but I can see the anger and disgust in his glare. "The senator made me a promise of twenty million dollars and since he's dead thanks to your fucking boyfriend, you're going to pay me." I don't bother responding. I've already tried to explain to Sebastian I don't have access to that sort of money. The sale of the shares was close to five million dollars. I offered that to him for him to let me go and he spat in my face. My eyes roll back in my head as my mind fights to escape.

When Weston used to rape me, I'd use my mom as well as my childhood memories as an escape, but now that Gio has become a huge part of my life and my heart, my mind immediately goes to him. My goal has been to not think about Gio. I refuse to let Sebastian take those memories away from me, but the more my body breaks down, the harder he hits me, the more terrified I become that I just might not make it to see another day, and that thought has me wanting to remember Gio, has me wanting to die with only the memories of our love in my head and heart.

Of our trip to the Bahamas. The way he would smile just for me. I mentally replace Sebastian's slaps and grabs with the gardens at the mansion. Of the art exhibit that now feels like years ago. I try to keep my thoughts on the day he found me in the basement, his promise to protect me. I remember the first time he told me he loved me. I wish I could die right here and now with the memories of him all around me.

Sebastian jerks away from me, jolting me from my only safe space—my mind. I'm thrust into the present. I can feel everywhere he's violated me. Everything hurts. It's as though my body no longer belongs to me. The only thing he can't ever take is my mind. He hasn't even backed up before I'm throwing up acid all over myself and the bed.

"You dumb slut!" Sebastian slaps me across the face. "Now you can lay in your own filth." He slams the door behind him and I close my eyes, praying that he kills me and gets it over with.

I'm not sure how long I'm asleep when I hear the door swing open. My eyes snap open and I see Gio stalking toward the bed—a sudden sense of déjà vu hitting me. For a split second, I wonder if I'm dreaming. He scoops me up into his arms and memories of him doing this very same thing six months prior hits me hard. "Are you real?" I hear myself asking.

"Yes, Aria. I'm real."

"You're saving me again," I choke out, raw emotion stuck in my throat. I let my eyes close, knowing I'm safe once again in the arms of Gio, and blocking everything around me out, I fall back asleep.

Chapter Thirty-Four

GIOVANNI

THE MINUTE I TOLD MY DAD I NEEDED TO FIND ARIA AND who had her, he sprang into action. I knew the only reason he was calling in any favors he had was because I had inadvertently agreed to let her go once she was found. He placed a call to Victor Lorenzo, Sebastian's father. It turned out, Sebastian had gone behind his father's back and made a deal with the devil himself, Weston Hightower. In exchange for helping him get Aria back, he would give him a piece of the trust fund, and with that money, Sebastian would be able to come to us to buy back their territory.

Victor ordered his son not to make the deal but Sebastian didn't listen. After he found out Weston was dead and his money train had come to a stop, he lost it. His dad told him to let it go and when he didn't, he pretty much disowned him. When my dad called and told him he was holding Aria, Victor was willing to throw his son under the bus in exchange for the ownership of the territory back. My dad, the businessman he is, agreed with the clause we can use that shipyard for all of our shipments at no charge.

Victor agreed and gave us the location to their Miami safe house. With a single call to one of my dad's enforcers, we were able to get in and out. Sebastian was killed with a shot to his head before he even saw it coming, and Aria was on a private plane back to Nevada with Dr. Fox waiting for us at the house.

She gave Aria a sedative so she would sleep and checked her out.

Tearing of her anus.

Sperm.

Bleeding.

Damage to the vaginal walls.

Dr. Fox had concluded that Aria had been violently raped in every way possible.

Aria's words hit me like a ton of bricks. *You're saving me again.*

I lost it. I went down to my office and destroyed it. The computer went flying into a wall, papers were thrown around. I don't know what else I did, but my knuckles were bleeding when Johnny walked in and sat next to me on the floor while I cried like a fucking baby.

You're saving me again.

I did this! I saved her and then brought her into this life. I swore to protect her and keep her safe and I broke my promise. In my world, people kill over broken promises.

Johnny sat with me in silence for who knows how long before I let out a sigh and got to work figuring shit out. I made several calls and called in a lot of favors, and while it felt like my chest was being crushed the entire time, making it hard to breathe, I knew I was doing the right thing. When I was done, I started to clean up my destroyed office, until Vivian knocked on the door to let me know Aria was waking up. I nodded and stood to go upstairs.

Now I'm standing in front of the bed, staring at Aria. Her eyes are open but they look distant and lost. She blinks slowly but doesn't say a word. She's the strongest woman I've ever met but even the strongest, break, and my girl is broken. I put a call in to her psychiatrist and she's going to be here soon.

I sit next to Aria on the edge of the bed. "We need to talk."

She looks up at me with unshed tears. "You don't need to say it. I already know."

"Know what?"

"Sometimes you have to love someone enough to let them go."

Rialto
Rialto

Chapter Thirty-Five

GIOVANNI

One Year Later

"GIOVANNI! EARTH TO GIOVANNI!" NATALIE WAVES HER hands in front of my face, snapping me out of my daydream.

"Yeah. Sorry. Just a lot on my mind. What's up?"

Natalie gives me the same look she always gives me when she catches me spacing out. "Your mom is here. She's at the bar having a drink."

"Okay, thanks." I stand from behind my desk and close the file I was supposed to be looking at but wasn't really paying attention to. That seems to be the story of my life this past year. My numbers are down, memberships have decreased, and I don't really give a fuck about any of it. I head out to the front to meet my mom, looking forward to having a drink more than conversing with her.

"Scotch neat," I tell Edgardo as I sit next to my mom, who's sipping on her usual fruity drink. I don't bother starting a conversation. She'll do it for me.

She places her drink down and turns toward me. "It's time for you to go."

"Go where? I don't have any meetings today." Edwardo places my scotch down and I pick it up, downing it in one large gulp before knocking on the bar top for him to get me another.

"To *her*, Giovanni. I need my son back."

I let out a humorless laugh and take a slightly smaller sip of the new drink in front of me. "What the hell are you talking about, Mom?" I take another sip and finish off the drink.

"I was wrong last year. I was thinking like the wife of a mob boss and not like your mother. I never should have told you to let her go."

"It doesn't even matter. She's halfway across the world and safe. What would I do? Bring her back here, into this life again? So, what? She can get kidnapped and raped again?" I wince at my own words and reach over the bar, grabbing the bottle of scotch to pour myself another drink.

"Natalie tells me you are drunk every day, Giovanni. We've all watched you self-destruct this past year. I thought you would come around but you haven't."

"What the fuck do you all want from me?" I roar. Members and staff turn their gaze on me, and I force my voice lower. "You wanted me to let her go, so I did. Dad threatened her. He wouldn't even help find her unless I agreed. I did what you wanted. What. More. Do you want from me?"

I take a swig straight from the bottle, not even bothering to pour it into the glass tumbler.

"Aria..." my mom says, and I cut her off.

"Don't you say her name! Her name is not allowed to leave your fucking mouth." I swipe the bottle and tumbler across the bar, both flying off the end and crashing to the ground. Edgardo jumps into action, without even giving me a second glance, to clean it up. This isn't the first, third, or probably thirteenth damn time glass has been broken at this bar. My elbows hit the bar top, my head going into my hands as I scrub my face in an attempt to calm down. "I'm sorry."

"I've spoken to your father and you're out."

My head shoots up at her words. "What do you mean I'm out?"

The rims of my mom's lids fill with unshed tears. "You are out of the organization."

"You're disowning me?" I ask incredulously.

"No." She shakes her head. "You will always be our son, and while your dad isn't happy about you leaving, he will come around. You're out of the organization. Mario is moving here to take over the restaurant and Casino and Nico is going to take over the bordello and any other business you have. Amber has agreed. They won't be living here, but he'll run the place with Natalie. We were wrong to put you in such a position. We had it set in our minds about you and Cecilia."

I hear what she's saying, but it all feels so surreal. I'm free. So many times I've dreamt about what I would do if I was free, but I never believed it would happen. Could I have walked away a year ago? Yeah, I could have, but Aria wouldn't let me. She told me she couldn't come between my family and me. She asked—no, she begged—me to let her go. So, I did. I let her go, and it feels like the day she walked out the door, with her bags in her hands, is the day my heart stopped beating.

"Do you think she'll want to see me? She was kidnapped and raped because of me."

My mom's built-up tears fall and she gives me a sad smile. "If she loves you the way you love her, the way I believe she loves you, I can't imagine she'd ever hold you responsible for what happened. But there's only one way to find out."

"Why are you doing this for me, Mom?"

"Because once upon a time I believed in the fairytale. I believed in the power of love. But somewhere along the way, I got caught up in your father's world of power and materialistic possessions and began to live a lie, telling myself those two things equaled love. I've told your father I'm done accepting him the way he is. I'm done turning my cheek while he cheats on me. If things don't change, I am filing for divorce."

My eyes widen at her admission. "You threatened to divorce Dad?"

"That's right. He says things will be different so we'll see. I'm not sure if it's too late for us, but I don't believe it's too late for you and Aria."

Chapter Thirty-Six

ARIA

"BUONGIORNO! CAFFÈ E PASTICCERIA PER FAVORE."

Francesca, the wonderful woman who owns the bakery I frequent daily, smiles and grabs my usual coffee and pastry. I hand her four euros and make my way to the outside patio to set up my laptop. I plug it into the outlet and connect to the Wi-Fi before taking a sip of the hot, caffeinated goodness.

"Aria!" Trevor calls out my name and waves. "I'm going to grab a coffee and then I'll join you."

I nod and reach for my pastry, taking a bite. The buttery flakiness melts in my mouth. I could eat this for breakfast every day. I came across this cute bakery my third day here in Italy. After spending the first two days crying, then spending over two hours video chatting with my therapist, whom I still talk to on a bi-weekly basis, she insisted I get out of the flat and explore.

When I left Nevada and stepped on the plane to Italy, I had no idea Gio had gone to such lengths to make sure I was taken care of, but that shouldn't have surprised me. I don't think there was anything he wouldn't do for me. One look into his eyes that night when he told me we needed to talk and I knew what he was going to say. I could hear it in his voice. He had no choice but to choose his family over me. What he didn't know was that I had made the decision before I was taken to walk away.

I guess you could say our breakup was a bit unconventional, probably because unlike most people who break up because they've fallen out of love with each other, we were breaking up because we were in love with each other. Gio gave me my space to heal but still constantly checked on me. A week later, I was packed and got on a plane, leaving my broken heart back in Nevada.

Gio gave me all the information I would need. A car service was waiting for me when I stepped off the plane and took me straight to the gorgeous flat he had rented for me in the heart of Florence. He had contacted an English-speaking art college, which was walking distance from my flat, and through whatever strings he pulled, he had me enrolled and starting classes two weeks later.

He got me in contact with a financial advisor to help me budget and invest my money, and he made sure Dr. Weisberg would continue to see me through video chat as often as I wanted or needed. All of this was put in writing, and the day I walked out of the bordello was the last time I saw or spoke to Gio. We hugged goodbye and I about lost it. He whispered that he would always love me and apologized for hurting me. I was too choked up to respond and so many times in the last thirteen months and seventeen days, I have wished I would have told him I loved him back, told him he didn't hurt me, he had saved me, and I didn't blame him for what happened with Sebastian. I didn't need to ask Gio if Sebastian would ever be an issue. I knew he was dead and would never hurt me again.

The first several months were rough to say the least. I spoke to Dr. Weisberg daily. I missed Gio. I missed his strong arms holding me. The last intimate touch I had felt was Sebastian raping me. I had nightmares for months where I would wake up in a cold sweat screaming and reaching out for Gio. Eventually the nightmares stopped and my life turned into a robotic schedule of school, study, and sleep.

At first, I would take pictures everywhere I went, trying to create memories, but my heart just wasn't in it. Dr. Weisberg found me a rape support group to join and I attended their weekly meetings. Now I only attend once a month because sometimes being there feels like it does more harm than good when I'm trying to move forward. And I think, for the most part, I've moved forward. I know it sounds crazy but I don't think I ever truly gave myself a chance to heal until I moved here on my own.

"Hey, what's up with the tears?" Trevor points to my face after setting his cup down. I met Trevor last semester. He's studying photography like I am and we hit it off straight away. Okay, maybe not straight away...but eventually I did give him a chance and we've become good friends.

Trevor knows pretty much everything that has happened to me and is used to my tears. Any time I think about Gio, they come, and even after over a year, they still come frequently.

"Just thinking." I swipe the traitor tears away, take a deep breath, and plaster a smile on my face. "Do you have any ideas for the presentation?"

"Yeah." His eyes light up. Photography is Trevor's passion. I would give anything to feel passionately about something again, but for right now I'm content with simply moving forward. "I was thinking we could call it one hundred strangers. I found it online and tweaked it a bit. We would approach a hundred strangers and ask if we can take their pictures, then make up what we think is going through their heads. Where they're from, what their story is..."

I'm listening to Trevor's idea when a chill runs down my spine, goose bumps prickling my skin. I scan the area around me, suddenly feeling like I'm being watched.

"Aria, are you listening?"

"Yes...no. I was listening, but I just got the weirdest feeling like I'm being watched, or we're being watched. I don't know."

Trevor looks around before shrugging. "I don't see anyone, but we can leave if it'll make you feel better."

"No, it's okay. I'm okay."

Trevor nods and goes back to telling me about his idea. I agree it sounds like a good creative project and we make plans to meet here tomorrow to iron out the details and map out the different areas we can hit up to find people who will let us take their photo. I tell Trevor I'd like to cover a bunch of different areas so we can hit different income divisions to get a variety of people, and Trevor agrees.

I throw my coffee cup and wrappers into the trash and pack up my laptop. I go by the store on the way to my flat and pick up ingredients to make a chicken salad for dinner before heading home. Taking the lift to the third floor, I step off and dig into my purse to find my keys. Once I have them in my hand, I look up and gasp at the sight in front of me, my bags hitting the ground. My hand comes to my mouth as the tears, for the second time today, come streaming down. Only this time, they aren't because of the memory of Gio but because of the man himself.

Chapter Thirty-Seven

GIOVANNI

Two hours earlier

AS MUCH AS I WANTED TO TAKE OFF ON A PLANE TO Florence the minute my mom planted the idea into my head, I couldn't. I had been neglecting my responsibilities for the past year and it wouldn't be fair to Nico, to leave him with the bordello like this. I spent the next week bringing everything up to date. I wrote down important names and numbers, let the members know about the change in management-slash-ownership, and tied up all loose ends. Nico asked if I planned to come back and I knew without even having to think about it, I would only be back to visit my family. My life wasn't here anymore.

He asked me what I would do if Aria had moved on. At first, I glared at him and told him to shut the fuck up. But then I thought about it and the fact that it could be a possibility. Just because I haven't been able to move on doesn't mean Aria wasn't able to. After some thought, I decided if she has in fact moved on and is happy, I'm not going to fuck it up. I'll walk away and leave her be. I also decided that regardless of what happens with Aria, I'm done with the organization.

The concept of letting her be was great in theory. But after I asked the doorman where I could find Aria, and he pointed me in the direction of a quaint little bakery about four blocks from her place that she apparently frequents often, I went in search of her. And just as he said, there she was sitting outside the bakery, only she wasn't alone. She was with a guy, smiling and chatting with him. And that theory of letting her be went flying right out the window.

She looked absolutely beautiful. A bit harder around the edges but nonetheless, still has breathtaking. Her hair was no longer golden brown but instead midnight black. In place of the light pink lipstick she used to wear, her lips were darker—the color of mocha. Her eyes were lined in black and she was dressed in skinny jeans, an off the shoulder sweater, and she was sporting tall black boots. Aria had only aged a year since she left, but her look of innocence was gone. Maybe it was the event that led up to her leaving or living on her own, but Aria looked older, more mature. She looked fucking amazing. My heart ached as I watched her interact with the guy she was sitting with. When she looked around, I was scared she might've seen me so I walked back toward her place and called Amber.

"I think she's seeing someone."

"What?" Her voice was raspy, probably from having been asleep.

I forgot about the nine-hour time difference when I called her.

"Sorry, were you asleep?"

"Umm...yeah, it's two in the morning here."

"I think Aria is seeing someone. I saw her with a guy."

Amber huffed out, clearly annoyed. "She's not seeing anyone, Giovanni."

"Then who was the guy with her?"

"I don't know. But I would know if she was seeing anyone. I've visited her several times since she's moved there and I talk to her at least once a week and she has never so much as mentioned seeing a guy. Now man up and go get our girl."

I hung up and made my way to her place to wait for her. I didn't have to wait long because not even thirty minutes after hanging up with Amber, the lift chimed and Aria stepped out onto her floor. And when our eyes locked, I knew I could never let this woman go again.

Chapter Thirty-Eight

ARIA

LOOKING DOWN AT THE BAGS I DROPPED, I BEND TO PICK them up, but Gio gets to them first. I'm able to snag a glimpse of him up close and he looks just as handsome as he did a year ago. He's wearing a pair of jeans, a t-shirt, and tennis shoes. He looks the most casual I've ever seen him. His forearms look solid, muscular like he's been working out, and his facial hair is just how I used to like it— just long enough to feel the stubble against my lips...and between my thighs. But he also looks sad. He has dark circles under his eyes like he hasn't slept recently and I immediately wonder if he's here because something has happened.

"Thank you," I say once he has all my bags in his hands. "Would you like to come in?" My words come out so calmly, I question my sanity.

Gio nods but doesn't say anything else. We enter my flat and I start to put the groceries away into the refrigerator to busy myself, my eyes constantly glancing toward Gio, who is leaning against the counter following my every move.

Once I have no groceries left to put away, I offer him a drink. "I have water, orange juice, white wine, and…" I look down and spot a beer in the back. "…beer."

"You drink beer?" Gio's brow quirks up.

"No, it's Trevor's." The words come out before I can stop them and Gio's eyes turn cold.

"The guy you were with at the bakery?"

"You were watching me?"

Gio doesn't even try to deny it. "I came here first and the doorman steered me in the direction of the bakery. We're going to need to speak to him about privacy. Is Trevor your boyfriend?"

I shake my head and pour myself a glass of wine, needing it to calm my nerves.

"Fiancé?"

I choke on my sip of wine, coughing to the point that Gio comes over to me, grabs my glass and places it on the counter, and pats my back. *Jesus, this is not going well.*

"I'm okay. Thanks." I clear my throat to get a hold of myself. "No, Trevor is just a friend from school. You didn't answer me. Would you like something to drink?"

He shakes his head and walks to the living room to have a seat. I follow behind and once we're both seated, I say, "It's been a long time and you're far from home. Is everything okay?"

Gio shakes his head again.

"Are you going to actually speak or should I keep throwing out questions for you to nod or shake your head to?"

He chuckles softly and that small laugh has my chest tightening, my eyes opening, and my heart pumping. It's like a switch has been flipped on, and all the darkness is now full of color and light.

"Fuck, I've missed your sass." His fingers come up, twirling a strand of my hair. "You died your hair black. It looks good on you."

"I needed a change." What I needed was the darkness to match my state of being. For the last year I've lived my life to the tune of black, white, and grey. The moment I was forced to walk out of Gio's life, my world lost all its color.

"I don't know what I'm doing, Ari." He shakes his head and gives me a half smirk. "I came here without a plan. Without thinking this through."

My head goes down and I mess with my hands unsure of what to do or say.

"Baby, look at me." Gio lifts my chin and gives me a small smile, one that has my heart quickening. It's been over a year since I've been with this man but one simple touch and he has my body going haywire.

"What are you doing here, Gio? What's going on?" My words come out serious, demanding an answer. He can't just come here, walk back into my life and fuck with my head and my heart. I won't survive it. It'll be hard enough once he leaves after he's said whatever it is he came all the way across the world to say.

"I need you close to me," he mumbles, and without even asking permission, he lifts me up by my hips and places me into his lap so my legs are straddling him. My hands go to his shoulders to steady myself and our faces are mere inches away from each other.

"I came here for you. I need you, Ari. *Sei il mio cuore.*" *You are my heart.* I gasp and shake my head as his words sink in.

"Don't do this, please." My head continues to shake as I will the traitor tears away, but it's no use. They build up and fall down my cheeks. Gio's fingers catch them before he cradles my face with his strong hands.

"I love you. You are my heart. I can't breathe without you, baby. I've tried. I can't do it. The day you left, my heart stopped beating. My chest closed in on me and it felt like I was suffocating. Every day it feels like it's a job just to get up and breathe. I need to breathe again, baby."

My tears fall harder with every word he speaks, each one hitting home. "I feel the same way," I choke out. "But nothing has changed." My tears turn into sobs as my head collapses into Gio's neck, his arms encircling me and holding me close.

"Everything has changed," he whispers. "I'm out, baby."

My head snaps up, my eyes meeting his. "What does that mean?"

"It means I'm out of the organization. At the request from my mom, my dad let me out. I'm here for you, for us. You're all I want, all I need." His lips meet mine, soft and gentle. He kisses me once, twice, three times before pulling back and leaving me wanting and needing more.

"What do you say, baby? I was thinking maybe I could crash here for a while until I figure my shit out. I'm currently homeless and jobless." He smirks and I laugh, the sound feeling so foreign but good.

"You're moving here? Like, for good?"

"That all depends on you...Will you have me for good?" This time it's me that initiates the kiss. My lips crash against his, my tongue seeking entrance. Gio grants me access, his tongue swirling around mine as we get lost in each other. The kiss is more than two lips gliding across each other. Two tongues entwining. It's two hearts finding their way back to each other. Two souls connecting. And for the first time in a long time, I feel like all the colors in my world are shining brightly.

Gio's hands move down my shoulders, grazing my sides, and land on my ass, pulling my body closer to him like even the few inches of distance between us is too much. My hips grind down on his hard length, eliciting a moan from me, a feeling of want I haven't felt since the last time I was with him. He breaks our kiss and smiles wide. "I want to make you dinner."

"What?" I bark out a laugh, completely confused.

"I never got to cook for you. I promised to cook for you and I never got to."

"Right now?"

"Yes, no more wasting time."

"That sounds like a plan but...I'm kind of thinking maybe we can work up an appetite first." My lips go to his neck, suckling on his skin. Gio shivers and lets out a groan as I run my tongue up the side of his neck until I get to his earlobe. I pull on it, then whisper, "I'm thinking maybe we could be the appetizer."

Climbing off him, I drop to my knees, spreading his legs enough so I'm kneeling in between them. His eyes widen, but he doesn't argue. I unzip his jeans and tug his pants and boxers down. He lifts slightly to make it easier for me. His dick springs free and it looks as mouthwatering as it did a year ago.

Fuck, I've missed this man something fierce.

It's hard and smooth and slightly veiny as it stands at attention needing my undivided attention. Then a thought hits me. How many women got to wrap their mouths around him and taste him? How many women got his attention while we were apart?

"Hey." Gio lifts my chin so I'll look at him. "What's wrong? You don't have to do this."

"How many women have you been with?" I blurt out.

"Since you left?"

"Yeah. I know it shouldn't matter but, I just need to—"

"Zero."

"What?" There's no way I heard him correctly.

"I haven't been with a single woman in any way since the day you left. You're it for me, Aria. Now, here's the thing. Just because I couldn't be with someone else doesn't mean I expect you to not have been with anyone. It's been a goddamn year, but I would rather not know. I just think it would be best—"

"Zero." I echo the same word, the same number he gave me.

"Thank fuck!" He leans down and pulls me into a standing position. "Take your clothes off now," Gio commands. So, I do. I peel each article of clothing off me until I'm standing naked in front of him, his eyes assessing me, and instead of feeling vulnerable, I feel complete, whole. I see the colors returning to the picture.

"*Bellissima,*" he murmurs. Gorgeous. "Fuck, you're just as beautiful as I've imagined every day for the last year." He cups my sex. "Are you wet, baby? If I stick my fingers into your cunt will you be dripping for me?" My God, I've missed his dirty talk.

"Maybe you should find out." I raise a brow as I spread my legs, earning a huge grin from him. He sticks a single digit in me, quickly finding out how damn wet I am for him.

"Holy shit, woman." He pulls his finger out and, gripping my hips, lifts me up and onto him, my pussy clenching around his hard length as he fills me completely. It's been over a year since I felt a man inside me, the last time being when I was raped. I focus on pushing those thoughts away and staying in the moment with the man in front of me, the man who holds my heart.

He must sense something is wrong, because he cradles my face in his hands and says, "Stay with me, Aria. It's me and you. I love you, baby."

I nod, my emotions getting the best of me.

"It's okay," he coos, wiping the tears away as they fall. "It's just you and me, for the rest of our lives."

I nod again, keeping my eyes locked with his. I focus on the soft brown in his eyes, the way they warm up when they find me, like deep chocolate and comfort and happiness all rolled into one beautiful man.

"You're in control, Aria." How he knows what I need, I have no clue, but it shouldn't shock me. He's always known what I need. His words hit me and all the horrid thoughts are pushed aside, and it's only Gio and me and our love right here, right now, in this room. My hands go to his shoulders, his to my hips, and I lift my pelvis up slightly, the feeling of his hard dick rubbing me in a way I've been craving. "That's it, baby. It's all you. Take what you need."

Gio pulls me into a searing kiss, and our lips and tongues make love as I circle my hips and begin to rock back and forth. I ride his hard shaft slowly, hitting spots I've only dreamed of hitting for the last year. This is exactly what I've needed for too long. His hands and tongue and dick in me, on me, all over me. I close my eyes and see the bright colors of our future. Blues and pinks and reds replace the gray.

When our kiss ends, I lick my lips, his taste lingering on me, making me want more. His mouth goes to my nipple as he licks and sucks on the hardened tip while one of his hands comes to my other nipple, pinching and pulling it, his touch sending sparks straight to my core. It's just us. No one else. I can't believe I ever went this long without him.

My movements turn frantic, my breathing becoming more labored as I ride him harder, deeper, my hips bouncing up and down on his hard length as my orgasm approaches. Gio must feel me clenching around him because suddenly he's taking over, his hips thrusting against me, hitting my G-spot over and over again until I'm screaming out my orgasm as my pussy explodes with pleasure around his cock, Gio following right behind me. My head drops to his chest in satisfaction. I had no idea how much I needed him until now, and I know in this moment, I never want to live another day without him.

"How soon until you can go again?" I giggle, but I'm serious.

I need more of this man. For the rest of my life.

Chapter Thirty-Nine

GIOVANNI

AS MUCH AS I WOULD LOVE TO STAY BURIED BALLS-DEEP in Aria all day, I also want to spend time with her with our clothes on. I want to talk and catch up and find out how she's been, what she's been up to. I want to know how school is going. I want to know about everything I've missed out on over the last year.

So, after we shower and get dressed, despite Aria's pouting face, I insist we go to the store so I can cook for her. Over the last year, I can't even recall how many times I had wished I had gotten to make a meal for her before she left. Now that I'm being given this second chance, I plan to cook for her every day she'll let me. She agrees, but only if I promise to be her dessert. My hard-again cock and I wholeheartedly agree.

We go to the grocery store and Aria pushes the cart while I fill it with the ingredients I need to make my homemade shrimp and chicken fettucine alfredo. After I order the shrimp from the meat department, I notice Aria has a huge smirk on her face, like she's trying to hold back her laughter.

"What's so funny?"

She giggles and shakes her head.

"Tell me, woman!"

"Nothing, it's just...this is so very domestic of us."

I raise one brow, needing her to further explain.

"Oh, c'mon. Back at home, you have a cook and maids and servants...and a bartender!"

"I was running a business."

"Yes, but you never cooked for yourself, and when was the last time you bought your own groceries?" She's got me there and she knows it.

I grab her by her curve of her hips and pull her into me. "This is a fresh start, *cuore mio*. I want this to be my home, *our* home. I want to do shit like this." My eyes graze our surroundings. "I want us to go grocery shopping together. I want to cook for you every day. I don't know what else normal couples do—"

Aria cuts me off. "Like doing laundry together?" She holds back her laughter. To her, this is funny. To me, this is everything.

"Yes! Like laundry. I want us to cook together and do laundry together...and I have no fucking clue what else, but whatever it is, I want us to do it all together."

Aria grants me a huge smile, her arms going around my neck in the middle of the grocery store. "I don't think I would ever call us *normal*, but baby, you can do laundry with me any day." She gives me the most adorable wink and I laugh out loud. Then she leans in and whispers into my ear, "Or we can just stay naked all day and not have to do any laundry." She gives the side of my jaw a kiss before backing up and grabbing the cart, leaving me with the visual of her walking through her flat naked.

"Let's get the groceries and get the hell home." I grab the end of the cart to speed her up, and she laughs, slowing me down. "New rule," I say in complete seriousness. "No clothing allowed inside our home. Ever."

Aria gives me a soft smile. "I like the sound of that."

"Of no clothes? Hell yes."

She shakes her head, tears filling her eyes. "No, well, yes, I like the sound of that, too. But I was referring to the part where you called it our home."

I lean over the cart and give her a soft kiss. "Our home." I repeat the words and she nods in agreement.

"Our life," she whispers.

"Our life...I definitely like the sound of that."

We get back to the flat, and after putting away all the groceries, I start preparing dinner while Aria sits at the island. We go back and forth talking about the past year. She tells me all about art school and how she only has one semester left after this one. I update her on Natalie and how she's now strictly managing the bordello, and how Holly and Sienna are both going back to school. Aria wanted to keep in touch with them but couldn't bring herself to, too afraid she would ask about me.

The only person she kept in touch with was Amber and they had a rule not to mention me. Amber and Nico are engaged and getting married next year, here in Italy. Aria is the maid of honor and I'm the best man. Mario is engaged as well and is planning to get married soon, and will more than likely have his wedding here as well.

I finish cooking the pasta and pour the sauce, shrimp, and chicken into the pot, mixing it all together, while Aria sets the table and grabs a bottle of wine. We sit down and I serve us both a plate.

"Oh my God, Gio. This food smells so good!" Aria takes a large bite, the cream from the alfredo sauce coating her lips, and moans loudly. My dick twitches not understanding that Aria is currently having a foodgasm and that moan, while hot as fuck, isn't for us.

She takes another bite and after swallowing, says, "Seriously, this is delicious. The way to my heart just might be through food." She laughs, taking a sip of her wine, then takes another bite. I smile, feeling genuinely happy for the first time in a long time.

"Come here," I say, suddenly needing Ari in my arms. She gets up and climbs into my lap. "Thank you."

Aria looks at me with a confused look. "For what? You made the dinner, silly."

"No." I shake my head. "You once thanked me for saving you, but the truth is, Aria. You saved me." I take her face in my hands and place a soft kiss on her forehead, on each of her cheeks, on her nose, and lastly on her soft plump lips. "Thank you, baby, for saving me."

Aria sniffles and shakes her head back at me. "No, Gio. We saved each other."

Epilogue

ARIA

Three Years Later

I JOLT AWAKE, SHAKING SLIGHTLY FROM A HORRIBLE nightmare. I don't get them often, but when I do, it takes a minute to remember that the darkness, which only appears in my sleep, is nothing more than a dream. I open my eyes and the brightness hits me, reminding me that the color is my reality. I roll over and notice the side where my husband should be sleeping is empty. I lie there for a few moments wondering where he is, listening for any voices. He got home late last night from the restaurant, and was up even later making love to me.

The smell of bacon assaults my senses and then I hear the most beautiful sound of a giggle. Grabbing my camera from the nightstand, I turn it on and head to the kitchen. Standing against the stove with only a pair of black sweatpants on, is Gio. With a spatula in his hand, he flips the bacon. Standing on a stool next to him is our two-year old daughter, Bea, who loves cooking almost as much as her dad does.

Snap.

Snap.

"Fluff them," he instructs, handing her, her own spatula. She giggles some more, taking the spatula from him and pushing the eggs around in the pan, knocking some out and onto the floor. She giggles as Gio laughs, picking them up and throwing them into the sink.

Snap.

Snap.

Snap.

I take several photos of them until it reads *memory full*. I must have put the wrong card into the camera when I left the studio after a session with a family yesterday. I click view and scroll back several pictures until I get to one I took years ago.

It's of the Giardino Delle Rose. A beautiful garden here in Florence. I can remember the picture like it was yesterday, yet it feels like forever ago that I took it. I was studying for a test and decided to have a picnic in the grass. The flowers were blooming, deep pinks and yellows. The grass was a deep shade of green.

The next picture is one I took during my weekly trip to the outdoor food market by myself. Ripe red tomatoes, purple eggplants. I flip through them, realizing these were taken during the year Gio and I were apart. I flip through each picture and it hits me that I created a life here during that year apart, filled with so many colorful memories. The problem was I couldn't see the color. I was lost in the grey, in the darkness.

The next picture is one I took of Gio and Bea eating dinner at the restaurant last night, both laughing at the camera. I click to the next photo. It's a selfie of Gio and me. He's tickling me in bed and I have my eyes closed, my head thrown back, and the silliest grin on my face as he snaps the picture.

I flip from picture to picture of us, laughing, smiling, and I end up at the ones I just took, of Gio and our beautiful daughter cooking in our kitchen. I close my eyes and take in a deep breath, pushing away the nightmares from my past. It's a struggle every day to live in the moment.

I open my eyes and exhale a deep breath. Gio is standing there, staring at me with the most gorgeous smile on his face, holding our daughter in his arms, and I can finally see it. The beauty in the darkness. The Rainbow that comes after the storm. The bright colors that make up my life when Gio is in it. To an outsider looking in, my story may appear dark. Gloomy. Black. Gray. Like a horrible storm that comes through filled with destruction, destroying everyone in its path. But to me, those colors are just the outlining of the bigger picture, because inside those dark stormy lines are shades of the most beautiful colors.

And those colors are my life.

ABOUT THE AUTHOR

Reading is like breathing in, writing is like breathing out. – Pam Allyn

Nikki Ash resides in South Florida where she is an English teacher by day and a writer by night. When she's not writing, you can find her with a book in her hand. From the Boxcar Children, to Wuthering Heights, to the latest single parent romance, she has lived and breathed every type of book. While reading and writing are her passions, her two children are her entire world. You can probably find them at a Disney park before you would find them at home on the weekends!